P9-DFP-410

Praise for THE PRAIRIE BRIDESMAID

"Salamon's talent shines in her lively and authentically depicted characters.... But the true highlight of the novel is the wit, cynicism, and insight that Salamon gives Anna.... Salamon's sharp prose and wicked wit imbue the novel with a tone similar to that of [Melissa Bank's] *The Girls' Guide to Hunting and Fishing*.... [A] worthwhile and entertaining read."

WINNIPEG FREE PRESS (top five bestseller)

"There's already buzz about the just-published novel about plucky Winnipegger Anna, a high school teacher in her early thirties, stuck in a toxic relationship—and not just because it happens to be very good. Observant readers will have noticed the sticker on the back of the book directing them to the novel's eponymous website, where they are prompted to enter a unique PIN and access a free download of the novel's soundtrack, a handful of songs by emerging and established Canadian artists.... [I]t's a helluva creative multimedia way to add depth and flavour to the act of reading: discover a favourite author, and also a new favourite song."

THE NATIONAL POST

"In reading this book, I was touched and inspired. It is original and well-written and points to a reality both relevant and poignant for women with whom I share a generation. Daria Salamon writes with wit and compassion and manages to dignify the thoughts, emotions, and sometimes treacherous turns that are part of growing up as women in Canada."

CHANTAL KREVIAZUK, singer/songwriter

"*The Prairie Bridesmaid* was funny, smart, and heart-wrenching all at once. The subject of emotional abuse is dealt with in depth, and anyone who has ever been in such a situation will surely recognize themselves in Anna's guilty feelings and neurotic coping mechanisms."

THE SACRAMENTO BOOK REVIEW

"[A] standout debut. Salamon has raised the bar on chick-lit with a thorny bouquet of razor-sharp wit, misguided relationships dripping with irony, and a heroine who for once is just as forlorn as the rest of us.... By giving her novel both style and substance, Daria Salamon writes chick-lit in a singularly groundbreaking way."

THE UNITER (The University of Winnipeg)

"*The Prairie Bridesmaid* is the debut novel of Winnipeg author Daria Salamon, and it's a good one.... Although some parts of the story are dark, the overall tone is light and there's plenty of offbeat humour."
PRAIRIE FIRE

"[S]ubversive chick-lit. Daria Salamon has written a funny, dark, quirky take on one woman's epic struggle with the harsh realities of adult life: angry boyfriends, dull colleagues and meddling girlfriends. Like U.S. novelist Lorrie Moore, Salamon deftly combines humour and pathos to great effect."
THE GLOBE AND MAIL

"Daria Salamon adeptly crosses genres and displays an abundance of literary savvy in *The Prairie Bridesmaid*. Daria manages an impressive balance between angst and wit, between a serious treatment of the ravages of a love relationship gone brutal and a humorous take on the vanities and shortcomings of a young woman who is mired in the muck of her own making."
MARJORIE ANDERSON, editor of DROPPED THREADS and DROPPED THREADS 2

"The book is funny, and hits on some darker topics, even though it's supposed to be lighter fare. The characters are believable and utterly Canadian.... [Anna] isn't perfect, which makes her relatable. She's witty and her voice is fully fleshed out and rings true throughout the book.... I look forward to reading more books by Salamon and am glad she's taken it upon herself to write wise, Canadian chick-lit."
GRAND PRAIRIE INK

"*The Prairie Bridesmaid* is a witty, sardonic, and touching story of self-discovery leading to liberation. Daria Salamon's writing is like a breath of fresh Winnipeg air."
NIA VARDALOS, screenwriter and star of MY BIG FAT GREEK WEDDING

"From the first page of *The Prairie Bridesmaid* you can't help but to care about Anna and her life. Although the tone of Daria Salamon's novel is cheerful, the story is darker and deftly told. Salamon is a skilled writer, keeping a tight rein on the emotional depth of *The Prairie Bridesmaid*. This is chick-lit for grown-ups. And it's good."
ALICE KUIPERS, author of NOTES ON THE REFRIGERATOR DOOR

the prairie bridesmaid

the Prairie Bridesmaid

Daria Salamon

KEY PORTER BOOKS

Copyright © 2008 by Daria Salamon

All rights reserved. No part of this work covered by the copyrights hereon may be reproduced or used in any form or by any means—graphic, electronic or mechanical, including photocopying, recording, taping or information storage and retrieval systems—without the prior written permission of the publisher, or, in case of photocopying or other reprographic copying, a licence from Access Copyright, the Canadian Copyright Licensing Agency, One Yonge Street, Suite 1900, Toronto, Ontario, M6B 3A9.

Library and Archives Canada Cataloguing in Publication

Salamon, Daria
The prairie bridesmaid : a novel / Daria Salamon.

ISBN 978-1-55470-054-7 (bound)—ISBN 978-1-55470-183-4 (pbk.)

I. Title.

PS8637.A5323P73 2009   C813'.6   C 2008-907526-9

The author acknowledges the generous support of the Manitoba Arts Council and the Winnipeg Arts Council.

The publisher gratefully acknowledges the support of the Canada Council for the Arts and the Ontario Arts Council for its publishing program. We acknowledge the support of the Government of Ontario through the Ontario Media Development Corporation's Ontario Book Initiative.

We acknowledge the financial support of the Government of Canada through the Book Publishing Industry Development Program (BPIDP) for our publishing activities.

Key Porter Books Limited
Six Adelaide Street East, Tenth Floor
Toronto, Ontario
Canada M5C 1H6

www.keyporter.com

Text design: Marijke Friesen
Electronic formatting: Alison Carr

Printed and bound in Canada

09 10 11 12 13 5 4 3 2 1

For Babas and Gidos,
both mine and Oskar's

Prologue

I'm at the bookstore in the self-help section. The Relationship section. The People Who Can't Get Along section. The People Who Want to Kill Each Other section. The Gimme a Fucking Baseball Bat section. The titles slam into my brain like a load of wet cement. *Ten Days to Self-Esteem, Walking on Eggshells, When Love Goes Bad, Leave Your Husband and Find Yourself for under $300*. I scan more titles: *Seven Steps to Taking Your Life Back, Ditch That Jerk, Dealing with Men Who Control and Hurt Women, Angry Men and the Women Who Love Them*. I don't know who writes these books or for whom. I decide they aren't for me. They're written for weak women, women who have lost control of their lives.

I reach for *Saving Yourself from Abuse*, gingerly, as though it's a disease that produces open sores. A butterfly tries to lift off from the peacock-blue cover. I thumb through the pages, uncommitted but intrigued as the chapter titles flip by: "You're Not a Bad Person," "Starting Over."

Hundreds of erect spines harnessing thousands of pages of advice. The self-help section is empty except for me. People across the aisle in the magazine section are gazing at articles about organizing desks and toning thighs, or flipping through glossy photos of Versace-clad women, who most certainly are in control of their lives. I need to leave. I'll purchase a few books, browse through them at home privately, and then return them tomorrow. No harm done. I select three books. As I'm walking away, a workbook, *Marching out of Abuse*, catches my attention, taunts me. I grab it. My arms are now full of self-help books for pathetic women.

As I approach the cashier, a boy steps directly in front of me. Breathy Craig. Craig is a member of the student writing group I teach at the high school; he writes the worst fantasy I've ever read. At first the group was a forum for a handful of adept writers. However, over the past few years, it has degenerated into a collection of misfits who want to avoid the school cafeteria, where they are regularly beaten up. They've conveniently developed passions that coincide with the noon-hour programs at the school. Craig is a close talker—he's inches away from my face. His front teeth are angled outward and caped in butter-coloured gunk. He smells like cat and blocks my path of escape with his scrawny frame.

Winnipeg is too goddamn small. There are over half a million people living in this city, but I still inevitably run into students when buying foot powder, pantiliners, or self-help books.

"Whatcha buying?" Craig always bleeds his words together. I can smell tuna.

"Books," I reply, hoping that the dragon he always writes about will swoop down and snatch him up, like it does the characters in his stories.

He stares at me bewildered and blinking, his arms—two fleshy ropes with knots tied at the elbows—dangling at his sides. He tilts his left ear to the floor and moves his lips as he reads the titles under my arm. *Shit. What kind of story can I feed this kid?*

"They're for the writing group. I thought we would do some

character development," I stammer, "explore some crazy characters." I juggle the books so the titles aren't visible. Craig's *Ring
in Arbour Day* T-shirt hangs down to his thighs and looks like it's
been sprayed with the contents of a mustard bottle. I don't ask
what the hell Arbour Day is. He scratches the matted curls on
his head.

The line has cleared and the clerk eyes me. I push past Craig.

"Oh, it's my turn. See you tomorrow." I know I'll see him
even though the group doesn't meet until Thursday. Most days I
get pinned to my desk listening to Craig's version of teenage
angst.

"Eighty-nine thirty-six," the cashier declares. Money I probably won't see again because I never actually return anything. As
I leave the store I spot Craig leafing through books in the self-
help section.

At home, I pour myself a glass of wine and peruse the books.
How did I get to this point?

I must have been away from school the day they explained
relationships. I was there in fifth grade when the boys and girls
were separated and shown videos. Mrs. Prystupa, in her bifocals,
explained to us girls what would happen when we got our periods. The boys said that they were shown videos about wet
dreams and masturbation. Girls learned that they would not
only bleed, but also be bloated, cranky, and irritable every
month for the next forty-odd years. Boys were taught how to
get themselves off.

In tenth grade we had to take part in a ritual aimed at dis-
couraging us from procreating. We were paired up with boys and
each pair had to carry a chicken egg around for a week without
breaking it. When it was my turn, I took the egg everywhere with

me; I decorated it with coloured felt markers and named it Sophie. My partner, Chris Timchuck, who wore a Toronto Maple Leafs jersey to school every single day, stored the egg in his locker during his shifts. On the last day of the project, Sophie rolled out of Chris's locker and splattered on the floor. The experiment worked, though, because I didn't get pregnant in high school—and haven't since, for that matter. They should have made us tote a pit bull around for a week to discourage us from getting into relationships with bad men.

No one ever talked to me about relating to the opposite sex: it was something we were supposed to intuitively figure out. The schools I went to addressed every other social issue: sex education, teen pregnancy, drinking and driving, and addictions. Some schools even dealt with homosexuality. It could have been slipped in some time after girls got the period talk and boys got the wet dream chat, and before the "Just Say No" campaign. Or perhaps that campaign could have been applied to men as well as drugs. Nobody ever told me about things like respect or communication, the anchors of a healthy relationship. My information came from my parents, the modern-day Honeymooners, and the pretty movies—*Pretty in Pink, Pretty Woman*. These movies taught me that on my own I could never be happy, that I needed to be saved. Mr. Right would lead me down a path of bliss.

And if a relationship *does* go awry—say, one's parents get divorced—it's usually never explained what actually went wrong, assuming the former couple even know. And it's not explained that sometimes relationships just *need* to end, and that it's *okay* to end a relationship. The relationship is simply labelled a failure and the breakup is coated in a lot of anger. And then everybody moves on—often into new relationships—without ever reflecting on what went wrong in the previous one.

I entered the relationship world thinking it was all based on how loudly those butterflies were beating their wings in my tummy. I could have used some warning at twenty-one when I met Adam and began my first serious relationship, a relationship that would last ten years and bring me to where I am now, consulting self-help books and consoling myself with cheap Merlot.

Divine Intervention

"So, Anna, this isn't a bridal shower for Sara," Renate says, shutting the front door of Sara's house behind me.

"What?" I'm holding my gift, wrapped in pink tissue.

"We're having an intervention," she declares as she leads me down the hallway.

"For you," Sara adds from her perch on the living room couch. "Sit down." I'm clearly overdressed in a new skirt I'd bought specifically for this shower. I even splurged for leggings. Renate and Julia are comfortably decked out in jeans and Sara lounges in her two-hundred-dollar yoga pants.

The living room of Sara's new suburban house is sparsely decorated. The whole place has the look of an air freshener commercial. It makes me jittery and afraid to touch anything, for fear my fingerprints will mar the clean surfaces of Sara's life. I'm the drooling dog; Sara will Lysol her living room when I leave. The white leather of the couch creaks beneath my ass as I sit down.

Sara, Renate, and Julia are my dearest friends. We spent days lingering at the shopping mall when we were fourteen and hours lying in our beds, twisting pink telephone cords around our toes as we squealed into the receiver, "He did not say that!" Now we convene for bridal showers and, apparently, interventions. We've drifted in different directions at times only to get washed back onto the shores of one another's lives. We are still moored together by the experiences we endured as teenagers.

What the fuck is an intervention? And why did they let me squander eighty-seven-fifty on matching yellow lace bra and panties? I drop my purse on top of the gift, a clear physical indication that the bra and panties will be returning home with me. Sara and I are roughly the same size—six—although Sara has purchased a size four wedding dress for her upcoming nuptials and has eaten only grilled chicken and grapefruit for the past three months in an attempt to fit into it.

"What's an intervention?" I ask casually as I curl my legs up under me.

"It's when your friends all think that your life is sufficiently screwed up that they try to help you change it." Renate grips my arm, sensing that I am formulating a plan to get out of here. She knows me well: I am scanning the room for exits. My skirt will slow me down if I try to run.

"You know you're not happy. We know you're not happy," Renate says, letting go of my arm. A huge diamond wedding ring gleams on her finger. Renate married her boyfriend of forever three years ago. The silk bridesmaid dress still hangs in my closet. She's earned her unofficial title as Relationship Expert. She casually stretches out on the couch, indicating we will be here for a while, and rests her hands on her swollen belly. She is pregnant with her second child. Her firstborn, two-year-old David, is cheerfully bashing pieces of Lego together in the corner. The Lego blocks are looking far more appealing than what's about to take place in my corner of the living room.

"You're not doing anything about it, so we are," Sara says.

She reaches over and picks some lint off my sweater. Sara is neurotic and she will pick apart my life the same way she attacks lint. Lint, I can tell already, is the least of my problems.

"This shit with Adam is not healthy and it has to end," Renate adds. "While he's away, we think it's your best shot at getting out."

"I read about interventions in *Marie Claire* magazine," Julia explains. Julia is usually my ally—I can't believe she's instigated this whole thing. Traitor. She barely glances up as she flips through the pages.

"Can I drink at my intervention?" I mutter.

"I don't know. Did anyone read anything about drinking?" Sara asks.

Julia flips through some more pages. "No, but I didn't see anything saying you couldn't."

"I guess so. I'll get you a drink. I'll get everyone a drink." Sara disappears into the kitchen. *Thank God. I don't think I could sit through this blatant intrusion on my life sober.*

"Can you check on Emma?" Julia calls to Sara. "I couldn't get a sitter so I had to bring her," she explains to me. "She's sleeping—I guess one-year-olds find interventions boring." Julia is lying on the floor and she rolls over onto her back. Her body, big and curvy in black capris and a T-shirt, stands out against the plush white rug, her mane of shiny dark hair spread out around her as she continues to read. Her daughter, Emma, is fatherless. Julia decided she wanted a baby without the hassles of a man. "I don't see why you can't have one without the other," she had said. Within a year Sara, Renate, and I were crowded around Julia in the delivery room as she screamed obscenities while pushing Emma from her womb and into the world.

"I sent him an email yesterday telling him I want to end it," I explain. "So there's no need for an intervention. I've already intervened for myself. Is there any food?" I try distracting them.

"How many times has this happened before?" Renate reaches around to the table behind her to a cheese tray and passes it to me. David runs over to the tray and helps himself to two fistfuls of cheese.

"No, really. This time I'm going to do it. I even bought books the other day." I toss a cube of cheddar into my mouth.

"We have to make this stick. David, in your mouth, not on the carpet." Renate scolds both David and me at the same time.

"Yeah, you can't go running back to him when he says he's having a nervous breakdown or that he can't live without you. Forget it." Julia tugs at an earring that grazes her shoulder.

"Has he emailed back yet?"

"Yeah."

"And?" Sara pokes her head out from the kitchen. She misses nothing.

I'm starting to realize that an intervention means invading your friend's privacy and choking her with unsolicited advice.

"He said he can't live without me. It's awful."

Renate passes me the tray again.

"Yeah. It's always awful. It's intervention time. Julia, what's the first thing we're supposed to do?" Renate reaches for the *Marie Claire*. Angelina Jolie, on the front cover, snickers as she flashes past.

"I don't know. *Marie Claire* made it sound so easy, but when I looked it up on the Net, I didn't really understand exactly what we're supposed to do." Julia, exasperated, pushes the stack of sheets that she'd printed from the Internet toward Renate. It's typical of my friends to throw an intervention without actually knowing what it is.

"Nice. Let me see." Renate rifles through the sheets. A dentistry degree has made her analytical. She reads, "*A critical element of emotional violence is to blame the victim for the violence.*

Exactly, every time Adam has one of his psycho spells he says it's your fault, you drove him to it. *Without support and solidarity, victims often feel that they are responsible for the emotional abuse they experience. They internalize blame.* Anna, this is so you. *As a result of the isolation they feel, the abuser often becomes their sole reference point. Support and solidarity are critical in providing the victim with an alternative way of perceiving the situation and of determining viable safety plans by which to exit the relationship.*"

"Must we use the word 'victim'?" I ask. I'm ignored. I take two cubes of marble cheese, shake them in my cupped palms, and roll them on the glass table as though they are dice. I toss them in my mouth. Two faint milky smudges are left to face the wrath of Sara's Windex bottle.

"Those sheets go on and on. *Marie Claire* made it sound far less complicated. We just lock her in a room until she agrees to break up with Adam," Julia snorts, still sprawled out on the floor examining her split ends.

"All this is saying is that we're supposed to help Anna so she knows that her situation is not normal and then we support her through getting out of it," Renate says. They might not even notice if I slip out.

"Duh. Isn't that kind of obvious? Did I need to print off twenty-six pages from the Internet to tell us that?" Julia asks. She's blocking the path to the front entrance, but there's a clear route to the back door.

"Well, then, why have you let her stay in this shitty relationship for so long if it's just common sense?" Renate snaps.

Renate had earned our envy early because she was the first to develop boobs and wear a real bra. By the time we were twelve, she had a shapely figure while the rest of us were still physically one-dimensional, barely filling out our white cotton training bras. She also had a boyfriend before any of us; he was fourteen. We listened longingly as she fed us the delicious details about what it was like to make out with a boy. Our own kissing experience was limited to dragging our tongues along the brushed cotton surface of a pillow.

Two days after Renate's thirteenth birthday, I squeezed her hand as we sat in the doctor's office waiting for the results of her pregnancy test. Somehow we hoped that these results would offer a different conclusion than the three sticks Renate had peed on in the girls' bathroom at school. We had taken a two-hour bus ride through prairie wheat fields to Brandon because Renate's mother was a pediatrician and Renate didn't want her to find out. The doctor confirmed that Renate was pregnant, almost four months. She had only had sex twice. She was hysterical—and Catholic. Paul, her boyfriend, refused to believe that Renate was pregnant, so Julia punched him in the face, leaving him with a fat lip and a loose tooth.

Within a week, because Renate was so young, the doctor waived the rule and performed an abortion on her even though she was into her second trimester. Julia and I sat in the waiting room of the clinic flipping through leaflets about high cholesterol and Pap smears while Renate had the baby sucked from her womb with a vacuum. When she emerged from the treatment room, her face was pale and her palms were red from gripping the bed railings.

After the abortion we went to A&W. I glared at Julia when she returned to the table with a tray of Cokes and Mama burgers.

Maybe she grew up faster because of her experiences, but today Renate's the one who has her life together—she was in a long-term relationship and finishing grad school while we were still trying to have relationships with men we met at shooter nights and figure out what we wanted to do with our lives.

Renate and I became friends with Julia when we called her fatso in fourth grade and she turned around and told us to fuck off. We were in awe. We had never heard anyone our age use the f-word before. We didn't even fully understand what it meant. Julia shared her Danielle Steel novels, introducing us to a world of wealthy, beautiful heroines and the scandals that plagued them. We imagined that one day we'd be like those heroines, but, so far, I haven't married a gorgeous plastic surgeon, nor do I play tennis all day.

Julia was the token rebel in our group. She was wearing makeup by the time she was twelve, smoking at fourteen, and she went out and got a tattoo on her shoulder for her sixteenth birthday. We also thought she was more worldly and exotic than we were because she was adopted. Our families were all dull, but Julia had a mysterious past that none of us knew about—even her.

For years, Julia battled a weight problem. She tried various fad diets, encouraged by her mother, and went through unsuccessful bouts of bulimia. While I was being dropped off at gymnastics, Julia was dragged off to Weight Watchers. One day, when she was nineteen, she decided that she was comfortable and sexy in her big body and she's been that way ever since. We think Oprah had something to do with it.

Sara returns to the living room with a tray of drinks. Finally.

"Sorry, I'm out of red wine," she says, handing out glasses of white wine. She sits down on the sofa with perfect posture and crosses her legs. Her pink toes are freshly polished and I think they might be painted to match the cushions on the sofa.

Sara, who was also in the same class as Julia, Renate, and me, slept over at my house almost every weekend when we were ten years old. She had slept over the night I got my first period.

"Sara, I got IT!" I squealed. This is the most anticipated but overrated event in a girl's life, although the night she loses her virginity plays a close second. At least sex gets better—periods remain painful and annoying.

Sara calmly extracted the kit she had prepared for this, equipped with pads, tampons, and clean underwear, even though she had not yet had her first period. She scrubbed the crimson stains from my panties while I practised walking around the room in my new pad. Her warm breathing comforted me that night as I fell asleep with a mixture of excitement that my body had finally made the passage into womanhood and the unexpected heartache in knowing that this process was irreversible.

Sara stopped sleeping over on the weekends when we were twelve. When I asked her if I had done something to upset her, she said no, her mom had kicked her stepdad, Joe, out, so she didn't need to stay over anymore. Joe used to smoke a joint as he drove us to soccer games when we were seven. We giggled and thought they were funny-smelling cigarettes. All of us girls packed into the back of the station wagon in our yellow soccer jerseys, our tanned, skinny legs tangled up like spaghetti. Sara explained, matter-of-factly, that Joe used to come into her room at night and slide his hand between her legs and rub his body up against her soft flannel pyjamas. Her own childhood, I realized, had ended long before mine and long before she got her first period. Sara had a string of "step-in dads," as she called them, because her mom never kept any of these men around very long. None of the others touched her, but one of them had a bad temper and one time we saw him catch Sara's mother by her blond ponytail and slap her across the face. Some of the other step-in dads were nice, but Sara didn't get attached to any of them. We would all make wagers for Slurpees about how long each would last.

Sara's tattered childhood has fed her need to neatly stitch together every loose thread of her adult life. Sara is an accountant living in suburbia, her perfect wedding is less than a month away, and she'll have 2.4 kids. Though she cruise controls her way through life and I'm careening down a slope with no brakes, we've managed to preserve an old friendship.

"I appreciate what you guys are doing, but I'm going to get out of this relationship," I tell my friends.

"Okay, go print off the email Adam sent you. We need to see it if we're going to help. That's where we'll start." Renate points at the computer.

"Isn't that kind of personal?" I ask.

"This has been *personal* for years. Go print it off," Renate says through a mouthful of chips.

"Fine." I have no choice but to go to the computer. I'm surprised that they haven't broken into my email account already.

"Mommy, I'm thirsty," David proclaims from the corner of the room. Renate retrieves a juice box from her purse, pierces it with a straw, and passes it to David.

I hand them the email I received from Adam yesterday. Renate rubs her belly as she reads the letter aloud. Sara sits beside Renate on the sofa, resting her chin on Renate's shoulder so she too can read the email.

To: annalasko@hotmail.com
From: adam_rp@hotmail.com
Subject: The End of Us

My dearest Anna,
I'm facing the finality of the end of our relationship. It's so hard. I guess I never realized that I might have to truly face life without you. I thought we were in this together—marriage, kids, old age. I think you are making a mistake. The person you are dumping is not me. I'd dump that asshole too. I wish you

wouldn't give up on me yet. When I put my mind to it, I can do anything. Even become the person I once was, if even for myself.
Adam

"You see?" Renate's head snaps up. "That's just crap! He's trying to guilt you again. Forget it, it's not going to work." *Already has.*

"It's the same old thing—excuses, then he begs you to come back." Sara smoothes a velvet pillow with her hand.

"I call bullshit." Julia sits up. "'I'm sorry. I'm sorry I treated you badly,' he always says and the following week he's fucking screaming at you again." Julia has not stopped swearing since the day we met her.

"Can we watch the language?" Renate gestures at David.

"Did you respond to this?" Sara demands.

"Well, yeah." I am forced back to the computer to print off my reply.

To: adam_rp@hotmail.com
From: annalasko@hotmail.com
Subject: Re: The End of Us

Hi Adam,
I've needed my thoughts and feelings to settle a bit. Yesterday was an awful day. I was sad after our conversation and still feel that way, but somehow today feels a bit better. I started chain-smoking. Cigarettes feel good.

"You started smoking again?" Sara interrupts. Now would be a good time for a cigarette, but Sara would attack me with an air freshener if I pulled out cigarettes in her house. Renate continues reading.

On the phone the other day, I felt that I could be totally hon-
est and I haven't felt that way in a long time. Ironically, we
were talking about splitting up, yet it feels like we are finally
understanding each other. You seem to be reconnecting with
yourself and getting back to the person you once were, the person I fell in love with.

"You called him, too?" Julia sucks back her wine, some of it drib-
bling down into her cleavage. Her bosom, full and voluptuous,
is usually accentuated by low-cut tops.

"He called me," I lie.

"This is way too nice," Renate snorts. "You are giving him
an opening." She continues to read my email.

I've felt really lonely and empty . . . but at peace. It's like I'm
finding strength for myself rather than pouring it into a difficult relationship. Does that sound selfish? I think by dealing
with the pressures of living together and trying to force the
relationship to work, we brought out the worst in each other.
I love you, but I don't want to go back to how things were.
Being apart has finally put an end to the ugliness that we are
both capable of.
Anna

I stretch out on the carpet against the wall as far away from my
friends as possible as they hover over the emails Adam and I exchanged. I close my eyes and shut out the comments that are
flung across the room at me. It's easy for my friends to pore over
these emails and bark at me to dump him. But I'm not simply
leaving a bad relationship. Adam is so much more than a
boyfriend or a lover. For ten years, we've spent every day together.
He's become my family, albeit a highly dysfunctional one. I'm

walking away from the moment we first met and all of the hopes and possibilities of that day.

I watched Adam over the top of my book as he strode toward me, a smooth spring in his step. I'd finished my waitressing shift and was settled at a table in the corner of the university restaurant where I worked. There wasn't enough light to read. I waffled from one text to another, killing the hours that lapsed between my shift and my night class. Adam was about to interrupt my studying—and my life. I didn't know that yet.

I'd taken his orders before for sandwiches and fries, or cups of coffee, but that was the extent of our conversations. Adam was a regular, always chatting with his friends or professors, standing, laughing with his arms folded at his chest, feet crossed at the ankles. I'd noticed Adam immediately and had developed a serious crush on him. He stood out from the American Eagle crowd who flooded in and out of the restaurant. He was a little shorter than the six feet I was normally attracted to, but with the way he carried himself, I could easily overlook a few inches.

I got to know his schedule—Tuesdays and Thursdays he came in at 10:30 a.m. for an hour between his classes and again in the late afternoon. He drank coffee—double cream, single sugar—and read the paper or one of his textbooks. Normally, I hated The Coffee Drinkers because they occupied tables and left no tips, but I had my co-worker trained to seat Adam in my section. Sometimes he worked on the crossword and after he left I would scoop up the paper and study the letters he'd printed cleanly and confidently in ink into the boxes. I interpreted his personality from these letters as though I were a handwriting expert. The dark ink indicated he was strong. Most of the letters were assuredly printed within the boxes, with the exception of a few that bled into the next box, suggesting he was neat but not obsessive, and the loop at the base of his Rs hinted at creativity. And his answers were almost always right—he was smart.

Adam stopped at my table. A flood of panic and delight.

"What are you reading?" He gestured to the French literature books spread out in front of me. Not "Hello" or "How are you?" Just a bold question. I loved it.

He wore muddy boots, fitted jeans that were ripped at the knee, and a faded Ramones T-shirt. Some days he wore a ball cap, but not today. Layers of brown hair hung over one of his eyes, fell onto his shoulders. His clothing and hair screamed artsy, but his T-shirt emphasized a taut physique; I'd caught glimpses of toned arms and had seen him toting around a bicycle helmet. This all suggested a layer of athleticism that was appealing and countered his artsiness. I could spend hours at my favourite second-hand store, lost in racks of dull clothing until I found a gem—a great coat or a pair of jeans. For me, Adam was one of these rare finds.

"French lit. I'm reading *Madame Bovary*, or trying to." I casually slipped the bookmark from page four to forty before I offered him the book.

"At least my books are in English." He smiled as he examined the cover with its swirling romantic letters. "Well, sort of." He gestured to the book under his arm. *Paradise Lost* was printed in fat, white letters. He leaned on my table and I tore at the napkin in my lap. I reached up and slipped the elastic out of my hair, hoping for soft waves to frame my face even though I knew it fell limply onto my shoulders. As I pushed a few dry strands behind my ear, I noticed I needed a fresh dose of chocolate colour.

Adam tilted toward me, his arms firmly planted on my table, suggesting he had conquered me at our first meeting. An early

warning sign I didn't recognize at the time. I knew he was about
five years older, more worldly, a little defiant. I loved these traits
and dating the rebel appealed to me. I should have recognized it
for what it was—some sort of rite of passage that girls are drawn
to—meaning I was supposed to have a bit of fun and then move
on. I was twenty-one and wanted to be wooed by a sexy and
rough-around-the-edges man. I had little knowledge or experience that would alert me to the dangers of such desires.

Adam eyed the brigade of Balzac, Zola, and Flaubert battling
for attention on the table in front of me. He seemed intrigued—
in a *this girl studies romantic foreign languages* sort of way.
These courses could work to my advantage, at least until I failed
them. Earlier in the semester I'd found a computer program on
the Internet that translated from English to French. I wrote my
six-page paper in English, highlighted it, and clicked *translate*.
Voilà. The program was designed for words and phrases, though,
not entire literary papers. Beside the *D,* my professor wrote that
I had an unusually poor grasp of the language for a student of
French literature and suggested that I switch my minor.

As Adam glanced at the titles, I did nothing to dispel the
myth that I could read these French books. They might as well
have been Turkish. I made a note to myself: Grab Turkish books
from library to further impress rebel.

"You're a French major?" Adam's eyes burrowed into me.

"Minor. English is my major," I replied.

"Mine too. I'm finishing my honours." The skin on his hands
was rough, but his nails were clean and smooth. I wanted to
touch them, lick them.

"I'm actually in education." I fondled the blue glass pendant
of my necklace.

"Ah, you're going to be a teacher." He leaned closer.

"I guess." I hoped this wouldn't turn him off. Teacher. One

of the most unsexy jobs, ever. Why couldn't I have been in film school or architecture? I had to pick the Faculty of Cotton Pants.

"You don't seem too excited about that."

"I didn't spend much time thinking about what I really wanted to do before choosing my faculty. Education seemed like an easy path until I figure out what I really want." I pushed the sleeves of my V-neck sweater up past my elbows.

I thought of education as one of those faculties that required a lot of enthusiasm and group work, but a limited amount of original thinking. I didn't want to drop out, though—it would feel too much like being held back in the second grade because you couldn't cut inside the lines. I chose, instead, to meander through my degree.

"How do you like Milton?" I nodded at the book under his arm, trying to steer the topic away from my lack of life direction.

"He's okay." He crouched down to eye level. I looked away. His knee was visible through the tear in his jeans. God, he had a beautiful knee.

"Have you read him?" he said, jolting me from my knee fantasy.

"No." I made another note to self to read Milton as soon as possible.

"Lots of heaven and hell stuff."

"I'm enrolled in Chaucer. An entire semester on the *Canterbury Tales*." Another course that had seemed romantic at registration time. Turns out Chaucer is about as romantic as an enema. As we chatted, all the blood from my body surged into my neck, my ears, my tongue. I knew I couldn't possibly be good enough, interesting enough for him—so I made things up. Little white lies. Suddenly I was shift supervisor at the university restaurant, I dabbled in Nietzsche, and I knew how to snowboard. Adam told me that he was a musician and that he played in a band. I said I went to shows all the time, hoping he wouldn't press the issue. The last concert I'd been to was Van Halen, years ago. Or maybe it had been that band with the one-armed drummer. Def Leppard.

"Which band do you play in?"

"Lugar Vandros. I'm the singer and guitarist. Have you heard of us?"

"Yeah," I blatantly lied. "I think I've seen you guys. You're good!" Taking the lie a little further.

"Writing and playing music is my life." Adam's hands clenched into a fist as he said "life." He suffered from passion. I loved that.

"It's great that you have something that you're good at."

"It's what I want to do. What about you?"

"I can't say there's anything that I'm really good at. I don't really know what I want to do." It probably wasn't the best idea to tell him that I was lacking in passion and devoid of talent, unless you count drunken karaoke.

"Maybe you just haven't found it yet. You will." God, he believed in me more than I believed in myself and he hardly knew me. He was perfect and he said all the right things. "You should come to one of our shows." Would this be considered a date? I was already in my closet picking out which jeans and shirt I would wear.

"I'd love to." I glanced at the clock on the wall. Five to seven.

"I should probably get to my class." Or I could skip the class, since I hadn't done the reading anyway, would never do the reading. Sorry, Chaucer. I slid my books into my backpack.

"Wanna go to a movie sometime?" Adam stood up, pushing the hair away from his eyes. *A date with the lead singer of Lugar Vandros!* I screamed in my head.

"Sure. I'll give you my number." I tore a piece of paper from my notebook and wrote it down quickly. I handed it to him, wishing I had better handwriting. He stuffed the piece of paper into the pocket of his jeans: it was a simple gesture given it was my fate he was holding.

"I love you and don't want to go back to how things were'!" Julia rereads my email in disbelief. "For fuck's sake! You need to tell him that you don't want to go back to him EVER," Julia insists. Over Renate's shoulder, David squeezes his juice box and a lovely arc of pink floats through the air and lands on the carpet. I wink at David, who scooches over so that his bum covers the stain, a little intervention souvenir for Sara's carpet.

"She's right, you need to be much more assertive," Renate adds. She glares at Julia. "And stop with the swearing."

"Okay. Sorry."

"No more wishy-washy emails like this." Sara grabs the email and rips it in half.

"Anna, do you want out of this relationship or not?" Renate reaches for my hand.

"Yes, but I feel bad about leaving him." The finish line of my relationship is just ahead—I can hear the crowd, imagine the relief I'll feel collapsing on the other side. Julia, Renate, and Sara are in the stands cheering, waiting for me to round the corner. Then the agony kicks in—blistered heels, aching calves, wheezing lungs. I never make it because I start listening to my body, listening to Adam. I slow down, start walking, and the finish line disappears. I stay with Adam—Julia, Renate, and Sara go home. Maybe next year.

"Were you happy in this relationship?" Renate massages my palm as she inspects my nails. "Stop chewing your cuticles." With her pregnant belly leaning into me, she gently squeezes my hand as she softly reprimands me, and I remember how maternal she is.

"No, not happy. I do want to end it. It's just that I read his emails and hear his pleas for another chance, and I fucking melt. I feel like we've spent so many years together, I owe it to him."

"You owe him nothing." Julia snaps her compact shut, having applied a coat of raspberry gloss to her lips. Her cheeks are round, the tone and shape of peaches. We always tell her she looks like Jann Arden.

"Don't talk to him on the phone, don't email. Just live on your own for four months while he's away and see how you feel." Renate returns her hands to her belly.

"Okay."

"Can we take a break from this intervention stuff for a while?" Sara interrupts. "I have some wedding things I need to ask you guys about." She spots the cheese smudges on the coffee table and briskly wipes them away with her napkin.

I sit up. "Sure. It's supposed to be a shower anyway." Under any other circumstances I would thump Sara for bringing up her wedding, but today I'm grateful for her obnoxious, self-indulgent interruption. I'd go skipping through a field collecting daffodils for her wedding if she asked me to.

"What's up?" Julia asks.

"We can't decide how to word our invitations," Sara says. "We want to say 'Together with our parents we invite you to attend the wedding of . . . ,' but his intrusive mother wants us to say 'Mr. and Mrs. Jones request the pleasure of . . .' But invitations aren't like that anymore." She brushes a stray strand of blond hair from her face.

Sara has spent fifteen hundred dollars on wedding magazines from which she plucks ideas that we, her bridesmaids, must implement. Every week it's something different: handmade chocolate, dried flowers, embroidered something or other. Being a bridesmaid should be a paid position—I'd be rich by now. For Renate's wedding, being a bridesmaid was an honour.

Perhaps I'm bitter because I was the one with the boyfriend. I had the most promising future as a bride. Something went very wrong and ten years later, instead of picking out shades of taffeta to be worn by my friends at *my* wedding, they are planning my breakup. I have established myself permanently as The Prairie Bridesmaid. And I have the taffeta to prove it. A few friends, a few cousins, and the dresses start to pile up.

"I can't remember how we worded our invites," Renate offers.

Emma starts wailing. Julia leaves and returns with her in her arms. The baby has puked all over her Winnie the Pooh blanket. Julia is not naturally maternal like Renate, but she could be the poster girl for single mothers. She's mastered it.

"Sorry, I'm trying to schedule her. She's not used to it yet." Julia absentmindedly tosses the blanket into the kitchen sink. Sara jumps up and chases after the pukey blanket. She spots David's juice on the carpet and sighs, exasperated. Children and their messes don't fit into her dry-clean only, white carpet world.

"We never scheduled David. We let him eat and sleep whenever he wanted," Renate says.

"That doesn't work if you want to have a life," Julia replies.

I stare at them blankly. I have not the faintest clue what it means to schedule a baby. I can barely follow a schedule myself. I dig my toes into the plush carpet. Last time I was here, I drizzled red wine onto the carpet, which is probably why I've been given white wine tonight. We've all been offered white, I notice.

"Anna, you're not going to bring anyone to the wedding, are you?" Sara turns to me as she scrubs out the juice stain on the carpet. "I've got to get my final head count to the hotel."

"I don't know." I can't believe they would force me to break up with my boyfriend of ten years and then point out that I will be dateless at the wedding. I have nothing to contribute to the discussion of weddings and babies. I pull clumps of mascara from my eyelashes.

"You should start dating. It's the best thing you could do."

"Do bridesmaids need dates? My date would be stuck by himself half the time anyway while I'm fluffing your dress and posing for pictures."

I reach for Emma's yellow stuffed daisy and roll it in my hands.

"Isn't it just a beautiful day?" the toy screams at me. No, I would not characterize this as a particularly beautiful day. "Daisies, daisies, the prettiest flower of all," it sings in a high-pitched tone. Emma starts crying again.

"I'm actually thinking of daisies for my wedding," Sara yells over the toy and the crying baby. The chaos is starting to wear on her. "Oh, Renate, I talked to the seamstress and she said she'll sew your dress with an expandable waist, so your weight won't matter." Sara insists that Renate be in her wedding party not long after giving birth.

"Oh, it'll matter." Renate's usually angular face has filled out and softened, and is always a little flushed. She wears pregnancy the way some women wear cashmere.

"Daisies, daisies, the prettiest flower of all," the toy blares. It's a scary-looking flower.

"Hey, I'm supposed to be the fat bridesmaid in this wedding party," Julia says over the screech of the toy that I can't seem to shut off. She lifts up her shirt, unclips her bra, and attaches Emma onto an enormous breast. Her nipple alone is the size of my entire boob.

Little David wanders over to the stereo, where he starts experimenting with the volume button and deafens us with Celine Dion. "The Power of Love." Perfect intervention music. Renate scoops him up and he launches into a tantrum, his howls competing with the singing daisy and the stereo. I feel around the bottom of my purse for a loose Advil, but at this point any pill will do. The whole scene is chaotic, but in a weird way I wish I were more a part of it.

My girlfriends seem to gravitate toward one another, their breasts filled with milk and life, talking about weddings and the philosophies of child bearing. Renate is already on her second helping of babies. They weave their problems into the fabric of their friendship. I have no threads to offer.

Maybe I prolong my relationship with Adam because it gives me substance and baggage that my friends can rifle through. The intervention was a generous attempt to help get me caught up. I should be married and starting a family, not clinging to a dead relationship, they might as well have said.

Next week I am having lunch with Colleen, a friend from university. She just opened her own consulting firm in Toronto. She doesn't want kids, and she disdains to spend more than a week or two with the same man. *Fuck and get out* is her creed. I make a mental note to seek out a group of friends who are entrenched in unhappy relationships with vacancy signs flashing in their wombs. I'll even offer to host the Christmas party next year.

"So, I've met this guy online," Julia announces.

"What? I thought you didn't want to date?" I ask.

"Oh, for fuck's sake, it's just for sex," Julia huffs back at me.

"Language," Renate sighs, for what feels like the twentieth time.

Sara rolls her eyes. "It's disgusting. Why don't you date someone that you actually want to be with?"

"Because not everyone wants to be a freaking bride and put their friends through bridesmaid hell!"

I'm glad Julia said it instead of me.

Sara's eyes well up. "What? Now you don't want to be part of my wedding?"

I guess coupling the words "bridesmaid" and "hell" together didn't quite spell it out for Sara. I wait, barely able to breathe. Will Julia tell Sara how she feels about this out-of-control wedding? The engagement parties, the showers, the wedding shows, the dress fittings. Will Julia tell her we've all just about had enough, and risk losing Sara's friendship forever? Renate, always the peacekeeper, intervenes. *Damn.* That would have been a good catfight.

"Come on, knock it off. We're all tired. It's been a long night."

"Anyway," Julia emphasizes, "I'm meeting this Internet guy, Phil, at a coffee shop on Tuesday night and I need someone to come just in case he's a freak or something."

"I, for one, didn't know you could have sex in a coffee shop," I mutter.

"I need to meet him, make sure he doesn't pack any weapons. And shut up," Julia blurts before I can get out a penis joke.

I know where this is all going before anyone speaks. I will be the one in the coffee shop, pathetically eavesdropping on Julia's date. I am the only one without a life—or so it would appear from the perspective of my friends.

"I'm up to here with wedding stuff," Sara says.

"Calvin is working nights. I'm not hiring a sitter for that. David!" Renate shouts. We all look at David, who is covertly draining the last of my wine into his mouth.

"Anna, why weren't you watching your drink?" Renate scolds me.

"I didn't realize I had to *watch* my drink." I'm annoyed that David has polished off my fresh glass of wine.

I arrive home to my dark, quiet house. The wooden floors creak as I walk in and lock the door behind me. I'm greeted by the musty smell that my house holds—the blended odours of those who've lived in it over the past hundred years. Sweat, curry, flowers, fresh bread, wet boots—these smells leak from the walls and wrap around me. Sara wrinkles her nose a little every time she walks in, but Mr. Clean could never eradicate the smells. She can't understand why I'd live in such an old, odour-infested house. The smells and colours of Sara's house are crisp, the lines are sharp and clean, while everything about my home—the wood, the walls—are warm and soft and a little sunken. My house honours the lives that have lived in it. I never feel alone at home.

I toss my keys onto the kitchen counter. There is no Adam asking me where I've been all night and no child sucking away my alcohol supply. I take a half-drunk bottle of red wine from the shelf above the fridge and I pour myself a glass, go upstairs to my bedroom, and try on Sara's yellow lace lingerie. I catch my reflection in the full-length mirror on the back of the bedroom door. Yellow doesn't really work with my olive-toned skin. My body is average early-thirties fare—my boobs are holding their own, my tummy is flat but not toned, and my thighs are always a little chunky regardless of how many squats I do. I wear a sweater, jeans, and a pair of boots well. But I don't have the hot, I-must-fit-into-this-wedding-dress body of Sara, nor do I have the soft, I-don't-care-if-my-abs-aren't-hard, look-at-my-beautiful-baby body of Renate or Julia. My body doesn't tell a great story—it just exists and chugs along, like me. I don't feel sexy, especially after I take a sip of wine and dribble it all over the pretty bra. I guess I won't try to return it.

I enjoy the silence of the house.

I pull on my favourite floppy sweater and crawl into bed. Adam made us the bed. He pulled apart a couple of cracked, discarded oak tables and spent weeks in the basement constructing it. He sanded and planed and screwed the beautiful bits of oak together. He was as determined and driven as the nails he used to pound the wood into place. This was his way of showing me that he loved me, pouring his imagination and heart into the construction of a piece of furniture for us.

This bed is where we should have held one another, whispering how much we loved one another. More often, though, it was where we would scream at each other until our heads hurt. The bedroom should have been our place of intimacy, but most of our arguments either started or ended in this cold room. It was in this bed that Adam yelled at me for the first time, and I yelled back. I can't remember what we fought about, but we were both shocked at what we were capable of. We both apologized and had that warm, blurry sex you have after a pissing match. But the arguments became our habit, and instead of a cozy place for sex, the bed became a place of silence. After our spats, the sorrys became fewer and fewer, and instead we would lie back to back, glaring at the ice-blue walls over days of numbing silence.

I curl up and drift off to sleep in this bed that I hate, wondering what Adam is doing.

Not Working Out

When I wake up, my head is throbbing. I roll over and reach my arm across the bed. Empty. Then I remember, and the monkeys start their acrobatics in the pit of my stomach. It's my own version of morning sickness, without the baby. Anxious. Confused. Uncertain. I reach for the package of cigarettes and lighter on the bed stand. I pull out a cigarette, light it, and draw the smoke into my lungs. As I exhale, the smoke obscures a photo of Adam and me on the wall above the bed. Adam is grinning for the camera, his tanned face shadowed by his Tilley hat and his arms wrapped around my waist. I gaze up at Adam through big sunglasses. There are trees and we look happy.

The throbbing creeps out of my skull and into my chest.

Ever since Adam left, mornings are the worst. When I wake up, my brain is not fully operating. All I can remember is that Adam's not here. He has taken a job working at a museum in Germany for six months. I encouraged him to take the offer. My friends think I'm supposed to be happy he's gone because they think it gives me a chance to reflect on the relationship, and, most importantly, a chance to get out of the relationship. Except that so far it's only given me a chance to be lonely and miserable.

I'm about to light another cigarette when I realize it's Monday.

Fuck. When Adam was packing for Germany, he must've accidentally packed my ability to keep track of time and days. I need to get to work. After a shower I feel a little better. I pull my wet brown hair into a ponytail and throw on jeans and a sweater. My eyes look grey instead of their usual green; they are puffy, marked with dark circles. I slather on eyeshadow and cake my lashes with mascara in an attempt to bring myself to life. It doesn't work. I have a few Advils for breakfast and leave for school, late.

I arrive at the high school where I work, and ease my enormous Plymouth Fury into parking spots twenty-one and twenty-two of a lot filled with Hondas, Nissans, and Voyager minivans. Buying a new car is on my to-do list this month. I've had to rent two spots because my 1965 beast can't fit into one. I walk through the cloud of smoke surrounding a group of girls with pierced noses and low-slung pants. Their hips are pressed against the wall as they talk to boys who flip skateboards with their feet. I pull open the doors of the high school and walk in, exhausted, as I am every Monday morning.

The polished floors reflect the numbing glare of fluorescent lights and rows of orange lockers, rubbed clean of graffiti by invisible weekend janitors. Clean slates for another week of sixteen-year-old anarchistic expressions of love, hate, fear, and hope. Blackboards etched with last week's math formulas and poetic devices have been wiped away with wet rags. Clean canvasses for another week of lessons.

I feel like a drugged walrus as I shuffle to my office, sure that nothing extraordinary will happen to jar me from the boredom of teaching. I've lost the ability or desire to create an engaging "learning environment." I can keep students reasonably entertained and occupied for an hour at a time, but it would take an impassioned revolution to revitalize the dull school system.

The moment I realized that the classroom was definitely not

for me was one afternoon when I was teaching a class of tenth-grade repeaters. They were behaving horribly—yelling, banging their binders. Their hands and desks were covered in ink sketches. I stood in front of them, impotent, trying to get them to identify a verb, and then simply begged them to stop shouting and throwing pencils at each other. The mayhem persisted, and I left to get a cup of coffee from the office next door. Out in the hall, the fire alarm caught my attention. Gleaming, it screamed *PULL ME! Pull me and I will pull you from your misery.* And I did. It meant I could get away from them for ten minutes. Later, the principal went on a fishing expedition to find and make an example of the guilty student. It never occurred to him that it might be a teacher.

I've pulled it more than once.

Like many teachers, I sustained myself for a few years with the idea that I was making a difference; not many of us, however, can hold on to this delusion for an entire career. Eventually we let go of the notion that we can make any difference. That's about where I am. A colleague told me not to worry about the faded idealism, that once you abandon all the *Stand and Deliver* crap, everything levels out and teaching becomes like any other job. Go in, fill out the insurance forms, or work the till—or correct a few *Hamlet* papers—and go home.

Students are milling in front of flipped-open locker doors that are plastered with pictures, mirrors, and magazine clippings, little shrines they've created to carve out their identity for all to see. Some are sitting on the floor furiously finishing math assignments, others are laughing. Two students are slurping on each other's lips, a sight I don't need first thing in the morning.

I arrive at my office, a closet-like enclosure that I share with the five other members of my department. My desk is a mess of dirty coffee cups, memos, student assignments, parking tickets, and supplies that I've hoarded from the supply room. To look at my desk, one might think there was a worldwide Post-it note shortage. When I took the job, I promised myself that I would teach for only a few years until I figured out what I really wanted to do. Seven years later, I found myself head of the English Department. School administration seems to put the most ineffective people into management positions to avoid the awful burden of fresh ideas.

Fred occupies the desk next to mine. No one knows how old Fred is, or what goes on in his classroom behind the shut door. I think he's seventy and that not a lot goes on. It would be my responsibility to find out and report anything amiss, but his students have been spotted carrying around Hemingway and Chekhov, muttering about failing, so I assume he's having some effect. I've gotten into the habit of curving his grades up by twenty percent to match the rest of the department's. It's rare for public school teachers to torture themselves by staying in the system for this long, but Fred has two ex-wives to support, even though both left him for other men. When he found out one of his children was the product of one of his second wife's many affairs, he still put him through an electrician program at the community college. Fred rarely shows up for department meetings—although to be fair, I rarely hold them—and he eats a bologna sandwich for lunch every day. Last week, Fred reported his car had been stolen from the school parking lot. It wasn't until lunchtime that he remembered that he'd walked to school that day.

Across from Fred is Ainsley, the English Department sex kitten. She has fiery red hair and may or may not have had a boob job. She moonlights as an aerobics instructor and was written up by the administration for appearing in a swimsuit calendar as Miss May last year—she's always struck me as more of an August. In her defence, it was a charity fundraiser for a local bar. At least she helps with the truancy problem the school has with teenage boys. Plus, male students are always trying to transfer into her classes, so teachers in the rest of the department benefit from having fewer students.

"Really fucking nice, Lasko," Angelo says to me as he comes through the door. Another teacher in my department. His black hair is gelled and slicked straight back. Tiny curls form at the base of his neck like little convicts that have escaped the hair product. He still wears Drakar cologne, left over from the eighties.

"What?"

"I had thirty people at my place Sunday at 9 a.m. Ha fucking ha." He takes off his leather jacket and tosses it on his chair. Angelo occupies the desk across from me. I try to knock him off his Greek god pedestal by regularly complicating his life. I advertised an open house for his place this weekend. Last week Angelo had his students dump the entire school's recycling into my car. I was cleaning paper and cans out of it for days.

"My mom didn't appreciate it, you know. She got all stressed out and her eczema acted up." Angelo still lives with his parents until he can find a wife who will take over his mother's duties.

Angelo's hiding out in the public school system in an attempt to evade the family restaurant business. With his gold chains and leather jacket, he hardly seems like teacher material. I entertain myself by starting school clubs on Angelo's behalf: fashion club, coin and stamp collector's club, noon-hour baking club. Angelo takes his coffee cup and leaves the office.

I toss my briefcase down on my chair, grab a stack of papers, and head for the office photocopier. I take the long route and slip in through the back to avoid the scrutiny of the secretaries, who have developed an inter-office rating system to assess the daily appearance of those teachers who stroll past their desks.

There is the standard Monday morning lineup at the copier of the ill-prepared. The usual suspects—Winfield, the art teacher,

Delores, the librarian, and Soon, from sciences. I wait my turn, listening to everyone's "How I spent my weekend" stories. Soon tells us that she got engaged. That tops my "I got drunk at my intervention" story. Soon straightens her silk blouse and flashes her left hand. Everyone pauses for a perfunctory inspection of the ring. There is something about women and engagement rings that I can't stand—the ostentatious flashing of diamonds that have been mined by one-armed children, the oohing and ahhing. I imagine Soon's hand in the paper shredder. I'm political when it suits my purposes. It's more likely that my anger stems from sheer jealousy. While I might be aware of some of the injustice in the world, I'm still petty.

As soon as it's my turn, the bell rings. I make the copies anyway.

The photocopier spits out duplicates of my handout on metaphors. As I'm collecting them, Harold, a social studies teacher, corners me. I'm only five-foot-six, but I tower over him. His eyeballs bulge as though they are trying to touch the lenses of his glasses and his head is shaved to disguise his baldness. *Do men actually think this works?*

"I've left two notes for you." He gives me a bitter stare.

"I know." I've been avoiding him for a week. When I was seven years old, collecting eggs in my baba's henhouse, I was once cornered by a vicious rooster. It blocked the doorway of the chicken coop and puffed out its blood- and wine-coloured feathers, scratching at the dry, yellow straw beneath him with his wrinkled claws. His glassy eyes flared with anger. I screamed, dropped the eggs I'd just collected from underneath one of his hens, and ran from the coop.

As I look at Harold, all puffed up with his cold stare, I think about screaming, dropping my photocopies, and making a run for it.

"I've asked you several times!"

"But—"

"By the end of the day, Anna." He waves his finger at me.

"Harold, wait—"

"I don't want to hear it. I want my mug back by the end of the day!" *Or what? You'll meet me out in the back parking lot?*

Last week I grabbed what I had mistakenly assumed was one of several orphaned coffee mugs from the staff room counter in my rush to inhale a coffee and piece of toast while racing to class. He saw me flying down the hall with the mug, *his* mug. It's an important souvenir from the Swift Current Social Studies Teachers' Symposium, he claims. I suspect, however, that Harold gets just as attached to his Bic pens.

Before I had a chance to return the mug, I found myself using it as a prop in a heated *Hamlet* lesson when it went flying out of my hands. It slammed onto the floor and shards of ceramic scattered across the room. I've successfully avoided Harold since. Until today.

"Anna, your students are waiting," Keith, my vice principal chides, as he passes. And with that I duck out of the copier room, leaving Harold fuming.

I stride down the quiet, empty halls catching scraps of algebra and cell division lessons that escape through open doors of classes in session. I turn the corner to see twenty students loitering outside the door of my classroom, like tomato plants wilting in the sun. Some are leaning up against the wall, others are stretched out on the floor reading *Catcher in the Rye*, desperately preparing for a test, which, until now, I'd forgotten I'd scheduled.

"You need a late slip," one of my students says.

"I need a coffee. Alyssa, can you run down to the cafeteria and get me a coffee?" I fish into the pocket of my blazer for some change. Nothing. "Tell Mrs. Hyshka to put it on my tab." Alyssa is one of those students who lives to impress her teachers. I take full advantage of her.

I unlock the door and my students file in.

"Do we have to have the *Catcher* test today?" John asks. I pretend to consider it. Most students are quite content when we skip a test; however, there are always half a dozen who have done the reading and are put off by their missed opportunity to earn a hundred percent.

"It's your lucky day, John. The test is postponed till tomorrow." Most of the class is pleased with my announcement, except Anton. Anton is brilliant and has been prepared for this test since the fourth grade. In fact, Anton regularly corrects me when I'm teaching. "Yes, okay, fine, Anton, the book was written in 1951, not 1953." The last of the students filter in, followed by a woman who looks about twenty.

"Hi," she says, as though I should know who she is.

"Hello." No recognition.

"I'm your student teacher. Liz. We met at the start of the semester?"

"Right," I say, vaguely recalling a conversation that took place months ago.

"I'm observing the class this week—"

"And next week you'll begin student teaching." *Aha*. Now I remember her. So far Liz has observed me show up late for class, send a student to buy me coffee, and cancel a scheduled test. Later in the day, since I've already manifested my total lack of professionalism, I could get her to contact the Social Studies Symposium and order a few coffee mugs.

"It's so great to be here," she says. She is perky, has wide innocent eyes, and wears a cardigan. These kids will maul her.

"Sorry we're getting a late start, I had car trouble." I sound like one of my weakest students when they forget an assignment. I don't have a lesson plan for today. Maybe my idea of having a "reading" class isn't so great in light of her presence.

Ted wanders into my room and slides his arm around my waist. My elbow locates his gut. He is the fifty-year-old ogler who teaches biology down the hall. Every morning, Ted comes into my classroom to borrow money and annoy me.

"And which movie will we be watching today?" he asks my class, which sends titters through the room. Ted has the aura of an over-the-hill Casanova but the appearance of a stuffed toy. His head and body are round, he seems stitched together—and plush.

"We're not watching a movie today, although we will be discussing the perverts in *Catcher*." I nod toward Ted. "I don't have any extra cash to lend you," I tell him. Ted's gambling habit usually leaves him broke by Monday morning, unable to pay his bills, buy food, or put gas in his rusted Toyota. Ted spots my student teacher, his eyes widen, and I think I can feel saliva dripping on my shoes.

"Don't," I warn him.

"I'm Ted," he says, taking her hand.

"I'm Liz," she smiles. "Student teacher."

"Charmed."

"Ted, I have a class," I sigh.

"Fine. By the way, great date Saturday night," he calls out to the room. He amuses himself by telling anyone who will listen that we're dating. Ted probably hasn't had a date in fifteen years. Excluding those he pays for. This whole myth about teachers being role models is laughable.

"Gross," one of my students mutters.

Alyssa returns with my coffee. All is well.

"Mrs. Hyshka says you need to pay your tab."

"Thanks, Alyssa. Sorry, that was rude of me, I should have had her get you one," I say to Liz.

She smiles brightly. "Oh, that's okay. I don't drink coffee." Of course she doesn't.

She is already seated, notebook open, taking notes. She could be the new role model, a poster girl for the profession, "Teachers Care" stamped across her perky face.

The Dating Shame

"Try to sit two or three tables away. I'm going to have a coffee with him. If he seems all right we'll set up another date. If it's no good, I'll get up to go to the bathroom. That's the cue that we're done. If we *really* hit it off, maybe I'll invite him back to my place." Julia hands me the car seat containing Emma.

"What do I do with Emma if you take him back to your place?"

"Can't you take her for an hour? I'm sorry, but I'm wearing out my goddamn vibrator."

I find a table in the coffee shop not far from Julia, who redoes her makeup for the third time. I set Emma beside me. She is sleeping, so I pull out a stack of *Grapes of Wrath* essays. I scan the first paragraphs of a few papers—it looks like most of them have done the reading and I'm in for a long night. The papers are moderately more interesting to mark if the students haven't read the book. I hate this advanced class. They are a bunch of future accountants and lawyers always quibbling for marks. I purposefully assign them books I never bothered to read in high school—*Tess of the D'Urbervilles* is on deck.

The door swings open and a tall guy wearing a Winnipeg Blue Bombers sweatshirt and jeans comes into the coffee shop and scans the room several times. The only people without companions are Julia and myself. He looks like he might head over to my table, so I promptly start rocking the baby's car seat beside me. He finally walks toward Julia. He and Julia tentatively shake hands as he sits down. The whole thing looks horribly awkward.

If I break up with Adam, it will be me meeting Internet losers in this coffee shop. The idea of starting to date again depresses me. That's one of the reasons I've convinced myself not to leave him. I could go to the trouble of finding someone, meeting his family, maybe even living with him, and in the end I still might end up with an asshole, an even bigger asshole than Adam. Isn't dating just a sham where everyone lies anyway? In the early years, Adam *was* a normal boyfriend. I guess he was good at lying.

A week after I gave Adam my phone number, I walked up to the guy working the ticket booth at the bar and smoothly said, "We're on the guest list." A guest list sounded important; I didn't know at the time that all that meant was I didn't have to pay the three-dollar cover charge to get into the bar, and that half the people there were on the guest list.

"Names?" he asked, bored.

"Anna, Sara, Renate, and Julia. We're all on there," I said. He stamped the backs of our hands with ink spiders and waved us through the door. The bar was different from the dance clubs with flickering lights and smoke machines where we normally hung out, sloshed, grooving on the dance floor to UB40 or Madonna. It was dark, except for a few neon signs hanging along the brick walls advertising beer, and smelled like cigarettes and stale pizza. There was a stage at the front and pool tables at the back. The place was half full. I liked it. Sara was disgusted and didn't want to touch anything. Renate said she could only stay for a couple of songs because she had to meet her boyfriend, and Julia was already settled in at the bar ordering beers.

We found a table and sat down. A few minutes later the house music faded, lights flared on the stage, and Adam and his band emerged. He wore jeans ripped at the knees and a Bob Marley T-shirt. He picked up his guitar, plucked a few notes, bent down, adjusted some knobs on his amp, and then the band launched into their first tune. Adam's stance was wide, like he owned the bar, and he rocked back and forth, flailing his hands on his guitar. Then he grabbed the microphone and launched into the song, belting it out in his gruff voice. His eyes were closed, his head tilted to one side, and his guitar hung loosely around his torso as he sang. His hair fell down over his face so that only his mouth was visible. I was in love.

By the middle of the set there were people dancing and I was even more in love. I begged my friends to dance. Sara flatly refused, and Renate said she had to call her boyfriend, so Julia and I attempted to bounce and sway to the music that was a little more *rock* than we were used to. Julia was a way better dancer than me—she committed herself to the songs, whereas I felt awkward and had to down my beer in an attempt to loosen up.

"Lugar Vandros, you're awesome!" a girl screamed.

Seeing Adam perform convinced me that he was the guy for me, and soon after I officially became his girlfriend. I attended all of his shows, dragging my friends along. Is it every girl's fantasy to date the singer of a rock band? I'm not sure. It was mine. Twenty-one and in love with a cliché. It was superficial, of course, and the novelty should have worn off after a few weeks. It didn't. Weeks became months, months became a year.

We took an interest in one another's hobbies, except that I didn't have any. This was how, one year into our relationship, I found myself huddled next to a hot fire, sipping tea laced with rum, beside a frozen lake, the last place I had expected to be in the middle of a prairie winter. Winter camping, Adam had called it, when he asked me to go with him. I was skeptical and I should have just told him that I didn't like winter. I'd have rather licked pond scum from the bottom of a canoe than freeze my feet sleeping outside.

Adam had purchased the necessary apparel for me for Christmas: rain gators that attached to my boots, a lamp that attached to my head. I thought I should try using the stuff at least once, so I agreed to go with him. I could already tell that I preferred frolicking around in my bathing suit in the hot sun to shivering in fleece layers by a frozen pond. Adam had all the latest gear. He looked like he had walked off the pages of *Outdoor Living* magazine. I admired that he could take the stage and be a cocky rock star in one moment and, in another, clad in a parka, toque, and mitts, be the Canadian Marlboro Man.

After a two-hour drive I found myself pitching a nylon tent on the edge of a snow-dusted escarpment. *Nylon? Was he kidding me?* The only thing that should be made of nylon is stockings. I could hear the dull gnaw of the saw as Adam ground it into a dead tree. Within a few minutes, he had a fire going, flames jumping out of the snow. I spread the mats and sleeping bags on the floor of the tent and tried to understand the allure of sleeping outside in February. I had hoped a cabin would appear through the trees as we parked the car and that all this bedding-down-in-the-snow business would prove to be a lame joke. There was no cabin. It was cold. Winter in Manitoba is not an Old Navy advertisement with everyone frolicking around in powdery snow, sporting brightly coloured wool mitts and down vests, the temperature a mere few degrees below freezing. Winter in Manitoba is minus twenty-five degrees, with a fierce north wind. Frostbite and hypothermia are nonexistent in those commercials; they are very real on the Prairies.

I planted myself on a rock and leaned into the fire, allowing the boozy steam from my mug to drift up my nose. Tall, stark birch and pine trees scattered around the campsite did little to break the force of the cold wind. Every so often one of these trees would dump a purse of snow from its branches onto my head. *Ha ha.* Even the trees were mocking me.

Adam returned to the campsite carrying a shovel.

"Voilà! Your skating rink awaits you." He jammed the shovel into the snowbank. He'd cleared some snow from the frozen lake, and a large patch of ice was visible. I reluctantly tore my feet from the warmth of my boots and crammed them into my cold leather figure skates while Adam loaded the fire with wood. I felt like a true prairie girl embracing the cold, the snow, and the ice.

We stumbled onto the ice in our skates. I thought I would show Adam my figure-skating moves—those I could remember. I quit skating when I was eight years old after I'd failed my skating test for the third time. After the judges deemed me incompetent to move to the next level—again—my mother signed me up for ballet, where she thought my abilities would be better appreciated. I tried to conjure up a skating move for Adam, but my toe clipped the ice and I fell.

We staggered around the lake, pushing each other around until I slipped again, pulling Adam down on top of me. He kissed me and I kissed him back. He slid his mitten-clad hand under my parka and sweater onto my breast.

"Is this how winter campers make out?" I murmured. He kissed my neck. His lips were cold, his breath warm. He took off his mitts and slid down my pants. Lying on my back in my skates, my bare butt on the ice, was not my idea of foreplay, but we made love anyway. It was cold and uncomfortable, and I was unable to climax. Afterwards, I tried to slide my pants up.

"I can't."

"What?"

My ass was stuck to the ice. Ah, so this is why children are not supposed to stick their tongues on metal poles in the winter and adults are not supposed to fuck on frozen lakes. Adam peeled me off of the ice, leaving chunks of my skin behind. We skated back to the fire and I tried to thaw my frozen flesh by turning my butt to the heat.

"I guess that wasn't such a great idea," Adam said, warming the pot of tea on the fire.

"I'm so cold." It was taking all of my energy just to stay warm. I wanted to go home, but felt obligated to stay. He was trying so hard to get me to like this insane hobby of his.

"Rum to warm up your rump," he said gently as he handed me the tea. Poor compensation for my sex-induced injury.

"Thanks." I watched Adam in his thick fleece mitts as he heated frozen chili in a blackened pot over the fire. He moved smoothly, oblivious to the cold. I didn't like winter camping, but I liked that we were here together and that he knew what to do and how to take care of me. He bent over to ladle the chili into our bowls. I caught sight of the curve of his neck.

"You're a trooper." Adam blew on his spoonful of chili as he looked up at me. "I'm really proud of you."

"Thanks." I felt warmer. We ate quietly under the stars that had started to appear.

"Are you still thinking about moving?" Adam asked.

"Yeah, I'm going to start looking."

"What do you think about moving in together?"

I swallowed hard and coughed. I hadn't expected this question.

At twenty-two, I was still living with my parents and was looking forward to finding my own apartment. Lately I had been suffering from domestic urges: I yearned to hang pictures, buy towels, and clean my own oven. Mom said I was welcome to clean hers anytime.

"It would be cheaper," Adam pressed as he twirled the spoon in his empty bowl. I thought about it as I spooned up the last of my chili. We could get a nicer apartment if we got one together. Adam was still living at home and he believed his family was having a toxic effect on him. Even though he was right about the economics of it, though, I still wanted to live by myself. But I went along with it the way I'd started to go along with everything else. I stopped listening to myself.

We moved in together, soon after returning from our camping trip, into an apartment Adam found downtown. A layer of my skin had been left on that frozen lake, and as the relationship carried on, Adam began to peel away my other layers, stripping me of who I was and moulding me into what he wanted me to be.

If Adam and I were bordering countries, Adam extended his borders to annex me. I learned a new culture and language, a world that included art and music that was, at first, alluring. But relationships between people and countries can only thrive if there is a healthy exchange of cultures and ideas. They learn together and grow together. The conquering of one country or human by another can only lead to resentment and rebellion. In time I would become deeply embroiled in the bloody battles of Adam's colonial country and I would eventually unhappily bear Adam's flag. For now, however, Adam's world was charming and I wanted to be part of it.

"Anna. Anna!" Julia is shouting my name across the coffee shop. "Let's go!" she yells as she stands up. Phil is still at the table, shifting in his seat, face red. I was under the impression he wasn't supposed to know I'm here. The whole place now knows I'm here. Obviously the date didn't go well. "Asshole," Julia mutters under her breath as she pushes her way out of the coffee shop. I stumble behind her, essays shoved under one arm, the car seat bumping into everything as I try to keep pace with Julia, Emma bawling away.

"Big. He said I was a lot *bigger* than he'd expected. Can you believe that? He might as well have just slapped my face," Julia says when we're outside. She is angry, but I can also tell she is on the verge of tears.

"That's obnoxious. Didn't you guys talk about your appearances online?"

"Yeah, I said I was Twiggy's larger, hotter sister. He said he has a thing for meatier women, but there's a little too much meat on me for him."

"Did he mention that he's kind of hair-challenged?" I say.

"Funny, he never got around to that," Julia says.

"Fuck him. This whole Internet dating thing is crap."

"The whole dating thing in general is crap," Julia moans. We walk toward her car. "Hey, speaking of assholes, what's happening with Nat? Same old?"

"No, it gets better." I rifle through my purse, pull out a letter, and hand it to Julia.

Natalia is my sister who moved to the Middle East with her boyfriend eighteen months ago. She doesn't stay in touch with anyone except me, and only as a perfunctory obligation to let us know she's okay. A few months ago she informed me that she'd married her boyfriend, Aki.

When we first met Aki, he'd been just another float in the parade of boyfriends who passed through Nat's life. She brought home all sorts of men—firefighters, business executives, cab drivers. Nat sampled men like they were Spanish tapas. One short-lived boyfriend was older than Dad, which made for an awkward Sunday dinner. Mom was disheartened when Nat broke it off with a pilot only to start dating her yoga instructor. Mom had set her sights on free air travel to Mexico, not tips on how to better stretch her calf muscles. Nat is beautiful in a way that you can't quite put your finger on. Her eyes are green and deep, she has a lanky boyish figure, and her shiny, straight hair looks like it's been soaked in olive oil. She was voted "most likely to marry well" in high school. God, I hope they don't still do those yearbook quips. I'm still bitter because I was voted "most likely to get lost in her own house."

Dad wasn't interested in meeting our boyfriends unless we planned to marry them—the dinners interrupted his Sunday Night Football routine. Nat wasn't deliberately tormenting us, or her boyfriends for that matter—she naively believed she might marry any of the specimens she subjected to our family dinners.

Natalia, as I did, missed the seminar on meeting men who are normal and treat you well. If I could be accused of staying with the same ill-suited man for too long, then she was guilty of recklessly fleeing from one boyfriend to the next. Until Aki.

Nat had brought Aki over to my parents' for Sunday dinner two years ago. She introduced everyone and there was a pleasant exchange of hellos, except on the part of Baba, my grandma, who'd simply grunted.

"Can I get you a beer?" Dad offered.

"No, thank you. I don't drink." Uh oh. Aki and Dad would have little in common. Dad's eyebrows looked like they'd just come in out of a windstorm at the best of times. Now, as he furrowed them, they formed one hairy line across his brow.

"Aki. What an interesting name." Mom passed around some cheese and crackers. She was wearing a little too much perfume, but it went well with her glittery shirt, which she made a few years back during her T-shirt-making phase. Pink lipstick. Red nail polish. She was all decked out to meet her daughter's latest boyfriend. She'd been taking the boyfriends a little more seriously lately because she was in the market for a son-in-law and, more specifically, grandchildren. When she opened the door and saw Aki, she knew immediately that he would not make for an acceptable son-in-law, nor be her ticket to grandkids.

Aki was Caucasian, in his late twenties, with sharp blue eyes. He might have been good-looking except that he'd shaved off all his hair and sported an unruly strawberry-blond goatee. I didn't want to stare, but I think there was even a little tiny braid in his beard. He had a triangle tattooed on the side of his neck. He wore khaki pants and a T-shirt with SOCIETY'S EXILE printed on it in large red letters. He wasn't Nat's usual type. I could tell Mom was flustered—this was the third time she'd stumbled around with the cheese and crackers. She might have been the Kraft rep if she wasn't our mother.

"Scott is his real name, but he changed it," Nat said.

"Oh, but Scott's such a nice name," Mom gasped, clearly hoping she might call him by his given name.

"Yes, that's right, I changed it. My name didn't reflect my beliefs," Aki added. He spoke softly and we all had to cock our heads to hear him, except Baba.

"You need to speak up. I'm going deaf," Baba complained.

Dad smoothed his eyebrows, to little effect, and Mom stuffed a piece of cheese into her mouth. It had never occurred to them that a name should reflect one's beliefs.

I considered *Anna*. My name was lazy, common, simple. It suited my beliefs just fine.

"Aki did his master's thesis in politics of religion." Natalia's voice was as high-pitched and cheery as if she were trying to sell us a set of encyclopedias.

"So, what do you do with a master's in politics of religion?" Dad asked as he cleaned out his ear with a toothpick, the same one he'd been using to spear pieces of cheese.

"I'm taking aspects of various world religions that I think are important and combining them to create a new system of beliefs."

"So, you're making up your own religion?" I asked. Nat's last boyfriend, a male nurse, now seemed more and more appealing. At least I could get my birth control pills for free. We had all started to regard each of Nat's boyfriends as a means to some sort of perk, benefits for having to sit through these painful dinners. I couldn't see how this guy inventing his own religion could better my life.

"Isn't that amazing? Creating a religion is such an ambitious and intelligent thing to do." Nat gazed at Aki lovingly. *I could think of better ways to pass my Saturday afternoons.*

"The larger purpose is to eliminate some of the political strife that exists because of belief systems. You see, many of them have striking similarities when you look past their conflicting agendas." *I sense a conflicting agenda between my family and Nat's boyfriend.*

"We're Catholic," Baba said. "There's nothing wrong with Catholics." She was into her third glass of Manischewitz. She won't drink anything drier than a six on the sweetness scale; this is the sweetest wine we could find for her.

"Well, they've been involved in their fair share of political and social turmoil." Aki's tone was patronizing.

"You mean because of those gays always trying to push their monkey business into the church?" she grumbled. Her pink blouse was covered in cracker crumbs. Baba follows politics, but usually has to invent facts to support her bigoted views.

"Where did you meet?" I interjected because I could see Nat was squirming.

"At a rally at the Legislative building to free political prisoners," Aki replied.

"Nat, I had no idea you attended rallies—or even knew what they were." Natalia is five years younger than I am and most of her excursions until that point had involved nightclubs, the Gap, and salons. I would have been considered the more socially aware of the two of us only because I knew what a blue box was—not that I actually used one.

"Well, I went with Crystal, who had to attend as part of her sociology assignment. I just went to keep her company. Aki was a speaker and Crystal had to interview him. That's how we met." Nat's long dark hair was pulled into two braids, which she tugged as she spoke.

Natalia meets Aki randomly at a rally she normally wouldn't even slow down for in her car. I meet Adam while studying for a degree I'm hardly interested in. Maybe it was sisterly intuition, but I could see Nat's future unfolding. I wish there was some system or equation we could use to make sure we were making the right decisions. Our futures are built on fluky passing moments.

"Dinner," Mom called from the dining room.

We arranged ourselves around the table as Mom emerged from the kitchen carrying a rack of lamb.

"Mom, didn't you get my message this morning?" Natalia gasped. "I left it on the machine." Her eyes were wide with alarm. Unless there was a recent lamb epidemic, I couldn't imagine what the problem could be. Mom always made her traditional lamb for new guests.

"No, I didn't have time to listen to the messages." The truth was Mom still hadn't figured out how to use the answering machine. Sometimes she calls me to check her messages for her.

"We're vegetarians." *God, this is so cliché.*

"Since when are you a vegetarian, Nat?" I asked.

"Since a month ago." I could have sworn she ordered a Reuben when we had lunch last week. Nat shot me a warning glare. So she was only a vegetarian in the presence of Aki.

"We don't eat *any* animal products," Aki practically whispered. *Oh, Jesus.*

"But this is marinated. It doesn't even taste like meat." Mom set the platter directly in front of Aki. She still seemed to believe that once this misunderstanding was cleared up, we'd all be happily gnawing away on lamb.

"Aki follows a raw food diet. Mom, it's all on the message I left." My mother's wide stare was interrupted by rapid, confused blinking. Martha Stewart had not prepared her for the likes of Aki. I was enjoying this.

"It's okay, the salad looks good," Aki said, reaching for the bowl.

"Don't eat. We haven't prayed yet," Baba scolded.

This should be good. The only prayer my family knows is the Lord's Prayer, and not even in English, only in Ukrainian.

"Maybe we should skip it tonight, since we don't all believe in the same thing," Nat interrupted.

"We're not eating until there's a prayer." Baba folded her hands in front of her.

"The food's getting cold," Mom complained.

Baba shut her eyes and started chanting in Ukrainian. *Otche nash, shho jesy na nebesah.* Dad stared at the muted football game on the television, squinting so he could read the score. *Nehaj svjatyt'sja Im'ja Tvoje.* Mom stared at the lamb. *Nehaj pryjde Carstvo Tvoje.* Aki and Nat held hands and smiled at one another. *Nehaj bude volja Tvoja, jak na nebi, tak i na zemli.* I took three gulps of my wine and refilled the glass. We can all find things to believe in.

"What's this raw food diet? What's wrong with cooked food?" Baba said when she finally finished.

"I prefer food in its purest form."

"What's the matter with you? I'm eighty-one and I've been boiling food all my life," she said as she tore into her lamb. It's true. There are few things that Baba wouldn't throw into a pot of boiling water. Boiled sausage. Boiled cabbage. Boiled milk. Boiled chicken feet. I've had the pleasure of eating all of that over the years. She'll often revive something mouldy or well past its expiry date by throwing it into a pot of boiling water.

"Aki, do you follow football?" Dad barely took his eyes off the game.

"No, not really." *Strike two, Dad.*

Mom set a bowl of raw carrots on the table just as Dad slapped the table with the palm of his hand. Touchdown.

"Nat, do you eat cooked food?" I asked.

"Yeah." She spooned mashed potatoes onto her plate. All of my biting comments had gone unnoticed by my sister. Her eyes dripped with admiration for Aki.

"She's working up to the raw food diet," Aki said, smiling sideways at her.

"Are you sure you two won't just have a small piece of lamb? It's so tasty."

"Mom, please, we don't eat meat." Nat set down her fork.

"Natalia, when you're done being a vegetarian, I've got some butchered chickens in the freezer for you." Bits of bread flew out of Baba's mouth as she spoke.

"No chickens next year," Dad said.

"I'll just get a few to butcher."

"No, you won't."

"Yes, I will," Baba insisted. And so began what is known as the Annual Chicken Battle. Dad tries to implement a chicken ban because of Baba's failing eyesight and every year she bribes someone to get her the chicks—usually me. Each year I tell myself I won't do it, but the bribes keep getting better and better. The battle goes well beyond the chickens.

Even though she doesn't drive because of her failing eyesight, every year she insists on renewing her driver's licence. Dad forbids her. I take her to get it anyway. This piece of paper represents her freedom and her identity. Then Dad drains the battery in her 1972 Pontiac.

"Maybe we could talk about the chickens later," I suggested, out of respect for the newly declared vegetarians.

"Who's ready for dessert?" Mom asked, as she brought out a vegan special—chocolate cheesecake. Nat looked at Aki apologetically.

We'd assumed that Aki was one of Natalia's phases. She was drawn to him because he seemed worldly and enlightened. Love or lust prevented her from seeing through his pretensions. She would not be able to live up to his righteous expectations for long. Boyfriends rarely lasted more than three months before she got bored and moved on—most toddlers have longer attention spans than Nat.

But then, at Sunday dinner the following week, Nat told us she had an announcement to make.

"Aki and I are moving," she said. She and Aki were holding hands. "We're going to Iran."

"Where?" Dad asked, still watching the football game.

"Iran," Nat repeated.

"Iran! Why the hell would you move to Iran of all places?" Dad said, finally taking his eyes off the television.

"For one thing, it's an interesting place. We can study culture and religion." Until a few weeks ago, I'd have bet cold hard cash that Nat couldn't point out Iran on a map.

"What about school?" Dad asked. *What about the degree*

I've been paying for? he might as well have said. When Dad agreed to pay for Nat's undergrad degree, he didn't realize she'd keep switching majors and drag it out for six years.

"There's lots of time for that. I want to see the world."

"So you're just going to drop out?" I asked, wishing I'd had the guts to drop out of education back when I was in university.

"For now." Nat's face was getting flushed. "I told you this wouldn't go well," she muttered to Aki.

"But isn't it dangerous?" Mom stirred her tea, the spoon rattling against the edge of her cup.

"Everywhere is dangerous, Mom."

"The East is perceived by Westerners as far more dangerous than it really is," Aki explained, his tone suggesting we were complete idiots for not immediately embracing their plan.

"You watch CNN. That's where you get all of this negative information. Half of it's not even true." Nat chewed on her silver chain.

"What about these guys blowing themselves up? Are they making that up?" Dad pressed.

"Dad, you're so . . . frustrating sometimes. They don't talk about the great things that are happening there. They never do. Western media is so biased."

"What great things are happening there?" I asked. Nat glared at me without answering. As I suspected, Nat could not tell me anything about the country.

"It sounds like you've made up your minds," Mom said. "When are you leaving?" She took a long sip of her tea without taking her eyes off Nat.

"As soon as our visas come through. We've already applied."

"Well, how long are you going for?"

"We don't want to put a time limit on it. We'll try and find work. I'm going to try and get a job teaching English."

"Months? Years?" Dad asked flatly.

"We'll see how it goes. We'll stay longer if we like it," Aki said, resting a hand on Nat's shoulder. At this, Dad did the unthinkable—he shut off the television in the middle of an NFL game. The only other time I can remember him abandoning a football game was when someone had called to say that my grandfather had died.

"I don't think you've even thought this through."

Impulsive decisions had always been part of Natalia's character. She quit horseback riding so she could take up ballet. This year she effortlessly transferred from nursing to sociology. She's slid from high fashion to hippie without batting a mascara-laden eyelash. And now she was leaving with Aki, whom she'd only known for a few weeks, to live in a place where she had never expressed any interest in going.

"We hardly know this fellow," Mom said, after they left. "More importantly, she hardly knows him. Can't you talk some sense into her, Anna? She listens to you."

"She's obviously made up her mind," I said. I would try to talk to her, but I knew by looking at Natalia, and the way she looked at Aki, that I wouldn't be able to change her mind.

"What do you think, Walter?"

"What the hell can we do? She's twenty-four years old. We can't very well tie her up, though I think that's what she needs. And this Aki, there's something not quite right about him." Dad's finger circled the rim of his glass.

"This is awful," Mom said. She chewed hard on the insides of her mouth, but tears still formed in her eyes.

A few days before she left, Natalia came to see me. We'd barely spoken in months since I'd tried to convince her not to go. A gnawing in the soft spot behind my rib cage had not stopped since she had announced she was leaving. I made coffee and we sat in silence on an old sofa I'd inherited from Baba's brother. Nat kept pulling at the loose threads on the sleeve of her brown sweater. Her fitted Gap T-shirts had been replaced with sloppy sweaters.

"I'd lend you some things for your trip if I knew when you were coming home."

"I don't know how long we'll be gone. However long it takes." She was curled up in a ball and looked as though she were cold. Probably the result of eating only raw food.

"However long it takes to what?" I set my cup down a little too aggressively.

"I dunno. Figure things out. Find what we're looking for. I'm leaving in two days, whether you accept it or not."

"I know."

"So, you might as well accept it." She was both defiant and pleading at once.

"Why are you going?"

"Because I want to. It's my choice. Maybe I'm going because I can."

"Nat, if you were doing this on your own, I'd be okay with it. But all of this seems to be driven by Aki."

Nat had always come to me for advice about everything from what she should wear to what she should study. I'd always made a point of allowing her to come to her own decisions. She's smart— other than that lime-green taffeta number she wore to her high school graduation, she usually made the right decision. Sometimes it just took her a few tries to get it right. The five-year age difference had allowed us to spin an intricate bond without being too competitive. This was the first time that Nat had not talked with me about a major decision; it was the first time I felt compelled to tell her that she was making a bad choice. I sensed a tear in our web.

"No it's not. It's me. The Middle East may not have been my idea, but it's what I want to do. Aki is like this vessel through which I'm finding myself," Nat explained.

My heart lurched. I had never heard Nat talk like this before.

"Vessel? What are you talking about? Why can't you be your own fucking vessel?"

"Anna, I thought you would understand. But everything Aki says is starting to make sense."

"What? What is Aki saying?" My voice was harsh and loud.

"That my family would try to prevent us from doing this. This is a side of me that you have never seen, so of course you would reject it." Natalia was usually chipper and easygoing, but now she was sullen and barely lifted her eyes when she spoke.

"Wake up, Nat. How did you think we would respond to you saying you are going halfway around the world, maybe never to return, with a guy you met a few months ago who, as a living, invents and preaches his own religion? It's a TV movie of the week. A bad one." I was yelling. Nat sat and stared at me coldly. "Fine. Go. I hope it all works out for you."

That was the last I saw of my sister. Eighteen months ago.

Mom, against her better judgment, had found out Natalia's flight number and went to the airport "to say goodbye." Instead, she grabbed her and wouldn't let her go until airport security had to tug her away from Nat minutes before her plane was to take off. At least her daughter had had tears in her eyes, Mom said later.

"What!? She's pregnant now?" Julia scans the letter.

"Yeah. This does nothing to help my cause to get her home."

"And she seems totally fine with having this baby," Julia says, still reading the letter. "God, wait till your parents find out!"

"They still haven't gotten over the fact that she married Aki.

How can I possibly tell them that she's knocked up?" I can't see the point, especially since they can't do anything about it and it will only devastate them. I've somehow managed to dig myself into a hole with my parents and it isn't even my life. Part of me wants to bring Natalia home, while the rest of me wants to kill her. I have to believe that eventually she'll come to her senses. But this has just gotten much more difficult and complicated, now that there's a child involved. I have no idea if Nat realizes that.

Fallen Angel

"Lorna will still see you. You'll just have to wait a few minutes," the receptionist tells me. I have just arrived at the therapist's office after work, twenty minutes late with a freshly purchased Starbucks coffee in my hand. After three consecutively missed appointments, I thought I should at least make the effort to appear, seeing that I've already spent three hundred dollars and haven't set foot in the place. I hoped I was sufficiently late that my appointment would be cancelled and they would ask me not to make any more. No such luck. As I take my seat, I glance around the room. It is painted in soothing pastel colours, I suppose, to calm the emotionally volatile people who frequent it. There are magazines cast about the room—all wholesome reading material: *Today's Parent, Psychology Weekly, Canadian Traveller, Vegetarian Times*. Not a *Vogue* in sight. I'm surrounded by apples and I need a bag of chips. I hear the door chime and I slink back in my chair, hoping there won't be stunned mutual recognition. A middle-aged man whom I've never seen before— thank God—rounds the corner and approaches the reception desk.

As I flip through *Today's Parent*, I steal glances at this man, trying to form a profile of the kind of person who requires therapy. Midlife crisis, I decide. He's having an affair with his secretary.

He wants to end it, but it's too passionate. His wife is kind and doting, but dull. The sex is no good.

Another chime. Another cringe, followed by the unfamiliar face of a young girl. Teenage pregnancy, I decide. She's not showing yet, so she's probably only a few weeks along. She doesn't know whether she should tell her Catholic parents. I've barely gotten started on her profile when a woman comes from down the hallway.

"Anna?" she calls. Teenage Pregnancy and Midlife Crisis look at me. Should've used a fake name. I stand up.

"Hi, I'm Lorna," the woman smiles. Lorna wears tan khakis and a pale blue T-shirt. Her mint-green cardigan matches the walls. She leads me down the hall to a room with cheap, floral-print furniture—attempts at comfort. She directs me to a chair as she takes the seat across from me. When I sit down, I am swallowed by the overstuffed cushions. I squirm, but they will not release me. A box of Kleenex sitting on the coffee table conjures up images of people in earlier sessions stifling sobs. Divorcees, widows, addicts, and suicide attempters reached for solace in these flimsy white tissues. Then Lorna extracts one.

"You'll have to forgive me," she apologizes. "I have a cold. How are you?" She doesn't seem to be harbouring any anger about my skipped appointments.

"Good," I reply. *Silence.*

"Why don't you start by telling me why you're here today?" *More silence.*

"I'm feeling pretty good, so I didn't really need to come today. I don't even know why I made the appointment in the first place." *Silence.*

"Okay."

"I mean, when I made the appointment, I thought I needed it, but I don't really think I do anymore." I'm doing a miserable job of explaining my way out of this room. I consider getting up and running out, but this woman seems nice, and I would probably still get charged for the appointment anyway. I sincerely hope that her other clients are better therapy recipients than me.

"Why don't you tell me why you made the initial appointment?" Her voice is patient and kind.

"Um, well, I think that I need to get out of this relationship I'm in. But I don't know. It's hard to explain." Uncomfortable squirming. "You're only hearing my side of it, so it's not really fair. Shouldn't you hear both sides of the story before you make some sort of judgment?"

"I'm not actually going to make any judgments."

"Oh." *Silence.* "How are you going to tell me what to do?"

"I think you'll figure that out on your own." I was under the impression that I was paying her because she has some sort of degree in fucked-up people, and can tell me how to fix my life. *Expensive silence.*

"Why do you, or did you, think that this relationship isn't good for you?" Lorna asks. I decide to divulge only a few details. I don't know Lorna that well.

"Sometimes he gets angry. And he tells me what to do, or who I can hang out with."

"It doesn't sound like a good way to live."

"No. I feel like I don't really have control of my life. He makes all of the decisions. It wasn't always like this. Our relationship for the first four years was completely *normal*, for the most part anyway. There were little things like him getting jealous of time I spent with my friends. But then slowly, things just started to get kind of weird." I twist strands of brown hair around my index finger.

It's hard to explain to someone how you handed someone the power to control your life. I barely understand how this could have happened myself. In the beginning I stood up for the few convictions I had, even though Adam was the much stronger force in our relationship. It was our second Christmas together in our apartment when our ideals first clashed.

"We're not getting a tree." Adam plucked at his guitar without looking up.

"I want a tree," I pleaded. We hadn't bothered with a tree the previous year as we'd escaped to Mexico for cheap margaritas over Christmas, but this year I'd envisioned us decorating our first tree together. I'd had no idea people could be "against Christmas trees."

"It's stupid. Thousands of them end up in the dump."

"Not if I take it to that wood-chipping place in the park after the holidays." Having my very own Christmas tree was one of the highlights I was most looking forward to about living on my own. So far there were a lot of unexpected lowlights—like scrubbing toilets and eating boiled hot dogs. When I was a kid, my dad, Natalia, and I would pile into the red, rusted Ford pickup truck and drive to what I thought was Christmas tree utopia, but was really a bush outside city limits where Dad figured we could cut down a tree without getting caught. I'd plod through knee-deep snow in the woods, stumbling to keep up with my father, while looking at dozens of trees.

"How 'bout this one?" he'd ask.

"No, that one, Dad!" I'd shout, pointing to the tree next to it.

"You think so? Well, all right." Dad would heave the axe repeatedly into the frozen trunk of the tree and tell us children to stand behind him as he gave it a final hoof with the heel of his boot. It would swoosh down onto the snow carpet in front of us. *Timber.*

We'd scrutinize the tree.

"There aren't enough branches," I'd finally announce. We'd carry out this ritual several more times, leaving tree corpses in our wake until Dad's back was sore from all of the chopping.

"We're taking this one. Let's go home."

"But..." I'd always protest. But Dad would already be dragging the tree toward the truck.

Against Adam's wishes I stood in my parka in the tree lot of the Home Depot, trying to pick a beautiful Christmas tree from all the wrapped-up mummies that loomed in the lot. I could barely tell they even had branches, let alone if they were worthy of the ornaments that I'd purchased. I'd spent most of my Christmas decor funds on coordinated red-and-silver decorations, so I had to settle for a cheap tree.

"This one here'll be a nice one," said a husky, bearded man in an orange jacket as he appeared at my side. It was a frigid day and the bristly hair around his mouth was frosted over, and frozen drops of fluid were clinging to his nose. I had difficulty accepting him as my consultant to help fulfill my vision of an elegant Christmas tree, but I considered the scrawny fir he had pointed out.

"How do you know it's nice?" I tried to warm my fingers by thumping them against my hips.

"Well, it's the same kind as that one, a balsam fir," he said, gesturing to a tree that had been unwrapped and propped up in a snow bank. Perhaps he regularly worked in the kitchen cabinet department and had been caught stealing screws and relegated to selling the trees because here he was, trying to tell me that all trees, like cabinet doors, look identical.

"May I have that tree then?"

"Well, no, that's the display tree." I knew that they had to unwrap fifteen trees to find one with beautiful and evenly spaced branches just as we had to cut down a forest of trees to find the ideal one when I was a kid. I knew that my tree would look nothing like the display model, but I didn't feel like arguing with the Home Depot guy, so I took the fir. I was tired from the argument I'd had with Adam about putting a tree up in the first place.

"Ya need a hand getting that out to your car?"

"No thanks." I dragged the crappy tree myself across the parking lot to my car. As I stuffed it into the trunk of the Fury, I heard a snap.

When I arrived home, Adam watched with folded arms as I dragged it up the stairs and into the apartment. I struggled to prop it up in the stand and it teetered as I tightened the screws into the trunk. Adam continued to lean against the wall, staring. His eyes were squinted as though he were willing the tree to topple over. But it remained as upright as Adam's moral stance on Christmas trees.

Adam's rigid beliefs didn't allow for exceptions or compromise. These convictions, along with his passion and rock star persona, are what drew me to him in the first place, but now his uncompromising nature was starting to drive a wedge between us. I understood and respected his philosophy about the environment—he'd been a tree planter when he was twenty. But my philosophy was that I couldn't tolerate the holiday season without a damn Christmas tree. I wanted to celebrate the traditions of my childhood and one of my favourite seasons of the year.

The top of the tree had snapped and hung down like a broken wing. I found a roll of duct tape and wound it around the stem a few times to reattach it. Decorations would conceal it. As the tree warmed up, the branches sprawled out thick and bushy, apart from one bald spot.

I was in the process of stringing garland through the branches when Adam passed through the living room.

"The lights go on first," he muttered. Clearly, his Christmas-tree protest was softening a little. I removed the garland and strung the lights through the branches. Just to annoy Adam, I had bought the kind that play Christmas carols. The tree emitted an off-key electronic rendition of "Joy to the World" whenever one of us walked within four feet of it.

I ate popcorn, sipped wine, and listened to Christmas music as I transformed the frozen mummy tree into my festive vision. Occasionally, Adam would come in, smoke a cigarette, and flip through a magazine. I knew he was watching me because he certainly wasn't interested in a preview of *Chatelaine's* spring trends. Perhaps it vexed him that I was doing something artistic and he could not participate because of his ideals, or maybe he found the whole spectacle hideous. I had forgotten to purchase a decoration for the top of the tree. I would have to go out the next day and find my angel. When I finished, I turned off the living room lights and the music, and watched the tree softly wink at me with its white lights until I fell asleep on the couch.

When I awoke the next morning, I opened my eyes to see that a creature had landed on top of my tree during the night. A gargoyle constructed out of rawhide bones for dogs, silver plastic hair clips, nylon stockings, and wire was perched on top of my beautiful tree. In the daylight, the sparkling ornaments from the previous night were dull, fearful of the creature.

I recognized it. By now Adam had enrolled in the fine arts program at the University of Manitoba, and one of his assignments that year had been to construct an art piece with items purchased from only a dollar store. He'd created this gargoyle, which until now had lived in the depths of the basement—for good reason. Now this creature was on top of my beautiful tree. As if this were not bad enough, Adam had strung lights through its bony frame and lined its pointy wire wings with more lights so that it was illuminated and exalted. Its eyes, two fierce red beads, glared down at me. My elegant tree had been turned into an outpost for one of Satan's disciples. But I would not evict the gargoyle: I didn't want to sabotage Adam's only act of participation in the Christmas tree. I actually thanked him for helping. We carried on as though the tree was meant only to be a perch for Adam's work of art.

With Adam still in school, I was beginning to notice a pattern. Adam never seemed interested in holding a job, only seasonal ones at best. Art and his music were his passions, he explained, and the drudgery of a day job distracted him from these pursuits. I had graduated from education and found a teaching job as Adam had learned the arts of sculpting, drawing, photography, and video. The passions that had initially drawn me to Adam were starting to irritate me, perhaps because I hadn't developed my own interests—other than tree decorating—and I felt obliged to support Adam's creativity. I had, after all, backed his decision to enrol in fine arts when he became depressed about his bleak career prospects.

"Professional artist wanted" rarely appeared in the classifieds. In the beginning, the life of an artist seemed romantic, but now it was getting expensive and clichéd. I probably should have encouraged him to find a job instead of signing up for another degree, which I had to pay for, especially a degree that didn't promise employment. His increasing moodiness was condoned and even encouraged by the Faculty of Fine Arts. Many of his school friends he brought home were either depressed or medicated. Adam was turning into a career student, someone who just keeps getting degrees because he doesn't want to face the real world. Maybe I was jealous. I couldn't do a fine arts degree even if I'd wanted to. Full-time employment wasn't glamorous. And full-time teaching was downright bleak. Adam stayed up late drinking beer and wine, talking Degas with his artist friends. I woke early, drank black coffee, and talked comma splices with sixteen-year-olds.

My girlfriends commented on my weird tree when I had them over for Christmas drinks.

"What's that on top?" Renate asked.

"I like it," Julia offered.

"It's kinda creepy," said Sara.

"Is that made out of those dog toys?" Renate's curiosity had her up on a chair inspecting the creature.

I remembered people complimenting Mom on our tree when they came over for rum eggnog and chocolate-covered cherries when I was a kid. I simply wanted people to tell me that my first Christmas tree was beautiful. The ugly gargoyle, however, stole the show. If art is supposed to provoke discussion, then Adam had sure been successful.

"When are you going to get rid of this tree?" Adam complained when he bumped into the tree two weeks after Christmas.

I should have taken the tree down right after the holidays, but I was so discouraged by the whole Christmas tree experience that I hadn't bothered. At the end of January the ornaments began to slide off the branches and shatter as there were few needles left to prevent them from slipping. After a few bulbs had smashed, I removed the lights and ornaments, the dead branches snapping off with many of the decorations. The gargoyle had long since migrated back to the basement even though I thought it would be more comfortable with this browning symbol of death and decay. The virtually needle-less tree remained in the living room for a few more weeks.

"I told you you shouldn't have gotten a tree," Adam grumbled. "When are you taking it out?"

"You wouldn't have been able to showcase your art thingy without my tree." I refused to acknowledge to him that I knew his creation was supposed to be a gargoyle. In mid-February, I finally dragged the brittle skeleton of the tree back down the stairs and planted it in the snow in front of the apartment block, where it remained until April. When the snow began to melt, the tree finally flopped over on the front lawn. The landscaping company removed it when they were doing spring yardwork. They dragged it to the back lane where it awaited its final journey to the dump. If only the Home Depot guy could have seen it.

That tree *was* us. I hung my hopes and large parts of myself on our relationship the way I hung lights and ornaments on that tree. But we've started to rot away like the tree, and I can't seem to unhook myself from this dead relationship.

How could I explain all this to a woman wearing khakis?

"How did things get weird?" Lorna asks.

"He just started acting differently and making all of the decisions. He always says that he loves me. And since I've put so much time into the relationship, I don't want to throw in the towel. And we renovated this house together. He said that if I just supported him, everything would be okay. And it was."

"But?"

"Supporting him means doing what he says. He gets these anxiety attacks when things don't go his way." It's strange to be talking about Adam and our relationship with a complete—badly dressed—stranger. I feel both relief and betrayal.

I tell Lorna about Adam's attacks and how he blames them on me. Just as easily as Adam convinced me that they were my fault, she explains that they are not. My brain feels like Playdough, which people can mould into whatever shape they want.

"And was he doing anything to help himself?"

"The doctors gave him meds, but he stopped taking them."

"Did they suggest therapy?" *She wants to double dip? Make money off both of us?*

"Yeah, but he would never go to a therapist. No offence."

"And so he wouldn't do anything to help himself, but he wanted you to make him better." Lorna extracts another tissue and blows her nose.

"I guess."

"It seems as though you are bearing a lot of the responsibility for his behaviour, and Adam is using this to control you." *This Lorna is smart. Why couldn't I have come up with that?*

"But I'm not a weak woman."

"No, I know that just by listening to you, but he has developed the ability to make you feel that way. Sometimes we just play the roles we've been assigned," she says.

"That's exactly it. It's easier."

"We'll delve into this more next time." Her tone has shifted, and she is suddenly less patient and more pressed. She closes the manila folder with my name on it.

What? We couldn't end the session. I was just getting started.

"Why don't you make an appointment for next week?" Lorna suggests. *Next week? What about now? I have time.* Lorna rises, a clear physical indication that she wants me out. And just like that, I'm evicted from my first therapy session. Therapy is like a good soap opera that leaves you hanging in the last few minutes so you have to come back for more. Even if deep down you know how it's all going to turn out.

Homesick

I come home from my session to find Buddy hanging around the yard, chasing invisible prey up and down trees and scratching the bark with his claws. His bony frame is covered in scraggly fur. I know he is waiting for me to feed him.

Buddy is the squirrel that Adam trained, named, and befriended. We could be running late for the movies, but Adam would still be on his knees, coaxing a wild, skittish Buddy toward him. I would shift impatiently, waiting, staring at Adam as he satisfied his need to conquer the neighbourhood wildlife.

"Buddy, what kind of name is that?" I scoffed, somewhat jealous of the attention that Buddy got from Adam. But when Adam moved to Germany, Buddy moved in. He's literally moved in. At first he just lived in the attic, but now he pretty much has the run of the house. I always wanted a golden retriever. Instead I have a pet squirrel.

When I walk through the gate, Buddy sees me and attaches himself to my shadow as I walk up the path to my house.

"Where you been?" he asks.

"None of your business," I reply as I climb the front steps and unlock the door to go inside. "Wait here." He would follow me inside if I didn't pull the door shut behind me. I've drawn the line at letting him have use of the front entrance. I return a few minutes later, changed into old jeans and a hoodie, with a glass of wine and a pack of cigarettes in one hand and a bag of mixed nuts in the other. I grab a few envelopes and a small package from the front mailbox.

"It's about time," Buddy complains as he sits up, preparing for his feast. Sometimes I feed him the nuts individually, and he presses his claws into my flesh while manipulating the nut out of the shell and into his tiny mouth.

Today I absentmindedly dump a pile of nuts in front of him and flip through the mail.

The package is from the Home Shopping Network and is addressed to Mom. She now has her Amazing Peelers and Super Stain Removers sent to my house, so that Dad won't find out about her shopping addiction.

There's a postcard from Germany. Upon graduating from fine arts, one of Adam's professors showed him a letter he'd received from a colleague in Berlin. There was a wealthy German constructing a museum and he was hiring fine arts students to help with its development and design. I practically filled out the application for Adam as he waffled back and forth, trying to decide if he should go. "It's only for six months. Of course you should go," I pleaded with him.

"Who's it from?" Buddy sees the postcard.

"Adam." I remove a cigarette and light it. Whenever I have to deal with Adam, I indulge in a cigarette. I've almost kicked the habit, like I have almost kicked Adam. But not quite. Lately I've been smoking a lot.

"Well, let's hear it."

"It's kind of personal."

"I'll just read it later anyway."

"*Anna, please don't throw away everything we have together.*

You can't do this to me. I'm different now. Everything will be okay. I promise. I love you. Please wait for me. Love, Adam." It's from the torture museum in Rottenberg. There is a picture of an iron maiden. *How appropriate.*

"Hmm," Buddy mumbles through a mouthful of nuts. I take three long swigs of my wine in an attempt to suppress the tears I can feel forming. I hate crying in front of Buddy. He thinks I'm weak enough without the tears. He stops eating, and we sit silently on the steps for a few moments.

"I'm thinking of moving." I know this news will not go over well with Buddy.

"You can't do that," he says.

"This isn't about you," I respond. "I don't think I can live here anymore."

"Stop being so dramatic." He devours his nuts. I inhale my cigarette.

"I'm not being dramatic. I find it difficult to continue living in this house. I have too many attachments to it and I can't leave Adam while I'm still living here."

"So you have a few memories. Big deal. Move on. Can you get the plain peanuts next time?"

"It's much more complicated than just memories, not that I expect you to understand," I reply. "His fingerprints are on absolutely everything—the wires, the pipes and paint, the fixtures. It's like I'm trying to dump him, but still hang on to *our* dream. It doesn't work." I stub my cigarette out on the paved step and flick it into the struggling rose bush. It lands on top of several others.

"His fingerprints are all over you," Buddy says. I stare at Buddy, who has momentarily stopped stuffing nuts into his mouth. "You can sell the house, but it won't help. You need to wipe his fingerprints off you. You're filthy. You reek of him. Why don't you just stand by your decision to leave him and get his stuff out of here rather than running away?" He finishes his last few nuts. "Got any more?"

"No, you'll make yourself sick again."

Adam and I decided to buy a house in Osborne Village that we could fix up together. I was tired of handing rent money over to the grumpy landlord with the sagging pants who lived below us in our apartment block. I was tired of the university students who lived next door, shouting obscenities at the television all night. I was tired of hauling bags of dirty clothes past the Corydon Avenue cafés to the laundromat down the street. My bank account actually had a surplus some months, and seeing as I seemed to stumble through life making decisions because they were logical or obvious, buying a house appeared to be the right thing to do.

I wanted an old house with a porch where I could sip wine in the shade of lofty elm trees. Adam was a revisionist—he wanted a battered house that he could shape into *his* uncompromised idea of perfection.

We were both interested in aesthetics; Adam's interest was naturally fostered by his degree in fine arts while mine was more superficially inspired by a degree in reading architecture and interior design magazines. As we embraced the search for our home, I also happily embraced all the clichés. *Home is where the heart is. Home is the most enduring of all earthly establishments. There is no place like home.* I convinced myself heartily that a home was all we needed to be happy.

The process of finding home sweet home was much like embarking on an addictive and all-consuming science experiment. Not only were other people's homes placed under a microscope for scrutiny, so were their lives. House shopping offered us a rare, if brief, glimpse into the lives of complete strangers. Our world didn't seem so abnormal.

A woman at a two-storey house on Mulvey Avenue waved us in as she barked at someone over the telephone.

"I'll be right with you," she said, holding her hand over the receiver.

"Can I show them my playroom, Mommy?" an eight-year-old boy asked.

"Fine, Michael. I'm on the phone," she snapped at him and turned to smile at us.

I expected Michael to lead us upstairs into a bright room with balloons painted on the walls and toys strewn on the floor. Instead, he led us down the stairs into a dank, grey cement basement. The boy's toys occupied one corner near one of only two small well windows.

"Wanna see something?" he asked excitedly. I anticipated a game or a trick, but instead he led us to another part of the basement where he lifted up a rug to reveal a monstrous crack in the foundation. He was obviously playing show-and-tell with all the house's flaws. He had taken enough people through his home that he knew how to evoke a response from his audience and maintain their attention, although that sabotaged his own chances of moving into another home. He needed attention even more than he needed a new playroom.

During a tour of another home, we stumbled upon a group of high school kids getting stoned, and in another house we saw two ferrets copulating. We met real estate agents so frantic to make a sale that we contemplated purchasing one just to end their desperation. I empathized with some of them after scrutinizing what they were expected to sell. We looked at derelict houses and seemingly perfect houses with cracks and flaws that couldn't be completely camouflaged. They were manifestations of the not-quite-perfect lives of the occupants of those houses. We looked at dream homes with stained-glass windows on Grosvenor Avenue, wondering how people could sell something so beautiful. Flawless houses that were within our budget were still, somehow, someone else's version of perfection. We needed to fulfill our own vision of a perfect home.

We finally went to see a solid, chunky house encased in faded blue siding on Gertrude Avenue, a wide road that abutted Osborne Street. The little shops of Osborne Village offered all the amenities that we would need—wine, bread, and coffee. It was a colourful neighbourhood shunned by the waves of people moving to suburbia. Some of the homes had already been adopted and refurbished, while other shabby houses like the one we were looking at pleaded to be transformed.

We wandered in.

The yellowed walls were saturated with nicotine and the bathroom carpet with urine. Yellow grime had scabbed over the windows, and the white enamel sinks had become grey; layers and layers of brown-crusted splashes in and around the toilet were accompanied by a sour odour. If it were not for the elements, the stove would have barely been recognizable beneath the caked grease. The woman who had lived here had been deemed unable to care for herself and committed to a home. Two weeks later she wandered into the river and drowned.

"We can't get this house. It's a fucking dump," I said.

"That's just the surface. Look at all the potential." Adam slid his hands along the surface of the bumpy walls as though he were looking for hidden treasure. This was classic Adam. He could transform anything with his vision. Vision and conviction were the qualities that I admired most in Adam—until he began to apply these principles to every aspect of his life, including me.

Adam pointed out the less visible treasures of the house.

Beneath the carpet, the dusty floors were original oak; beneath the strata of lead paint the woodwork was original turn-of-the-century. Under the grey grime, the pedestal sinks and clawed tubs were beautiful and from another time; under the glossy, chipped paint there were glimpses of a splendid carved banister.

We walked through the living room and into the kitchen. Wooden steps from the kitchen led up to a little loft that Adam immediately identified as our bedroom.

"This house could be amazing," Adam said, looking up at the bevelled ceiling.

By the end of the week, he had me convinced, and I took out a mortgage and bought the house. He would commit vision and manual labour to the house, while my contribution would be mostly financial. We spread a blanket out on the floor and split a six-pack of Budweiser. I had imagined champagne, but somehow the house didn't seem worthy of champagne—yet.

We tore the place apart, ripping down walls, making new rooms, and taking out windows—some accidentally. Since I was devoid of any carpentry skills and my painting prowess wasn't needed until there were actual walls to paint, I was mostly in charge of grunt labour. I carried endless boxes of laths and plaster down the stairs and returned with armloads of drywall and lumber. I filled fifty-nine bags with the peat moss insulation I removed from the attic, excavating families of deceased squir-rels—Buddy's ancestors. I was convinced that the fumes I inhaled while attacking the layers of lead paint with a heat gun and chemicals would dull my ability to think.

At first it was exciting and fun, but as the months wore on and the money wore out, there was little improvement to the toxic dump; in fact, it looked worse. I reached my threshold. One day I sat down in the middle of the floor and threw the full-blown tantrum of a four-year-old.

"I can't do this anymore. I hate this fucking house. I hate these floors and these windows. When will it end?" I raged and cried, while the workers we'd hired to do the wiring stepped around me gingerly and carried on. I threw scraps of wood that surrounded me at the walls to reinforce my point.

Eventually, a year later, the house began to look beautiful— glossy wood floors emerged, the walls became smooth, and rich oak framed the doors and windows. But for two years it had absorbed every bit of energy and every spare moment we had. I became increasingly disenchanted with the endless renovations, but that only fuelled Adam's tireless determination to create the perfect home.

"You're a quitter. Why don't you want to do this?"

"Because it's not fun anymore. We bought this place two years ago and we still can't live normally. You are possessed by renovations."

"You have no patience." He kicked a sheet of drywall, which snapped in half.

"I had two years of patience and it's officially run out." I was bored with the dream. It was like a playground that I'd long out-grown, but was still forced to play in every day. I would spin around and around on a merry-go-round that had once enchanted me until I needed to throw up. Then I was forced to get back on.

As beauty was restored to the house, our relationship began to deteriorate. It became as stained and ugly as the toilet had been when we first bought the house. We scraped at one another the way we scraped at the walls.

Our relationship needed renovation, but somehow, as diffi-cult as it was to repair the house, it was easier than repairing the relationship. This time the Home Depot could offer no help. We were wood and stone, mortared together by a crumbling dream.

Now that I am considering putting my house on the market, I wonder, when people come to inspect it, will they see the traces of what once was, the cracks in the surface, the cracks in *my* surface? Or will they ask themselves, "Why would these people sell this beautiful house?" If nothing else, at least I'm discovering the answer to that question. Nothing is ever permanent. The home cannot be constructed externally. It makes more sense to pour the home into oneself rather than oneself into the home. Who needs a state-of-the-art kitchen with stainless-steel appliances when all you really need is a can opener?

"This house keeps me tethered to Adam," I tell Buddy, who is busy cleaning his tail.

"House and home are not the same thing. You need to make this house your home. It's never really been yours." Buddy's right. But that's why I need to sell it. It would force me to figure out what I really want, rather than trying to paint over past mistakes. This is something I could pay Lorna another hundred bucks to talk about.

A long white truck crawls up the street and stops in front of my next-door neighbour's house. Two men in navy uniforms emerge from the truck and knock on the front door. Within a few minutes furniture, appliances, and boxes are being carried out the front door.

"God, even they're moving!" I say.

"Good riddance," Buddy mutters.

"Why?"

"I used to live there until they moved in and sealed up all my holes. That's why I had to move in here."

The couple who live there have been my neighbours for six years. There is no "For Sale" sign displayed on the groomed lawn. I feel betrayed. They can't just leave. Shouldn't they let me know first? I suppose they weren't really obligated to discuss their plans with me since we've never exchanged more than the obligatory "hello." They moved in and immediately began fervent renovations on the house just as we had finished ours. Gertrude is a street of renovated dreams.

You poor souls, I thought to myself at the time, *do you have any idea what you're getting into?* My chaotic relationship with Adam prevented me from meeting my new neighbours. I was positive that some of our verbal blowouts were audible to most of the neighbourhood, and I never wanted to say, "No, we can't come over for a drink because we haven't actually spoken to each other in three days. But maybe another time."

As they worked on their house, I felt drawn to them, watching them altering rooms, replacing windows, and painting walls. I heard banging and pounding regularly. The sounds ripped into me, aggravating my wounds, tearing scabs, exposing fresh sores.

I was also treated to the occasional flash of nude flesh passing by an unveiled window. They both had nice asses. While rinsing the dishes, I'd catch a glimpse of a tender embrace; meanwhile, another night, their dinner might be interrupted by the slam of our front door. These things connected me to my neighbours, even if we didn't speak. The home is intensely private. Within our home, we feel protected from the outside world by soothing walls. Neighbours, by sheer physical proximity, occasionally pierce these barriers of privacy. Even though we have never spoken, I know my neighbours.

The movers are hurrying back and forth with armloads of boxes. I become obsessed with finding out why they are leaving. I'm paranoid. I know I could mow the grass a little more regularly, but it never grows beyond a foot and this is hardly reason for them to move. Had they planned to renovate and resell for profit all along? No, he seemed too meticulous when I saw him attaching an awning or fixing the porch. They seemed to care too deeply about every detail to be sloppy profit mongers.

As the truck swallows tables, sofas, lamps, and mysterious boxes, my curiosity becomes unstoppable. I walk past their house to the store to purchase a coffee, a newspaper, a muffin, a juice— all separate trips, of course, fabricated in order to uncover this mystery. The movers become suspicious of me and begin to keep an eye on items on the sidewalk.

I realize that I haven't seen his wife in months. Not only that, but he's stopped his incessant renovations. They must be separating or divorcing. They too had adopted that whole bullshit dream-home philosophy, but the relationship must have disintegrated, leaving nothing but a beautiful empty house and two aching hearts. Broken dreams.

I can't take it anymore. I need to prove my theory before they are gone forever. I traipse over and find Mr. Fix-it in the garage. He is on a ladder pulling items down from the rafters. He does have a nice ass.

"Hello," I say, as I realize I don't even know his name. I jam my hands in my pockets.

"Hi there," he replies. His jeans are smeared with dust and dirt and his blue T-shirt sticks to his damp chest.

"So, you guys are moving?" I try to sound casual. He is obviously busy and doesn't need me around stating the obvious.

"Yeah."

"I didn't realize your house was even up for sale."

"We sold it to friends." He tells me the price, in case I was curious.

"Were you planning to sell it all along?"

"No, my wife got a job at the University of Waterloo, so we have to move." It turns out she is a professor and left two months earlier to start her new job. He works for a bank. I'm jealous of their happy ending.

"I don't have a job yet, so I stayed back to tie up loose ends."

"And pack?"

"Yeah," he smiles. Mr. Fix-it obliges my request to peek inside the almost-empty house, as my only previous glimpses have been with my face plastered to my window. He gives me a quick tour and proudly shows me some of his handyman prowess. I express my condolences about having to abandon such beautiful handiwork. I realize now, looking at him, how Adam must feel leaving our carefully crafted home. *Anna, please don't throw away everything we have together. You can't do this to me.* Adam's words echo in my head. I stand helplessly, my hands still stuffed into the pockets of my hoodie, sad for Mr. Fix-it and sad for Adam. They are watching their homes drift away. Mr. Fix-it, however, is willing to let it all go because he grasps what is important in life. I'm relieved that he'll soon be reunited with his wife. Like most people, they have put their love and determination to remain together ahead of their home. Adam and I compromised our relationship in pursuit of a vain dream—our house.

Not getting to know Mr. Fix-it and the professor was a missed opportunity. Adam always scoffed at the idea that geographical location should dictate friendships, but perhaps we might have learned something.

"Ian Jones, by the way," he says, extending his hand. I shake it.

"Anna Lasko. I had no idea we were trying to keep up with the Joneses this whole time." Awkward laughter.

I walk back home, resolved that I'll get to know my new neighbours, those who end up sharing our fence. I go down to the basement and rummage through my own boxes until I find the box marked "kitchen stuff." I tear it open and dig through it until

I extract a bread pan, another one of my grandmother's donations I thought I would never use. I'll bake banana bread for my new neighbours when they move in.

Shotgun Family

I turn onto the long gravel road that leads to Baba's farm. One side of the driveway is lined with stately elms that sprawl upwards. Their branches, with newly sprouted leaf buds, linger in the air as though waiting for a ride to take them back to the urban upper-class neighbourhood where they belong.

On the other side of the driveway, the trees have been infected with Dutch elm disease, leaving the leafless branches cracked and brittle. Baba refuses to treat the trees; she doesn't want to interfere with "God's work." In a few years, the disease will spread and all the trees will die. But at least Baba won't have interfered.

I try to visit Baba most weekends. She's eighty-three years old and refuses to leave her farm to move into a retirement home. "So I can sit and watch some old fart drooling and shitting himself? No thanks," she says.

As I park the car, I notice a flaccid, black-and-white lump on the doorstep.

"It's okay, she's dead." Baba strides toward me, her speed defying her stooped, aged frame. Her voice is husky and raw, like she's been calling bingo without a microphone her whole life. She has a rusty spade in one hand and the leash of Butch, her dog, in the other. Seventy years of baling hay, butchering pigs and

95

chickens, fetching and milking cows, shovelling grain, and digging potatoes have left her with tough, gnarled muscles that wrap around her brittle bones. Her friends are having hip replacements while she continues to saw and prune trees taller than her house.

Butch tugs her in the direction of the doorstep.

"Siddown, Butch," she yells at the dog. "She wants to go and eat her."

"Her?" I glance in the direction of the carcass.

"I was having breakfast this morning and when I looked out the window, I saw her right there on the step, eating out of Butch's dish," she explains. "I don't buy dog food so the goddamn skunks can eat it."

"You killed it?"

"I got out the twenty-two, opened the door a little, pointed the gun through the crack, and shot her square in the head. She hardly bled." She thrusts the spade into the ground. Dad has asked Baba not to use the gun after she blew out two of the windows in the barn shooting magpies, but Baba, like a vigilant gatekeeper, must protect her farm against scavenging animals.

She ties Butch to the door of the white wooden milk house, walks to the doorstep, scoops up the skunk carcass with the shovel, and disappears around the corner of the house. I hoist the econo-size bag of dog food she'd asked me to buy out of the trunk and lean it against the milk house. I rub Butch's thick brown fur as she sniffs at the bag.

Butch is unaccustomed to wearing her leash, a frayed rope that's been tied around her neck. Baba has had many dogs over the years, all of which ultimately fall victim to the teeth of combines, the wheels of cars, or the occasional box of ill-placed rat poison. She refuses to name the dogs anything other than Butch or Toby. When she speaks of a past dog, nobody knows which Toby or Butch she is talking about. She has had this Butch for an unprecedented six years—she got her after the last Toby fell into a well someone forgot to cover.

I slip into the world of the farm as though it were a comfy, old black rubber boot. The yard is wet and brown with smudges of green. Most people hate spring in Winnipeg. The streets are brimming with grey-brown salty slush that eats away at expensive shoes and renders all cars—beaters and Volvos alike—equal by coating them in muck. People awkwardly navigate puddles and clogged sewers, performing a ritualistic spring dance. Little boys construct boats out of paper and plastic straws and race them along these temporary canals. Basements flood; a sump pump is prized.

Spring is glorious on the farm. Patches of black field show through the snow, crows are muted by the sounds of other birds. Blue occasionally flashes in the thick grey sky. A playful teasing of things to come can be found on a spring trek around the farmyard. I'll take a romp later if I can convince Baba to part with her rubber boots for half an hour.

I go inside and make coffee. Baba comes into the kitchen as I am setting out the filled mugs on the table. We have been drinking instant coffee out of the same mugs for twenty years. My addiction to coffee and my predilection for soap operas can be directly linked to Baba—I was introduced to both at the age of ten. We would sit on the couch in the living room, sipping our coffee, watching the beautiful people having affairs with one another's spouses. Baba would often yell at the TV, calling them stupid, while telling me to cover my eyes.

"She didn't even bleed," Baba repeats as she sits down, reaching for the obituaries section of the paper. She wears her torn brown plaid shirt and her blue polyester pants. "Oh, Mary

Potovich died," she says. She is conducting roll call, a summary of the deaths and ailments of all her friends.

"Who's that?"

"You know who that is," she says, annoyed. "They used to live on Smith's farm when we first came to Manitoba. They moved to the city years ago." She digs out some mud caked beneath her nails.

"Oh, them," I say, feigning recognition.

"I heard Mrs. Bailey is getting an eye operation. I've been waiting months for that operation. How does she get ahead of me? I need another doctor." Talking with Baba is like playing pinball—she pings from one topic to the next.

Her head bends slightly forward to meet the cup as she sips her coffee. Her hair is a frizzy mixture of brown, grey, and blond. I take her to have her hair cut, curled, and coloured every year before Christmas. By spring her hair is back to its usual mix. Baba refuses to pay to have it done more than once a year.

"Eye surgery won't help you. The doctor told us that last time. Remember?"

Baba's world is becoming murky. The doctor confirmed last year that an eye disease will leave her blind within a few years. But her spirit and body refuse to deteriorate at the same rate. Blindness looms, threatening to take her away from the farm where she has been happily planting carrots for over fifty years. Dad sold all of her animals, except Butch, when she was first diagnosed, so her ark is devoid of life.

"Lena hates the home she moved to—food's terrible. Wishes she hadn't left her house. I'm telling you, I'm not leaving this farm until I can't see a goddamn thing." She closes the obituaries.

My grandfather died twenty-five years ago, and Baba has been on the farm by herself ever since. Some of her friends tell me she has grown belligerent from being alone for too long. She'd tell them to go to hell if she knew. She's pleasant enough with me, but then again, I'm not trying to sell her anything or bilk her out of her money. My close relationship with Baba, and I suppose my tolerance of her, has a lot to do with my fascination with the past. Baba is like a relic left over from another life; she really doesn't fit into the world anymore. I love that. Her words, ideas, belongings—everything is from fifty years ago. When I'm with her, here on the farm, the tightness in my chest eases.

"You want to make *perohy*?" she asks, already pulling flour out of her cupboard. *Perohy* are the Ukrainian perogies that I've been making and eating for as long as I can remember.

"Sure."

"What's new with you? Have you heard from your sister?"

"No."

Natalia hasn't written much lately because she needs to remain focused on her present life and can't be distracted by home-sickness, she says—or Aki says. Aki took her away from us and all that remains is the meaty, bleeding hole in our hearts. Part of me is confused, part is angry, and another part is jealous. Even if her decisions are screwy, at least she had the guts to get off her ass and do something with her life. I just sit in Winnipeg, spinning my wheels. At least when you leap after something, regardless how stupid it is, there's the rush.

"I'd like to know what Natalia's doing," Baba says as she mixes the *perohy* dough.

"We all would."

"I worry and it gets my nerves all worked up. Doesn't she know I'm going to die soon?" *Here we go.*

"You're not dying."

"I'm going to die and she won't be at my funeral." At the

rate Baba is going, no one will be at her funeral because she will have outlived everyone. She talks a lot about her funeral, like a six-year-old might talk about an upcoming birthday party. It's an important event for her. I've tried endlessly to point out to her that she won't be around for it, so it's really not worth looking forward to it. She says that I'm missing the point. When you reach your eighties there just aren't that many things to look forward to anymore and this happens to be one of them. Dying just has to be one of the highlights of life.

Baba punches into the *perohy* dough with her crooked fingers. Her skin is tough and loose except where it stretches over her swollen knuckles. She picks up the ball of dough and stretches it out and slaps it back down on the counter, sending a spray of flour into the air. Her rough brown hands slide over the smooth, pale yellow surface of the dough.

"My hands are numb. I can't feel the texture," she complains.

"Looks good to me," I say, although I couldn't tell the difference between Playdough and *perohy* dough.

"Come feel it," she says. My hand sinks into the soft, sticky lump. The dough is soothing as it folds around my fingers and I leave my hand immersed in its softness. I would climb inside of this ball of dough if I could.

"Well?" she grunts.

"It's soft," I reply, pulling my hand out of the dough.

"Good. Roll it out," she says, handing me a wooden rolling pin. "I can't understand your sister. We came here so our grandchildren would have a better life. I left Ukraine when I was twenty-one. I had just married your *Gido* when I was seventeen and we lived with his family for four years. I wanted a fresh start without the in-laws so we left for Canada. When I kissed my mother goodbye, I knew I wasn't going to see her ever again. And

I didn't. Canada was far. Another world. There was no future for us in Ukraine, everybody was so poor, starving. We left so our children wouldn't have to leave their families. I can't understand why Natalia would go halfway around the world when we came all the way here so she would be safe and happy."

"I guess she had her reasons for leaving." I roll the dough into a huge pancake.

"We work so hard. And for what? Do you think she'll come home? The dough needs to be thinner."

"I don't know." I keep rolling.

Maybe Natalia is following in Baba's footsteps, trying to find her own new beginning. Baba's dream was for herself, and she just assumed that her family would carry on the same dream. We're all editing and revising those dreams that have been handed to us by our parents and grandparents and making them our own.

"Butch dug a big hole under the house today. Someone's going to die," Baba says. She has a system for predicting the future. Weather. Births. Deaths. The death of her sister was foretold by Butch digging a hole beside the barn. Sometimes she's right. She predicted the flood of '97 based on the grazing patterns of her cows.

We spend the afternoon trapping blobs of potato between the seams of the dough and then dropping them into a pot of scalding water.

"What about Adam? You hear from him?"

"Once in a while. He's fine, I guess."

"Is he still your boyfriend?"

"I dunno."

"I like him." Adam was earthy and not afraid to get dirty when he came to the farm. He dug potatoes and helped Dad haul grain. He was the closest I had ever gotten to a farm boy.

"I don't think he's my boyfriend. I miss him, but we weren't very good together, you know."

"Relationships take work. Life with your *Gido* sure wasn't easy. I hung on because he's all I had. It certainly didn't help when his parents showed up from the Old Country to live with us. And his mother practically took over the farm, ordering everyone around. And on top of it all, we had to work to pay off their debt as well as our own. To think I came here to get away from them and then they followed us. The buggers."

"How long did they live with you?" I dropped the last *perohy* into the pot.

"Until they died. And your *Gido* died before his own mother." I remember another woman living on the farm with Baba when I was a kid. She had no teeth, only quivering pursed lips. She had only a few thin strands of hair left on her head, and always wore a babushka tied loosely under her chin. Nat and I would always try to make it fall off so we could see her bald head. We called her Little Baba. I couldn't imagine that slight woman, who barely spoke, ordering Baba around.

"There were times when I just wanted to up and leave this place. Or at least crack her over the head with a canning pot."

"Do you wish it had been different?"

"Sometimes I wonder. I think life might have been easier. We had to work so goddamn hard for everything. Farm life."

Baba is the human embodiment of the Prairies. I almost expect she'd bleed cow's milk if cut. Once she left the Prairies to visit her cousin in British Columbia. She couldn't stand the mountains, not being able to look around and see the sky everywhere. It was like suffocating, she said. She needed to be home and look out her window where the fields stretched endlessly toward the horizon.

I can't imagine Baba anywhere but on her farm.

"What do you want to take home today?" she asks later as we're eating the slippery, buttery *perohy*.

"Nothing. I have *perohy*."

"Well, I'm trying to clean out my house."

"I don't need anything."

"No one is going to do it when I die. I've got so much. Dishes and bedding. You need bedding?" she insists more than asks. The last set of yellowed sheets she gave me ripped in half when I tried to tuck in the corners. She is beginning her purging and getting-ready-to-die routine.

"Not really."

"What are they going to do with all this stuff when they find me dead? I don't have long left, you know." In the past year my closets have been filled with floral embroidered lunch cloths, pots that were ancient wedding gifts, glassware with the birds from each province painted on them, and lamps made of Popsicle sticks. She even gave me a box of Kotex pads from the 1950s. Lately, I've been making regular deposits at the Salvation Army on the way home from the farm.

"You're not dying and I'm not taking anything today," I say as I put our plates in the sink.

"Nobody knows when it's their time to go, Anna. Anyway, I've got too many damn plants. Here, take some of these aloe vera plants. Maybe you can sell them at work." She hands me two plants, thick with long, green pointed fingers reaching over the edge of the plastic margarine containers. "Wait, I've got a box." She rummages through the closet and pulls out a box and proceeds to fill it with several plants. "You can probably get three dollars apiece for them. Ask for five for this bigger one."

"Okay," I say as I put on my jacket.

"See you next week. And we'll go get some chickens," Baba says.

"What?"

"I want to get about thirty chicks from the Hutterites for butchering."

"Dad'll kill you." And, more importantly, kill me. *You may be ready to go, but I'm not.*

"I don't care. He can go to hell. I'll call the Hutterite colony and tell them we're coming next Saturday. And we should probably start on the Easter eggs soon."

I walk to my car carrying a box filled with *perohy* and aloe vera plants. I got off easy this time.

Night Crawlers

A beam of light pierces my window and disturbs the darkness of my bedroom. It flickers. I get out of bed, go to the window, and pull back the curtains. A dark figure lurks on the front lawn and the beam of a flashlight jumps around on the grass.

Did I lock the door? The light continues to leap from spot to spot and my heart keeps tempo. I wish Adam were here. I walk quickly and quietly downstairs and take the phone from its cradle. Through the front window I can see a second dark figure on the lawn.

I punch 9.

I punch 1.

Then the beam of light slides across one of the prowlers' faces. It's Mom. I throw on the living room lights and open the door.

"What the hell are you doing?!" I call across the lawn.

"We thought you'd be sleeping," Mom sings out. She is holding a bucket. Dad raises the light, and the beam finds my face.

"I *was* sleeping." I shield my eyes. "What are you doing?"

"Looking for worms," Dad says, returning the light to the ground in front of him. My eyes are adjusting, and I can see that he has my garden hose in his other hand.

"At one in the morning?"

"Well, they only come out at night. You got night crawlers here. Huge ones!" he says. Them or the worms, I wonder. "Your lawn is a gold mine." He bends down and plucks something from the ground.

"I almost called the police!" Part of me wishes I had called the police. My parents have to learn some boundaries.

"Here, Ethel, got another one." Mom holds the pail up for him so that he can drop his prize in the bucket.

"We didn't mean to scare you. Why don't you put some coffee on?" Mom suggests. *Because it's one in the bloody morning.*

"Okay, but don't bring those things in the house," I warn.

"You should see the size of them. Come over and take a look!" Dad is hunched over in the grass. I really don't need to see the worms, but I oblige him so he's not disappointed by my lack of interest in his latest hobby. I walk across the cool grass, the lawn lumpy under my bare feet. A dozen worms squirm in an inch of soil at the bottom of the pail. Retirement is the worst possible thing that could have happened to them. *And me.*

"Here, hold the flashlight, Ethel." Mom takes the light and Dad picks out a worm and holds it up.

"Look how long it is. It's got a flat head. Those are night crawlers all right—great fishing worms." The wet, brown worm is lethargic and slowly curls its pinched body in an attempt to free itself. It looks as impressed as I am to be drawn from its home at this late hour. My dad drops it into the bucket. I wish I wasn't barefoot.

"That's great." I go inside to make coffee instead of telling them to go home to bed like normal people. Several minutes later we are at my kitchen table.

"Have you heard from Natalia?" Mom asks, her voice hopeful. Walter and Ethel cannot sleep for worry about Nat. This partly explains why they're digging up worms on my lawn in the middle of the night. They can't understand how a daughter they love could just forget they exist. Nat's dismissal of them from her life has sparked a pain that I can't even understand, let alone soothe. I try to be the good daughter and fill their void with forced laughter and pleasantries. We're getting quite good at the act, though it's admittedly futile—like covering a canyon with Saran Wrap every evening as if it would keep the rain out.

"Anything?" Mom asks again, clutching her mug. There is a faint trace of mud on her cheek. When I finally told them that Nat had gotten married to Aki in a Muslim ceremony last summer, Mom cried for two days. It never occurred to her that one of her daughters would get married without her presence, let alone her knowledge.

Mom's own wedding to my dad had been a disaster. She grew up in Edmonton and when she reluctantly agreed to have her wedding in Winnipeg, she didn't realize that she was consenting to Baba planning the entire event. Baba, the frugal Eastern European Wedding Planner. By the time Mom arrived, even her dress had been ordered.

When Mom's dad suffered a stroke a week before her wedding and she pleaded to have it postponed, Baba declared that it wasn't possible—the deposits were non-refundable. Baba had turned into the overbearing mother-in-law she herself had been forced to live with.

So Mom stoically walked up the aisle alone and wed Dad. They ate breaded chicken in the basement of the Ukrainian Catholic church. Instead of white-gloved waiters pouring wine for guests, people reached for the cheap bottles across the table, trailing their sleeves in bowls of buttery cabbage rolls made by Baba's friends. It was the perfect Manitoba Ukrainian wedding, except that it wasn't what Mom wanted, and her father was lying in the hospital a thousand miles away.

Mom has always wanted to participate in her daughters' weddings, having largely missed out on her own. She knows my own prospects are pretty bleak at the moment.

I keep my own sadness buried deep within and maintain the pretense that my life is fine. They don't know that Adam and I are almost through. They don't know that the world I have spent the past decade building is falling apart. It's like I am constantly shining a flashlight into the crack between the bottom of the door and the floor, so my life appears warm and normal from the out-side hallway. I try to shield my parents, but parents can sense unhappiness in their children the way a mosquito senses the blood of a nearby fat thigh. Nat's offering up a pretty good diver-sion for now, but I'm pretty sure they're on to me.

Natalia's emails are sporadic and I still haven't told Mom and Dad about the baby. It annoys me that I'm forced to purée and strain information so my parents don't choke on the details of her life.

"No. I haven't heard from her." I set a plate of stale cookies on the table. Mom sends Nat emails daily and receives no responses, probably because Mom begs her to come home and offers to have Aki arrested. I wish Nat would reply, if only because it took me a month to teach Mom how to send an email. Mom thinks Nat doesn't respond because email doesn't work.

"So, are you going fishing tomorrow with all these worms?" I turn to my dad.

"No, not tomorrow. I just wanted to see if the worms were here. I was right, your lawn is so lumpy I knew it had to be infested with worms. They only come up at night when it rains." That explains the garden hose. "I could probably sell them." He leans back and rests his arms behind his head.

There is a noise upstairs. Buddy.

"Shhhh! Everybody quiet." Dad leans forward. "Do you

hear that?" He jumps up. Buddy has also been awakened by my parents' late-night visit. He usually doesn't start his burrowing routine until at least four in the morning.

"Yeah, don't worry about it. It's just a squirrel." *Dad, meet Buddy. Buddy, meet your demise.* Dad goes to the stairwell, pressing his large frame against the wall, listening, feeling for movement.

"You gotta squirrel? Do you know what kind of damage they can cause?" He slides slowly along the wall, like he's searching for explosives.

"He's no trouble. He just needs a place to sleep."

"Those buggers can chew through everything. They start chewing through wires and they can cause fires."

"But she says he's not causing any damage," Mom says as she bites into a cookie. She's been a reluctant witness to Dad's obliteration of many nuisance animals over the years, skunks being his personal favourite. She pours herself another cup of coffee.

I guess they're staying.

My father has always addressed the smaller, inconsequential problems in our lives, such as rodents or stalled cars, as though he were attacking an anthill with a sledgehammer. But when Aki came into Nat's life and took her away, Dad barely said a word. I knew that he hated the idea of Nat going to the Middle East and he wanted her to change her mind as desperately as the rest of us, but he was unable to tell her. I've always sensed that Dad has never entirely approved of my relationship with Adam, and he's never uttered a word about that either. But he rages against the prospect of a squirrel chewing through a few wires. I guess dads are better equipped to deal with electrical wiring than their daughters' more complicated emotional wiring. Sometimes I think Nat might have listened if Dad had said something, anything.

I'm hoping that Buddy will stay inside the walls and not introduce himself tonight.

Scratch.
Scratch.
Scratch.

Buddy is busy working at his usual spot inside the stairwell wall. I take the opportunity to give Mom the package that arrived from the Home Shopping Network.

"There's a grill on the way," she whispers.

"What?"

"Yeah. Just sign for it when it comes. I'll pick it up." She presses her index finger to her lips.

"We'll have to set a trap and catch the little bugger," Dad mutters. He hikes his slipping jeans up around his stomach.

"No, we won't."

"You can't have a squirrel chewing through your walls!"

"So, what are you going to do? Kill it?"

"I'm telling you, those things are a nuisance. They're as bad as raccoons and skunks."

"Maybe you could use a live trap," Mom suggests. She is only mildly interested in the squirrel as she flips through magazines. Dad gets a twinkle in his eye when there is a pest to be conquered. The worms will be safe for a while.

"I'm pretty tired." I stretch my arms over my head and yawn. Too tired to tolerate Dad's militia plans to obliterate Buddy, who has become suspiciously quiet.

"We should let her get back to bed," Mom says, dragging my dad away from the wall.

"It's gonna start breeding, and you'll have a houseful of squirrels on your hands. You want that?" Dad ties his muddy shoes. This is simply not true because I know for a fact that Buddy is not looking to get into a relationship right now.

"Good night. Thanks for the coffee." Mom hugs me.

"I'll figure out how we're going to handle that squirrel and

I'll call you," Dad insists.

"Don't forget your worms," I say as I shut the door after them.

I return to bed, but I can't fall asleep. I toss and turn.

"Can't sleep either?" Buddy asks from the entrance to my bedroom.

"Did you get into the coffee beans again?" I ask.

"He thinks I'd be stupid enough to chew through electrical wires? Puhleeze."

"I wouldn't take it personally."

"He wakes me up, and then he compares me to a raccoon!" Buddy shakes his tail.

"Don't worry about him."

"He's going to try and kill me. That I need to see."

"Just be quiet when he's over."

"But this is my house too. Whose side are you on anyway? You have to stop being such a pushover."

"Oh, you mean like when I let you move in here?"

"That's not what I meant. Besides, I would've moved in anyway. You have to start standing up for yourself."

"Okay, can we finish this tomorrow? I'm really tired."

"Fine. Can I sleep in here tonight?

"No. Good night." I hear Buddy's claws tap along the floor as he makes his way back to his hole.

Dress to Kill

Sara sits erect in an armchair at the seamstress's as Renate, Julia, and I are swaddled in peach satin. The dresses are loosely stitched, mostly held together with the aid of straight pins that are cold against our backs. If we stand close enough together, we look like window dressing—or Thousand Island salad dressing.

"Peach is possibly my worst colour, next to mauve," Julia whines.

"No, I think mauve is your worst colour," I say, wriggling in my material.

"You guys look great," Sara offers.

Elly, the seamstress, slides from Julia's dress to mine.

"At the last fitting you were busting out of this dress, but now you're swimming in it." She tugs at the material. Sara eyes my peach figure disapprovingly.

"Sorry, I've been stressed." Lately all I can seem to consume is either cheesecake or coffee—caffeine and fat are my only food groups.

Elly pinches my waist sharply. I look like a stick next to Renate's pregnant belly and Julia's voluptuous curves.

"You have got to get control of yourself. Please don't spoil this wedding," Sara pleads.

"Okay."

"Stop smoking for God's sake. And keep eating."

"Okay." I tear at the cuticle on my index finger with my teeth.

"And stop biting your nails. You need to look good for the pictures!"

Sara's right. My hands are starting to look really mangled and deformed. It's a meter that aptly indicates how much stress I'm under. Sara's wedding alone makes them look like they've been chewed up by a lawn mower.

"I'm not going to kiss you anymore until you stop chewing your nails," Adam announced one evening, about two years into our relationship. He'd begun to change things about me. He viewed me in much the same way he did the house, his art, or his music. I was something he could reconstruct into his vision of a perfect girlfriend.

"It's disgusting," Adam complained.

"I know. I can't help it." We'd be watching TV or driving somewhere and my hands would be mashed in my mouth. My teeth are a gnawing machine and my nails, my fingers, and, occasionally, my toes all fall victim. The finely honed machine isn't satisfied until the cuticle has been torn away and there's blood, and not truly content until blood is dripping from more than one finger or toe simultaneously.

"Fine. I'll stop."

I tried everything to break this habit. I sat on my hands, or had people remind me when they caught me chewing on my fingers. I tried dipping my fingers in gasoline and other disgusting substances, but I inevitably acquired a taste for them.

Binge-eating. Drinking. Gambling. Smoking. Nail-biting. Bad

habits that signal larger emotional problems. I ripped into my hands and made them look how I felt. Smoking and nail-biting were pastimes I took up more avidly as the years went by to deal with my inability to live up to Adam's expectations. He always seemed to be disappointed in me about something: I spent too much time with my girlfriends, who had started to annoy Adam; I didn't spend enough time renovating our house; I dressed too provocatively—early on he had liked the way I dressed, but now a pair of boots and a knee-length denim skirt from the Gap were considered too sexy.

"It's such a gross habit." Adam glared at my hands.

And so The Kissing Strike began.

I didn't view the strike as the cruel act it was—withholding his affection to punish me. Rather, I believed he acted out of love. I thought it was a great incentive to not chew my hands because I liked to kiss. I thought it would be one of my easiest but greatest feats ever, and for the first day it was.

But then the gnawing machine kicked in and forced me to choose between it and kissing. I began to sneak chomps while I was at work, out for the evening, or when Adam wasn't looking. I would take care not to draw blood, not to draw attention to my hands. I began having to hide my fingers because I desperately wanted to be kissed.

Unfortunately, the gnawing machine was not an expert in delicacy and care, and the traces of blood and missing chunks of my skin could be detected by even an untrained eye, let alone the eye of an expert, like Adam.

"I sure would like to kiss you." Adam smacked his lips. "But look at those hands," he chided. I felt even worse about myself and eventually the gnawing machine completely reclaimed my hands.

Adam would still have sex with me. Without kissing.

The Kissing Strike went on for months until Adam made the

mistake of sharing his philosophy on the merging of teeth and hands with a friend, who told him he was nuts. Adam decided soon after that he wouldn't catch any grisly disease and he revisited my lips. But kissing was never the same.

"I'm going to make an eating plan and you're going to follow it. You're pretty, Anna, but lately you're looking so washed out. I want you to look your best for my wedding."

"Sara, the world does not revolve around your goddamn, fucking wedding!" Julia snaps. Sara starts crying. Bridal tantrum #37.

"I'm sorry," she blubbers, "this whole thing is just really stressful, my mother-in-law is driving me crazy, and nothing is going right. Even these dresses won't fit. All I'm asking is that you stay the same dress size for two months and don't chew up your hands. Just look *nice*. It's not too much to ask, is it?" Tears streak down Sara's cheeks. Even when she cries Sara still looks perfect. When I cry, my eyes redden, mascara bleeds down my face, and I look like a drunk raccoon.

"Okay, I'm sorry. I promise I'll be the same dress size for the next fitting. I'll get my shit together and I will look normal for your wedding." I hand her a tissue. At least I'm not promising to *be* normal.

"Why don't you just sew her dress like Renate's?" Julia suggests. I look at Renate, seven months pregnant. Yes, sew me a maternity dress, please. And perhaps an anorexia dress too so that I'll have options the day of the wedding.

"I can sew an expandable waist, I suppose," Elly says.

"I won't look seven months pregnant at your wedding, I promise."

"It will need to be contract-able as well," Sara tells Elly. "I can't believe this, Anna." She is no longer sobbing, she just seems defeated, like her cheerleading squad has just lost the provincial competition.

"We'll have to schedule another fitting before I start the detailing," Elly says, looking at me.

"Do we all have to come?" Julia asks.

"Yes. I want to see what they all look like together when they fit properly," Sara says.

"I need a drink," Julia says as she struggles out of her dress. She looks at all of us. "And I need to talk to you about something important."

"I've decided to try and find my birth mother," Julia announces. We are sitting under a heat lamp on the Earls patio. I light a cigarette.

"What?" Sara says, shooting me and my cigarette a dirty look. I wait for her to slide in a comment that maybe Julia should wait until after her wedding before trying to locate her mother.

"That's fantastic," Renate says. "Why now? I've been trying to convince you to do this for years."

"I know, I know. It's not really for me. It's more for Emma. I kind of want her to know who her grandmother is. Actually, Anna, you've sort of inspired me with your relationship with your baba."

"How's the search going?" I ask.

"I have an appointment next week with the agency. It's pretty simple: it's either in my file or it's not, depending on what my birth mother wanted."

"Will you meet her?"

"I think so. But I have to sit through some bullshit coun- selling session first before they'll tell me," Julia complains.

Julia is trying to uncover her past and I am trying to escape mine. Will finding out where she came from affect Julia? "Fuck, no," Julia would say if I asked her. I don't know yet the extent to which the last ten years with Adam has affected me. I do know that our present selves are the sum of our pasts, even though we spend the better part of our lives trying to distinguish ourselves from it.

"What's going on with Adam?" Julia asks, sucking on her margarita. A girl, probably twenty, in tight jeans and a white T-shirt, keeps showing up every three minutes, asking us if we're okay. *No, not okay. There's more to life than appetizers and drink refills.* She wouldn't be so perky if she knew what was in store for her for the next decade. Bad boyfriends. Horrible peach weddings.

"Nothing new, really. He wants to move back in and try to work things out when he comes home."

"And you've said NO, right?" Julia asks.

Is this part two of the intervention? I wonder if the dress fitting was even real—it could have just been a pretense to back me into a corner again.

"I've thought about selling the house anyway, so there'd be nowhere for him to move back to."

"Right around the wedding? Won't that be hectic?" Sara asks innocently, flipping through her day timer.

"Change the locks." Renate pokes at ice cubes in her Diet Coke.

"I'll get it all sorted out."

"Uh huh. I'm sure you will," Sara mutters, still flipping through her day timer.

"I'm going to book you in for a massage next week. When can you come in?" Julia asks. Julia is a massage therapist, possibly the best occupation for a friend to have.

"How about Tuesday afternoon? I'm calling in sick." I've already booked my substitute teacher for that day. All of my friends have occupations that I take full advantage of. Renate fixes my teeth and Sara usually does my taxes, although this year Sara has made it very clear that she would be too busy with the wedding. She points out each year that, financially speaking, my life is a nightmare and that I should be saving a lot more for my future. *What future?* Every year she sets up an RRSP account, which I inevitably drain for shoes, coats, bags, and wine.

I swallow the icy dregs of my margarita. When the bill arrives I slide my Visa card onto the little black tray. What's another thirty bucks out of my RRSP savings?

I'm a Bad Poem

The following morning I arrive at work, unload the box of Baba's aloe vera plants from my trunk, and take them into the office.

"Good morning," I address the secretaries, who all take an immediate interest in the plants. I scribble "FREE PLANTS" with a marker on a sheet of paper and tape it to the box. They flutter around the box like butterflies.

"Morning, Anna."

"Morning. The plants are courtesy of my grandmother. Help yourself."

Some people grow marijuana, my Baba harvests aloe vera and I peddle it at work.

"Fred says he needs help with the DVD player," Debbie says, examining the plants. "These are nicer than the hostas you brought in last fall." After she gave me the hostas, Baba claimed her neighbour dug them up and stole them when she wasn't home. Her occasional memory lapses and her conspiracy-theory personality sometimes drive her to make ridiculous accusations.

I head upstairs to observe Liz, the student teacher. I take the long way so that I can avoid passing Harold's classroom. The replacement mug hasn't shown up yet.

I sit at the back and watch Liz deftly execute a poetry lesson. She's lured the students out of their usual catatonic state
with salacious trivia: that poet H.D. was engaged to Ezra Pound,
but broke up with him because she was a lesbian, and that Dylan
Thomas died at the age of thirty-nine from alcoholism after a
drinking binge in New York City. It's a cheap way to entice them
into a poem, like the way movie companies capitalize on the lewd
behaviour of film stars to sell movie tickets. Funny how scan-
dalous sex tapes and DUI charges seem to surface just before the
premieres of really bad movies that, without the exposure, would
otherwise flop. It works. I wish I had thought to teach poets with
seedy pasts. Liz has them keenly dissecting "Do Not Go Gentle
into That Good Night."

Liz has been pumped full of energy and fresh ideas by the
Factory of Education. I too remember pulling all-nighters, planning riveting lessons back when I thought my presence in the
classroom made a difference. Liz has been teaching for only two
weeks. She'll learn.

I glance at her lesson plan as she floats around the room. She
thinks these students will write poetry. I doubt it. As well as the
keeners, she's requested to teach this English class of tenth grade
repeaters because she "enjoys challenging situations." Right off
page two of her résumé.

Liz has asked to see my mark book after class so we can discuss assessment practices and include some of her marks. My book
is mostly blank. I had more evaluations, but I forgot to record
them, so now I'm making up assignments and filling numbers in
the columns while I'm supposed to be evaluating Liz's lesson. Suddenly, my students have delivered speeches, written memoirs, con-
ducted surveys, and completed group projects. I write "Peer
Evaluation" into the next blank column because I remember that
was a hit with last year's batch of eager student teachers.

Liz is passing out a handout that says "bio-poem," whatever that means. I haven't been paying attention to the lesson, so I've no idea what this is all about.

"Valerie," I whisper to the student next to me. "Can I see your notes?" Valerie hands me her poetry notes. A bio-poem, apparently, is a worksheet disguised as a poem. I decide to write a bio-poem for Liz.

First name:	Liz
Who is:	honest, fun, nauseating
Lover of:	overhead projectors, dogs, and church picnics
Who feels:	energetic, excited, nerdy
Who finds:	eating healthy and lots of rest important
Who needs:	herbal tea and crafts
Who gives:	handmade Christmas presents
Who fears:	people with tattoos
Who would like to see:	worldwide poetic literacy
Who enjoys:	reading and camp counselling
Who likes to wear:	socks with sandals
Resident of:	Faculty of Education
Last name:	Fields

That was fun, so I complete a poem for myself. Harold comes to the door and I slink down in my chair and motion to Liz that I'm not here. She deals with Harold. I compose a poem.

First name:	Anna
Who is:	tired, scattered, sex-deprived
Lover of:	abuse, coffee, and cheap wine
Who feels:	emotionally explosive
Who finds:	drinking and cigarettes comforting

Who needs:	love, understanding, and therapy
Who gives:	very few tests
Who fears:	Sara's wedding, prohibition, and Harold
Who would like to see:	harsher sentences for offenders of domestic violence, greater selection of cheap wines at the liquor store
Who enjoys:	long walks in the park, toenail chewing, and self-punishment
Who likes to wear:	her heart on her sleeve, men's underwear
Resident of:	Starbucks
Last name:	Lasko

"How is your poem coming along?" Liz asks me, as though I'm one of the students. The entire class is engaged in writing poems. She's succeeded. *Damn her.* I usually have to take them to 7-Eleven once a month in order to get them to do anything. She circulates around the room helping students with the passion and poise of a good teacher. I am starting to like Liz, even though I want to hate her and her shiny mane of blond hair.

I excuse myself to go and help Fred with the DVD player. It took five years, but I'd finally taught him how to work the VCR when the school replaced them all with DVD players.

The bell rings, finally. I just step out of the classroom when Craig corners me, breathing heavily in my face.

"We're meeting today, right?" he asks, slurring all his words together in one desperate breath. If he wasn't so nerdy I'd swear his slurring was a result of a Dylan Thomas-esque drinking binge.

"Uh, yeah." I would much rather spend my lunch hour driving around in my car, smoking cigarettes, but I don't have the heart to cancel the meeting three weeks in a row. I turn around, unlock the door, and slump down in my desk.

The others trickle in after him: Goth Girl Lesley, Julio the love poet, Jenna the fan fiction writer, and a few others whose names and weird behaviour I have yet to learn. Before anyone has had a chance to sit down and get out their lunches, Craig launches into his opening monologue, running his words together as usual.

"So I'm at the part where Argamyte is battling the Master Dragon. This is page 187 of the second book of *The Chronicles of Argamyte*." He takes a bite of his sandwich and continues to talk. Gobs of peanut butter and bread fly out of his mouth and land on the floor. Craig was home-schooled during his formative years and just this year has resurfaced in the public school system. He's an intelligent boy, but "his habits and behaviour reflect his limited socialization with other teenagers," or so his file reads. The kid's weird.

"But the thing is that the Master Dragon is trying to kill Argamyte because Argamyte is close to finding the pearl and needs to end the Master Dragon's reign of terror." Goth Girl rolls her eyes. Nobody really knows what's going on in Craig's writing or in his head. He believes that we're all riveted and lose sleep waiting to find out what happens next. *I need a cigarette.*

"Okay, I'll just read. *Argamyte can't yet see the Master Dragon, but he can hear the sonic beating of his fierce wings. Argamyte scans the empty skies as the beating draws closer. He clutches the vial of shape-changing potion in his hand given to him by Olf, the deaf owl. Can Olf be trusted? Or is Olf trying to thwart his plans to find the pearl? Argamyte cannot know.*"

Is there such thing as a deaf owl?

"*Two glaring eyes emerge out of the grey skies. Argamyte is pinned against a tree and the Master Dragon is heading right for him. The tree shakes from the force of the Master Dragon's wings.*" Craig stops reading.

"Is it hot in here? I'm hot," he says, wiping the sweat from his forehead. We all stare at him in disbelief as he takes off his shirt. He continues to read his story. His pale, pimply chest is concave above his little potbelly. This is more of Craig than any of us need to see, especially while eating.

"*The Dragon snatches Argamyte with his curled claws and drags him up toward the sky. Argamyte closes his eyes, fearing the worst. When he opens them again, the Master Dragon is circling over the swirling Pool of Doom. Not the Pool of Doom! Argamyte thinks. The black oozing liquid burns his eyes as he looks at it. Argamyte has never known anyone who has seen the Pool of Doom and lived to tell about it.*" Craig finishes and looks up hopefully. We all wish that the dragon would just end Argamyte's misery and Craig would end ours. Sadly I identify with Argamyte and feel like I'm about to drop into my own pathetic little pool of doom. It can't be good when I am identifying with Craig's freaky fantasy characters.

"You've got something caught in your braces," Goth Girl says.

"I, I liked it," Julio stutters. "I think that . . . th . . . that you co . . . could describe Olf and the Master Dragon more, b . . . but . . ."

Come on, Julio, spit it out. I need a cigarette before afternoon classes start.

". . . it was re . . . really suspenseful. It . . . it had good imagery."

"Yeah, I'm really good at imagery," Craig agrees. Homeschooling forgot to teach him modesty.

"I don't really like fantasy that much," Jenna says.

"Jenna, what have you been working on?" I ask. Jenna writes fan fiction about the has-been musical group Hanson. The three pubescent singers are characters in her invented tales. The writing group is a forum for her to cultivate her delusions, the kind most people keep confined to their own heads.

"A story, but it isn't finished."

"I, I have a poem," Julio says.

"Great," I respond. "Let's hear it."

Julio clears his throat and stands up. He paces as he reads, stutter free. He must practise before a mirror.

> *She sits by the lake, her soft eyes gaze out,*
> *Quietly breathing and whispering his name,*
> *She waits for him, tears fall onto her ivory hands,*
> *She is beautiful in her torn dress,*
> *Waiting for her man.*

Goth Girl rolls her eyes. Julio sits down. *I really need a cigarette.*

"I thought it was okay," Fan Fiction says. "But I wouldn't use the word 'beautiful.' It's too cliché."

"Maybe it could be a little longer," Craig suggests.

"I cou . . . could write another stanza."

"Why don't you do that for next week?" I suggest. "Lesley, have you anything to read today?" I need to speed this meeting along.

"I'm not really in the mood to read," she says, slumped over in her desk. I'm disappointed—I was really looking forward to one of her angry occult poems.

"Ms. Lasko, I was wondering when we were going to use those books you were buying at the bookstore?" *Thank you, Craig. Why don't you run through the titles so that everyone will know I'm in therapy and buying self-help books?*

"We'll get to those next week."

"Because I really think that my character Argamyte could

benefit from one of those books." *I'm in the company of Argamyte. Maybe the Master Dragon could put both of us out of our misery.*

"Have you got anything to read?" Julio asks me hopefully.

"Uh, sure." I read off a few stanzas of an Adrienne Rich poem that I'd copied out during Liz's lesson. I'd never read my own writing to these kids. Usually I never have any, so I've gotten into the habit of reading poems that I like, passing them off as my own. They haven't caught on yet. Today I read a few stanzas of "Snapshots of a Daughter-in-Law."

"I liked th...that one," Julio says. The bell rings. So long cigarette.

I'm heading back to my office when I'm halted by Harold's angry voice.

"ANNA." *Shit.* I had Liz order him a new mug and an extra one for me just to annoy him. *Look, I didn't attend the Swift Current Social Studies Symposium, but I got a mug!* I turn around. At least I'll be able to tell him something.

"Hi, Harold."

"Anna, you are behaving like a child. How many times do I need to chase you down?" His face contorts. "I'm going to come with you to your room right now to retrieve my mug."

"Harold, I broke it."

"You broke it!" His eyes are bulging again.

"I ordered you a new one and I was hoping it would show up by the time I saw you and then I could just give it to you."

"Very disappointing. It's not just about the mug, you know. It's your inability to face me, to accept responsibility, to tell the truth."

Shame. I am four years old. I have peed behind the couch again and Mom has just found it. She scolds me and tells me that is not how little girls are supposed to behave. And now Harold looks at me with eyes that say I'm a disappointment to his profession.

"You are a coward, Anna!" he says, and stomps away in his cheap rubber shoes. He's right. I continue on to my office to check emails and wait for the day to be over.

There are emails from Adam and Nat, Renate, and one from Sara, the subject line reading "wedding emergency." There is a wedding emergency every three days. Renate wants to know if I've heard from Adam, but technically I haven't opened his email yet, so I tell her that I haven't. I reluctantly open Sara's next.

To: annalasko@hotmail.com;renateenns@msn.com;
julia_onewoman@hotmail.com
From: sarasoda@yahoo.com
Subject: wedding emergency

Ladies,
There's supposed to be a surprise shower for me Friday night at Jeff's aunt's. Can you guys be there? I'm sorry about the short notice, but I need you there. Can't do this by myself.
It's at 1026 Kilkenny Avenue. It's a conservative crowd. I know this is a pain in the ass. Last one, I promise.

This is the fifth shower we've had to attend, not including the one we threw for her. The first one was in a church hall with 125 women and the bridesmaids had to deliver lengthy speeches about Sara, Jeff, and their undying love for one another. At the next one we had to wander around with coffee and lemon squares for three hours on a Friday night, and at the one after that we had to sing karaoke love songs—while sober. Sara has said "last one, I promise" about the last three showers. I doubt this will be the last one.

To: annalasko@hotmail.com
From: adam_rp@hotmail.com
Subject: How are you?

Anna,
There are always things I want to say, but then I can't remember
them when we talk. This is a nightmare and it's killing me because
the only person I want to talk to and who understands me is you
and I'm losing you. Talking to you really makes me feel better.

Funny, because every time I get an email or phone call from you,
Adam, I feel physically ill.

You can't leave me. You have to trust me. I love you. I love you
too much to let you go. You know we can't end things like this.
I know that I can change.

Reminder to self: In the future, don't open Adam's emails without alcohol and/or cigarettes in hand.

But then I think maybe I can't change and I really am that
small, insecure asshole, and you should never look back as you
break free from me. But that can't be me. I know I wasn't always
like this, so if I can change into a rotten person, why can't I
change again, to someone worthy of a loving mate? It may be
a risk you are unwilling to take. I, however, have to bet on
myself. When I get focused on something, nothing can stop me.
I know I am seeing with clear eyes for the first time in years,
and I see you, a person I love so dearly.

Adam's emails are always epic. I should stop reading now. But I
can't. This is about where I start to crack.

Don't think of our rotten last couple of years—that's not us. And don't think of those times and judge if we are right for each other or not. That isn't who we are or who we can be. We're both so much better than what we've become. I don't think any two people are "right" for each other. They either make it work or they don't. It's all in the hands of the couple. I do know that I choose you over anybody to spend my life with. Not the life we had, but the life we can make. We're both extremely determined people, and if we are determined to make the relationship work and be happy together, we won't fail. I hate failing at anything. I'm just telling you what I think and feel. I hope it doesn't make you uncomfortable.

Just a little.

Well, apparently I had a bit to say. I just meant to say a quick hello. Adam

To: adam_rp@hotmail.com
From: annalasko@hotmail.com
Subject: Re: How are you?

I'm sorry this horrible breakdown of our relationship is happening. I don't know what went wrong. I love you and I miss you and I hate this life without you. I feel lonely and empty and sick all the time.

Delete. Delete. Delete. Delete. Delete.

I don't know what happened to us. I know that you are not that person you became and I know that you can change back. I am waiting for you to come home.

Delete. Delete. Delete. Delete. Delete.

> I'm glad that you're not the person you were when you left for Germany. I know that you can and will find yourself again. It's scary to think of the future without "us," but we have to. It's the only way to get out of this rut. Somewhere along the way we both lost sight of what's supposed to be important in a relationship.
>
> Love,
> Anna

Send.

Dammit. Why did I have to say "love"? My inbox is showing one more unopened message. It's Nat. I reluctantly click *open*. I used to be optimistic that in one of these emails Nat would tell me that she's coming home, but it never happens.

> To: annalasko@hotmail.com
> From: natalialasko@hotmail.com
> Subject: hi
>
> I'm sorry that I haven't written much. I've made choices that you don't agree with, and my life is pretty different from what it was before. I don't really expect you to understand.
>
> I'll start with Aki. He has taken a second wife. I can just imagine your reaction to this. It's perfectly acceptable within the Muslim faith, which we're both practising. I'd always thought that I would be enough, but Aki said that his second wife is a good Muslim woman who deserves a good husband. He's doing her a service. I haven't met her and probably won't.

I'm sure he's doing her several services.

He loves me, I can work if I want, and I have everything that I need. When you think about it, Adam had only one partner, you, and he treated you badly. I will never have to endure that, even if my situation is not ideal. I think of all my friends and the infidelity and secrecy. At least this is out in the open.

When in Rome . . .

Leaving would be tricky, even if I wanted to, which for now, I don't. I gave up my visa when I started teaching English here and I haven't been able to get it back. Once I have the baby, it will become even more complicated and difficult to leave.

I miss you and Mom and Dad and Baba. How are they? That's why I don't open Mom's emails anymore. I can't. I did for a while, but it's too hard. In the last email I opened, she actually asked me if I was tied up in a basement.

Well? Are you?

I gather you still haven't told them about the baby. It's probably for the best. Life is much simpler and in a lot of ways more meaningful for me now. I'm not caught up in all that drivel I used to be so consumed with. I've made choices that for now can't be reversed. I'm looking forward to motherhood. I wish you could be here. If this doesn't sound like the old Nat, well, I feel like I'm ten years older now. Older than you! But it's still me. I've seen a lot of awful situations here.

By my old standards, my life sounds pretty bad, but it's really okay.

Love,

Nat

To: natalialasko@hotmail.com
From: annalasko@hotmail.com
Subject: Re: hi

Nat,

Aki has two wives and you're one of them? Are you off your fucking rocker? And don't worry about abandoning your parents. It's really no big deal.

Delete. Delete. Delete. Delete.

Nat,

I understand that you are living in a different culture and they play by different rules over there, but I can't help but feel that you are making a mistake in staying there. Perhaps I'm not getting why Aki needs more than one place to put his dick. Don't worry about Mom and Dad; they won't give a shit about their first grandchild anyway.

Delete. Delete. Delete. Delete.

Nat,

I support you in whatever decision you make. God knows you've respected my screwball decisions. I get what you're saying. I don't think there is such thing as perfection anymore, just different ways of manipulating problems so they can fit nicely into everyone's lives. But for the record, I DO think the two wives thing is nuts and you are a brave woman to be able to handle it. I won't lie—your decisions have caused everyone a lot of pain around here, but it's your life, I guess. Don't stop writing. And just say the word if you want me to haul your Muslim ass out of there.

There is a bang at the office door as I finish Natalia's email.

Talk to you soon,
Anna
P.S. You'll be an amazing mother.

Send.

"You wanna go grab a drink and some food?" Ted says when I open the door. This means that he is clean out of money, and I will be buying him dinner, which right now is fine by me because it'll get me away from these emails. They keep inventing more methods of communication—email, cell phone, text messaging—clearer, more convenient ways to deliver bad news.

"Do I ever." I'm glad it's Ted. He's my hassle-free buddy, other than the fact that he's twice my age and often hits on me. Our relationship is not complicated by weddings and interventions, troubled sisters, and bad boyfriends. Just beer.

"You seem like you'd be an easy lay right now."

"Long day. Don't push your luck. It'll have to be a fast drink. I have a therapy appointment in an hour."

"You're still wasting money on a therapist? Money you could be lending me?"

"You can't even eat you're so broke cause of your dirty little habit and you're giving me shit?" Ted is a degenerate gambler and there are few people left on staff to whom he doesn't owe money. He's always grateful when they hire new teachers. Fresh bank accounts to tap. He owes me money too, but at least I don't have to explain to a husband where the four hundred dollars went that was supposed to pay for little Cindy's ballet lessons. I am under no illusions that I will ever see that money again.

Ted chooses gambling over school; teaching just supports his habit—barely. For me, alcohol and bad relationships monopolize my time and energy. Ted and I don't bother using the public school system to camouflage our pathetic personal lives, which is another reason we're unlikely friends. I see teachers as having excessive personalities, making them poor role models. They fly under the wire because most thrust themselves into work— coaching basketball, directing drama productions, decorating bulletin boards, or marking homework twenty hours a day. School *becomes* their addiction—neurotic, freaky behaviour that has been spun into a "Teachers Care" campaign. But often in- telligence and good judgment, if we have any in the first place, stay in the school at the end of the day. Teachers are human, with human problems. Ted and I have long accepted that.

We go to a pub downtown and order beers. Ted orders chicken wings and a plate of fries. I'm not hungry, but I know I should eat something. Sara will never forgive me if I've lost even more weight by the next bridesmaid dress fitting. I'll have to eat lots of cake at the shower.

"So what's up?"

"What isn't? It's all this crap with my sister and Adam."

"Oooh. Adam is with your sister now?"

"Shut up."

"Let me guess, your sister's not coming home, and Adam is coming home."

"Ugh. I don't want to talk about it. I'll have to do it with Lorna later anyway. What's going on with you?"

"Is Lorna hot?"

"In a Julie Andrews sort of way."

"Pass. Nothing is new except that asshole punk administrator has decided to evaluate me."

"You need to do a better job of flying under the wire. If you kicked fewer kids out of your courses, you might not get evaluated. You could be completely inept, but still get promoted, like me."

"That's not going to fucking happen. These kids are allowed to mouth off and swear and do whatever they want. They smile smugly and those administrators put them right back in our classes. These kids are out of control."

Ted stuffs fries slathered with barbeque sauce into his mouth. He has good teeth, but not because he takes care of them—quite the opposite. Ted was so hopeless at cleaning his teeth that, upon the dentist's recommendation, he had all his teeth pulled and replaced with implants. He picks a bit of chicken from between the false teeth.

"Look at us. Look at their parents. Everyone says these kids are so rotten and out of control. I wonder where they get it from?" I muse.

I think the veneer of being in control—at work or in our personal lives—is the thin slippery skin of an onion. Beneath are the meaty layers—who we *really* are.

Living in the Projects

"What were your relationships like before Adam? It might help us determine why you're tied to always satisfying him and why you feel guilty when you can't meet his needs." Lorna's wearing a pink jumpsuit. One reason I attend my appointments is so that I can see what she'll be wearing. I wonder how someone so inept in fashion can be in tune with life. It makes me skeptical.

"I really didn't have any serious relationships before Adam. A few flings in high school. On my very first date, when I was fifteen, the guy took my hand and stuck it in his crotch. I lost my virginity in the eleventh grade to a twelfth grader I thought I loved. The day after he fucked me, he got back together with his girlfriend. The closest thing I had to a relationship was when I was the official 'other girl' of my manager at Wendy's." I was the envy of all the other cashiers and burger flippers. The Chosen One, I liked to think of myself. He courted me with better shifts, slightly inflated paycheques, and after-hours tours of the restaurant. I believed that love could bloom out of the grease of the fast-food world. Together we would rule Wendy's. Thankfully, I realized there was more substance to a Wendy's Classic Grill than there was to our relationship, though it took me over a year to figure this out.

"I moved on from all that bliss into my relationship with Adam. Somewhere along the way I forgot to pick up confidence and self-esteem, especially when it came to relationships. It amazes me that people can develop normally in one aspect of life and be completely stunted in another. I see it all the time in my classroom. These smart, articulate girls partner up with complete jerks. One girl's mark dropped from an A to a C when her boyfriend transferred into my class. I kept her after school one day to ask her what was going on and she *actually* told me it wasn't worth the hassle he gave her when she did better than he did on assignments. I wanted to chuck my entire box of chalk at her until I realized I could chair the club of women who let men control them."

"And no other meaningful relationships to break this pattern?"

"No. When I met Adam I thought the relationship was great. I tried to satisfy him because I wanted to, especially because he loved me and cared for me. God, I'm spewing such passive crap."

"Not at all. You're still primarily motivated by his needs, though." Lorna sits across from me, legs crossed, palms facing up. She must do yoga.

"Well, I'm trying to get away from Adam, but I keep falling into the same trap."

"It sounds to me like you're caught up in a cycle of thinking that existed long before Adam. Do you ever stop to please yourself?" she asks. What exactly is Lorna getting at here? She wants to know if I masturbate? "Fulfill your own happiness, do things for yourself instead of always for Adam," she clarifies.

"That's the thing. Whenever I started to do that, I'd get the 'You're a selfish slut' lecture and the 'Please don't do this to me, I can't live without you' crap. I hated it. I would feel so guilty I'd just do whatever he wanted. It was easier. And in all fairness, I think later on in the relationship I started to change the rules and

didn't worry as much about satisfying him. You might say I'm a late bloomer. But the point is I bloomed, right? I get it now and I know what I want. The problem is that it doesn't fit with what Adam wants. I feel bad for him because he started dating a nice girl, a passive girl who didn't know what she wanted. I remember thinking to myself, *I'm going to make this guy happy.* I don't really feel like doing that anymore. Most of the time, I don't care if he's happy because what makes him happy usually makes me feel miserable. For example, he's happiest when I stay home all the time with him. And that's boring. My life feels like being forced to play Scrabble using only two- and three-letter words. I've developed a great vocabulary, but I'm not allowed to use it."
IT'S ALL TOO BAD AND SAD. AND HAS TO END.

It wasn't until a few years into our relationship that Adam's severe temper surfaced. I let it slide because the anger was always cloaked in the rationale that it was *because I love you.* I treated Adam's angry outbursts as isolated incidents at first, but they became more frequent and more intense, and the cause of these outbursts was always pinned to me. He progressed from blasting me with insults to weird behaviour. I learned that in order to keep Adam calm, I just needed to change who I was. And for years, I did. This was easier and more appealing than walking away from someone that I loved.

It was hard, however, to *always* live up to Adam's ideal Anna, and inevitably the real me would sometimes break free, setting off land mines in our relationship.

I awoke one morning, about four years ago, to find that Adam, in one of his panic-induced fits of rage, had welded my car keys, sunglasses, and cell phone onto a chunk of scrap metal from the basement. He was punishing me for going out with friends the previous night. If the medium he chose to use were not my personal things, I might have admired his creation. It glistened as it caught the morning sun. At least his fine arts degree had some practical applications.

Adam had drilled holes through the lenses of my sunglasses, and although my car keys were still usable, they were inseparable from my cell phone and the scrap metal. I was forced to tote around a one-foot-square key chain for several days. Answering my phone with all the new attachments was awkward. Showing my phone to the phone company sales clerk and explaining why I needed a replacement was even more awkward.

"I'm sorry. I didn't mean to wreck your stuff. I do love you," he casually commented later that day.

The apology wasn't an end to an episode as much as a signal that soon the cycle of anger would begin again.

Adam continued to fanatically renovate and sculpt beautiful mirrors and dressers that he would present to me as gifts. The nicer our home became, the more infrequently we left. I began to realize that in renovating the house, we weren't creating a home where we could entertain and feel warm and safe. We were building me a tower. Adam thought that if he made the tower beautiful enough, and filled it with lovely things, perhaps I would forget about the outside world and eventually I would just want to stay. But inside the tower I was slowly running out of air.

When the house was more or less finished, Adam and I moved on to other projects—bungled attempts to find fulfillment in stable places even though our foundation was rotting. I was always anxious and found things to do that would fill my days and not piss off Adam.

Adam refinished antique mirrors; I took up jogging and ran a half marathon. Adam recorded a CD of songs about me; I rearranged the furniture. Adam finished his fine arts degree; I went back to school to get my bachelor of arts. Adam started playing hockey; I trained for triathlons and took up yoga. These activities filled the holes in our lives for a while.

When I stumbled across scrapbooking, I decided that was what would save us. One afternoon, after calling in sick, I was sprawled out in my flannel pyjamas, flipping television channels. I happened upon the Life channel. A woman was building a paper shrine around her photographs while another woman enthusiastically assisted.

"You know, Carol, the beauty of scrapbooking is that you can make it as elaborate or as simple as you want. You are in control of the direction of your scrapbook." Finally, something I could control.

The reason my relationship was such a disaster, I decided, was because I was storing all of our memories in plastic storage bins. They needed to be enshrined and exalted like Carol's photographs. A lack of respect for our memories had led to the ruin of our relationship.

I went to the craft store and exchanged a hundred-dollar bill for various pairs of scissors that cut in zigzag patterns, cutouts of trees and birds and hearts, a package of stiff coloured paper, bottles of glitter, double-sided tape, and non-acidic glue. I purchased everything that Carol from the Life channel said I would need, and a few extras that were suggested by the clerk at the craft store.

I laid out my materials on the kitchen table and then sifted through the shoeboxes filled with photos. Adam and me splashing in the waves in Mexico. Adam and me riding our new bikes. Adam wearing his Value Village suit and his dad's tie, and me wearing a hideous teal silk bridesmaid dress at Renate and Calvin's wedding. I found a picture of Adam and me camping, our faces illuminated by a fire. The tops of our heads were cut off because we'd set the camera on a timer. Nothing a little scrapbooking couldn't fix. It was a worthy memory. I selected a sheet of stiff black paper and a pair of jagged-edge scissors. I cut the edges of the photo into the shape of a campfire and placed it onto the black paper. I created a border of flames around the photo from bright orange paper. In the text box I wrote in neat capital letters: ADAM AND ANNA'S FIRST WINTER CAMPING TRIP AT TULIBEE FALLS.

I spent the entire day enshrining photographs. I pasted a picture of Adam and me at the beach onto sunny yellow paper. What wasn't in the picture was that later we got into a fight and I took the bus home. The pictures were tucked into frilly borders and nestled among cutouts. As the day progressed, the background became more important than the photo, and the memory was all but smothered. I exalted the photos—the same way that I magnified our good memories in my head as an attempt to justify the continued existence of our relationship.

"You ruined the pictures," Adam said when he saw the scrapbook. I realized he was right. They were hideous. It would have made an excellent project if it had been done by a fourth grader. Scrapbooking wouldn't save us after all.

Adam continued to squash any inclination I showed toward growth or independence. I was almost thirty, yet I was still expected to play the role of the naive twenty-one-year-old he met in that university café. It was only a matter of time before I would completely snap and do something to provoke Adam.

"You're allowed to change the rules. When you were younger, your need to please started at a sexual level. As you've gotten older and into a long-term relationship, your need to please has moved into emotional and psychological contexts. Your relationship has moved to more dangerous situations of suffering and consequences when you try to assert your independence. Ultimately you have to empower yourself to live the life you want to live." Lorna is starting to make sense. I love her, pink jumpsuit and all.

"That's exactly it. My brain knows I've had enough—it's time to move on. But then my guilt kicks in. What will happen to him? He needs me and says he can't live without me. We've built this life together. We've spent ten years together. I make all these excuses and before I know it, I've talked myself out of leaving for the hundredth time. I don't know how to break out of this." My eyes start to sting.

I will not cry in therapy. I will not cry in therapy. It's so hokey. Lorna crosses her legs; her socks are also pink. *Good God.* You can't wear solid pink from head to toe and be taken seriously. Well, you can if you're on a Saturday morning program, but then the only people taking you seriously are all under the age of four.

"It sounds like you're in the relationship for all the wrong reasons. You feel bad. You feel guilty. You've never actually said to me that you love him and that you want to be with him."

"I don't love him anymore, but I can't seem to stop saying it because it's habit and that's what he wants to hear."

"And it's all he hears. You're not responsible for his happiness or his life."

"I know."

"You have to start living for yourself. You're trying to break free of a cycle where you've endured abuse for completely normal and acceptable behaviour. You need a plan to deal with his emails and calls. You need to tell him before he comes back that he has to find somewhere else to live. If he moves back in, then you'll be caught in the cycle again, where you can't think clearly and you are living for the moment, for survival. Move his things out if you can."

"But it's his house too."

"Well, both of you can't live there, and if he moves back in, you know he won't leave. You can resolve what happens with the house when he returns, but both of you cannot live there. Do you understand? You need to be absolutely clear about this."

"I think so."

"You know what you need to do. Make another appointment if you forget."

If I can afford it.

Waiting Rooms and Showers

I sit in the doctor's office flipping through *Maclean's* as Baba natters away at me. She's decked out for the appointment in a navy skirt and a twenty-year-old orange blouse. I have a good relationship with her on the farm, but when we occasionally venture out into public for shopping excursions or doctors' appointments, I try to limit my connection to her by dropping her off and taking a really long time to park, or burying my head in a magazine.

"I wish these parents would control their kids," she announces in her stage whisper, perfectly audible to the entire waiting room. Two children race their toy trucks on the floor, using our feet as obstacles on their racecourse. I ignore her, trying not to encourage her public commentary. "Go ask that nurse how much longer it's going to be." She insists we show up forty-five minutes early for her appointment and then badgers the nurses about having to wait. Sometimes we show up without an appointment. She still pesters the nurses about having to wait.

"Let's just wait a few minutes and then I'll go ask. Here, do you want to read a magazine?" I try to pawn her off onto *Maclean's*.

"I can't read a goddamn thing. My eyes are no good today. All they put in those magazines is garbage anyway." I go back to the article. "So, is there anything good in there?" she asks. I haven't gotten through a single sentence.

I am no stranger to waiting rooms. I've spent years in them with Adam.

"Let's go," Adam demanded. We were at Sara's twenty-seventh birthday party. His chest started to heave and he held his head in his hands. He couldn't breathe, he said, everything was spinning and he thought he was dying. We went to the hospital.

We spent much of the following year in the waiting areas of emergency rooms and clinics, trying to figure out what was wrong with him. I sat beside Adam as he morbidly imagined his dramatic exit from this world.

"We didn't find anything," one doctor announced, scrutinizing a crisp sheet with a murky grey-and-white image of Adam's brain. Adam was disappointed. For twenty dollars they let him keep the snapshot of the inside of his head.

He didn't have a tumour, but his chest continued to heave and his world continued to spin. The final prognosis: Panic disorder. Anxiety attacks. A malady that had no medical treatment and little value in the medical system, an illness that doctors swept to the side for therapists and psychologists to treat. There was no cure; there was only the Valium offered by another doctor who tried to rectify every single ailment with prescription drugs. Adam was handed an umbrella to shield himself from the hurricane in his mind.

"Mrs. Lasko," the doctor calls. My head snaps up. Baba rises, pulling her black purse toward her chest. She wraps her arms around it and clings to it as though we are surrounded by convicted purse snatchers. She walks toward the nurse, scowling at her.

"You come with me," Baba instructs me. The doctor follows us into the room as we sit down.

"What can we do for you today?" he asks brightly.

"Everything aches. My feet are swollen and my hands are numb." *In other words, she's eighty-three years old. Can you fix that?*

"That's probably the arthritis, unfortunately. We can try some new pills."

"Pills don't help," she self-diagnoses. Her shoulders stoop slightly, but she tries to hold her head up high.

"Why don't you sit up here and I'll take your blood pressure." He pats the crisp paper on the examination table. The walls are papered with before and after pictures of hearts and lungs and livers affected by fat, smoke, and alcohol, respectively. I think I have an idea which one is my liver.

"There's nothing wrong with my blood pressure." I wonder why we are here since she rejects every single one of the doctor's suggestions. The doctor wraps the black band around her arm and pumps it up. Her knee-high nylon stockings have slid down, and are bunched around her ankles.

"She's still cutting her own grass and blowing her own snow," I say to dispel any notion that she is incapable.

"Because I don't get enough help." She still clings to her purse as she sits on the table.

"Seems like you're doing okay," the doctor says. "Blood pressure is just a touch high."

"That's from all of those kids running around in the waiting room."

"Mrs. Lasko, you're in good shape, except for a few aches and pains. You should keep doing whatever it is you're doing."

"What about my eyes? I can't see. It's getting worse."

"We'll leave that to the eye specialist. It says here you have an appointment with him in a few weeks."

"These appointments are useless," Baba announces on our way out, her words audible to the entire waiting room. "And I remember when kids used to sit quietly by their parents, not all this tearing around."

Like Adam, she has again been denied the grim diagnosis she wanted.

I deposit her back at her farm and head home to get ready for what I hope will be Sara's last bridal shower.

When I arrive at the shower, late, Sara is already seated, wearing a pink skirt, surrounded by a throng of older women who are cooing over the details of her wedding. Julia drags me into the kitchen, where Renate is standing awkwardly beside two women engaged in a heated debate about the proper way to repot a hibiscus plant. Renate is bursting out of her sweater. Her baby is due in a week.

"I'm fucking Métis," Julia announces. The two women scurry out of the kitchen.

"What?!" Renate blurts through a mouthful of crinkle-cut carrots.

"I had my meeting with the adoption agency today."

"And you're Métis?" I ask.

"Yeah, can you believe that?"

"It's great," Renate enthuses.

"This totally changes who I thought I was," Julia huffs.

"It explains your hair, now that you mention it," I say, running my fingers through her long, smooth dark hair. "I'd kill for hair this straight and shiny. It all makes sense now. There's always been something kind of exotic about you—I mean in a good way." Her icy blue eyes, deep olive skin, and dark hair are suddenly explained. My second-generation Ukrainian Canadian heritage doesn't assign me an exotic look. "And how does this change who you are? You're you."

"I don't know, Anna. Gee, what if I told you you were fucking Hindu?" She swats my hand away.

"You get to inherit this whole new culture. It's amazing," Renate says, her eyes glinting with excitement.

"I have to think about it. I don't know if I want to be Indian."

"You're French too," I add. "It's so cool."

Sara enters the kitchen, about to rip into us for not mingling with the other shower guests.

"Julia's Métis!" Renate blurts out.

"Huh?" Sara is clearly thrown off her wedding game momentarily.

"Yeah, I just found out at my adoption agency meeting."

"Oh." Sara glances at her watch. "Well, can we talk about this later and do this shower thing now?" As we follow Sara back into the living room, she adds, "We'll have to talk about the tax stuff, Julia. You'll get some good tax breaks." Sara, always the practical one.

"And these are the ladies in peach," Sara announces to the women congregated in the living room, gesturing at us. We are offered non-alcoholic punch as we slip into our seats. The absence of liquor promises to make the night that much longer.

"Don't remind us about the peach," Julia mutters. It will be nice when Sara returns from the wedding planet she's been abducted to.

"I don't even know a single Métis person," Julia whispers to me.

"Louis Riel." I've suddenly remembered my eighth grade history. "He's Métis."

"Ladies, ladies." A plump woman is trying to get our attention. "How about we start things off with a game?" The announcement is met with gentle claps and warm sighs. "My name is Doris and we're going to play bridal bingo. The idea is to go around the room and find all the answers to the questions in the squares on this piece of paper you'll all get. The questions are all about Sara and Jeff. It's a great way to get us all mingling and to get to know our little bride-to-be."

"How is this bingo?" I ask Julia.

"I dunno." Julia rolls her eyes. "But it's better than trying to wrap a present using oven mitts." This was the activity of choice at the last shower.

"So when do you get to meet your birth parents?" Renate asks.

"It's just my mother. No father was ever listed in my file. I don't know. I have to decide if I even want to go through with this," she says, tugging her fitted sweater down past her hips. The sweater reveals some nice cleavage and a few soft rolls.

The women flit around the room. Julia, Renate, and I know most of the answers, so we don't have to mingle much, and we're a source of wisdom to the bridal shower enthusiasts.

"Do you know where their first kiss was?" Pauline asks. I'm pretty sure that it was in the guys' bathroom at a Halloween social at the Convention Centre. But Renate informs me that Sara would like us to go with ice-skating at The Forks Market. I don't think Sara has ever ice-skated in her life.

"Skating at the Forks," I mutter.

"This is a dumb game," Pauline grumbles. "It isn't even bingo." I like Pauline.

"I'll go with you if you decide to meet your mom and want support," I offer to Julia.

"Thanks. I really want Emma to know her," Julia sighs.

"I can't imagine how hard it must have been for your mother to have a baby and then give it up," Renate says. Her hands stroke her own belly. "I couldn't do it."

Julia turns to me. "Hey, speaking of babies, have you heard from Natalia lately?"

"Yeah. Still pregnant. Still two wives at last count. She seems like she's just kind of resigned herself to accepting it all. How can she be happy?"

"Hmmm. Sounds kind of familiar," Renate chimes in.

"Ladies, we have a winner," Doris announces. She hands a Tupperware salad spinner to an excited recipient. *I should have tried. I could use a salad spinner.* We move on to a contest to see who can peel the most hard-boiled eggs in thirty seconds. Julia wins a roasting pan, and then she's dragged off to the kitchen by Doris to whip up some egg salad. We are left to suffer through about seven more games. We then have to haul around tray after tray of cake and cookies to women who say "Really, I shouldn't" due to various diets, but load up their little plates anyway.

When it's time to open the gifts, we develop an efficient assembly line. Julia passes Sara the gifts, usually correctly guessing what each one is as she passes it into Sara's manicured hands. I record the person's name and the gift onto a chart that Sara has made, along with my own personal comments.

Name	Gift	
Helen	tea towels	(how original)
Doris	salad bowl	(fourth one)
Edith	embroidered napkins	(not on the registry)

Renate gets excused from having to do much, seeing as she's about to have a baby and spends most of her time making trips to the bathroom. Being in the middle of a public breakup has, so far, excused me from nothing.

"I don't remember my showers being this bad," Renate says.

"They weren't." It's true that when she was married three years ago, I was the maid of honour and had to help organize these showers. But that wasn't the worst part. Adam was turning totally psycho by that point, and I didn't have the heart to tell Renate, in the middle of her wedding preparations, that my world was falling apart.

"Let's go," Adam snapped. We were at Renate and Calvin's Jack and Jill shower, which I'd insisted we both attend. I felt warm from the fire and the wine, and my belly was rounded by the food. Candles and laughter flickered around the room. Renate and Calvin looked happy. I was envious.

Adam's panic attacks happened randomly, but inevitably disrupted whatever we were in the middle of. A cart filled with soup, pasta, and vegetables would be abandoned in a grocery store aisle; half-drunk lattes and conversations with friends abandoned in restaurants—we were at the whim of his increasingly frequent attacks.

"What? I can't leave. Renate's my best friend and I'm her maid of honour. I'll meet you at home," I said, handing him the car keys. I was not in the mood to cater to one of his fits.

Adam grabbed the keys and left. I finished my glass of wine and then three more before I took a cab home at midnight. The door was deadbolted. I hit the doorbell, breaking the silence of the house. A few minutes later Adam stomped down the steps and opened the door. On his way back up to the bedroom, he turned to glare at me mid-stairway.

"How dare you?" His hair was dishevelled, like he had run his hands through it a thousand times, his eyes wide and angry.

"What?" I asked, knowing full well he was irate that I had not trailed home immediately after him.

"My heart has been racing for three hours and you don't even give a shit!" He squeezed his head with the palm of his hand.

I walked past him up the stairs to the bedroom. There was a pattern to these rages and I thought that maybe I could skip our twisted waltz that evening. No such luck.

He followed me to the bedroom, shouting his preferred insult: "Selfish slut!"

"What did I do?"

"It would be nice if I was with someone who supported me."

"I do."

"Yeah, how? By going out and getting drunk with other men?" Jealousy and paranoia lured the panic out from deep within Adam. Like a driver impaired by anxiety, he swerved toward me. He was inches from my face and his hot breath hit me as he yelled.

"This is the first time I've stayed out with our friends in months." I sat down on the bed. Since Adam's panic attacks had begun, we rarely went out anymore; he hardly left the house. If I did leave, he would badger me about where I was going and with whom to the point that I didn't bother going. I'd thought Renate's shower was a good enough reason to break the pattern.

"My heart was racing and I felt like I was gonna die, and you were out having a good time. How can you have fun when I feel like this?" he yelled.

"What am I supposed to do?" I yanked the covers from the bed. "Stay in the fucking house all the time?" I craved sleep, but I knew he wasn't going to let me.

"Why am I not enough for you?" He was no longer yelling, but hissing through clenched teeth. "If you loved me, you wouldn't do this to me. Selfish. That's what you are." The walls and the furniture were swirling around me. I was scared and drunk and exhausted all at once. The contents of my skull were mushy.

"Was it at least worth it? Did you have a good time talking to your new boyfriend?"

"Who? Who is my new boyfriend? Renate's fiancé?"

"His brother. I saw you two laughing. What were you laughing about?" I didn't even know Calvin had a brother. I had no memory of talking to him, but I was too tired to refute Adam's stupid jealousy.

"Was it me? Were you laughing at me?"

"No."

"It sure looked like you were having a good time and would rather be there than here!" He yanked his pillow off the bed, turned, and went to the couch downstairs. My shaky breathing interrupted the stillness of the bedroom.

We didn't talk for two days. He stomped around the house in silence, and I tiptoed, the wood floors creaking with each tentative step. The stillness was oppressive and more volatile than the argument two nights before.

"Do you want to see a movie?" Adam tugged my ponytail gently, finally breaking the silence on the evening of the third day. This was part of the pattern too. He had to make up with me; I had to forgive him. Only then could it start all over again.

"Okay." I set my book down, relieved that it was over for now. He leaned over me to reach for the movie section of the paper. I could smell the mint gum he was chewing.

We saw *Anger Management*. Fitting.

"I'm sorry about the other night." He put his hand on my knee as we sat in the car after the movie.

"It's okay."

"I didn't mean the things I said. It's just that my heart starts racing ..."

"I know." I slipped the key into the ignition and turned it.

"I felt alone and I just needed you."

"I know." I shifted the car into drive. I was relieved that it was over, and I could once again walk around the house normally. At least until the next time. I wasn't stupid. I knew there would be a next time.

It's almost nine o'clock by the time Sara finishes unwrapping all of the shower gifts and the alcohol-free shower is finally ending. Renate can't lift anything because of her belly, Julia is too worked up about being Métis to be of any use, and Sara manages to disappear anytime there is manual labour to be done—and besides, her heels are so high that carrying a toaster would surely cause her to topple over—so I am left to carry all of the salad spinners and cake platters out to her car. I'm exhausted by the time I get home and *finally* pour myself a glass of wine, vowing never to attend another bridal shower, especially one without booze.

Spring Fever

I sit on the steps with Buddy, drinking coffee and reading my Saturday paper, when a rabbit pokes its head through the bushes in the corner of the yard.

"He better stay away from my stash," Buddy says.

"I don't think Little Rabbit Foo Foo eats nuts."

"I know that guy. He'll eat anything. You should clean up your yard. Rabbits like unkempt yards, you know."

"I like rabbits."

"They're nothing but trouble," he mutters. "I didn't want to tell you this, but sometimes I'm embarrassed to admit that I even live in this yard."

"You don't live in the yard, you live in *my house*."

"You're splitting hairs. You know what I mean." Buddy's right. The yard is a mess of weeds tangled with last year's dead leaves. The grass has been overrun by clover, and the grape vines strangle the surrounding peonies and tulips. The untrimmed bushes reach out in every direction, and the lower branches have flopped down onto the lawn. Weeds trace the cracks in the pathway leading up to the house. Adam has left his green thumb print on the yard, but it is haggard and messy from neglect. I decide to clean it up—it will be the first step toward getting my whole life in order. If I clean up my yard, maybe I'll be okay.

I'm determined to eradicate the weeds. My yard will not be an embarrassment to Buddy and a haven for rabbits. I tug at the gnarled weeds and chop away at the bushes, attempting to give them shape. I rescue the ferns and daffodils, suffocating beneath the creeping charlie. At the end of the day, my palms are blistered and the dirt is so thickly caked beneath my short fingernails that I can't scrub my hands clean. When I inspect my work, I'm entirely disappointed. There's little difference. My lawn and my life—both hopeless. I call my sympathetic mother to tell her how frustrated I am with my yard and to let her know there are a few more shopping-channel deliveries awaiting her pickup.

"People spend years on their yards. You can't expect to get it done in one day. Did the steamer show up yet?"

"I think it came the other day."

"I'll be by to pick it up soon." Mom's yard looks like a Walt Disney picture book.

The next day, my Sunday morning ritual of smoking cigarettes and reading is interrupted by a high-pitch grinding noise that surely grates on the nerves of the entire neighbourhood. I peer out the window to see Dad, in his green coveralls, amid a self-created leaf tornado. I stub out my cigarette and go outside. Dad is circulating around the yard with the gas-powered leaf blower strapped to his back. He's extended the sides of the bed of his truck upward using large pieces of rotting plywood. It's prominently parked in front of my house. Mom emerges from within the truck smiling, armed with a rake. She is wearing capri pants with rubber boots even though it hasn't rained in weeks.

"We thought we'd help you out," she yells over the leaf blower.

"I'm going to blow them into piles, and you two start loading them into the back of the truck. Just throw them in there; don't worry about bagging them," Dad orders. He has a gas-powered yard appliance for every occasion—leaf blower, mower, weed whacker, tree trimmer.

We obediently load the leaves left over from last fall into his plywood coffin. I've no doubt that this incident will solidify my reputation in the neighbourhood as a hillbilly.

In an hour, my lawn is cleared of last year's foliage, and I'm completely nauseous from the flatulence of the gas-powered blower. Dad lowers the machine down onto the truck bed and slides his arms through the shoulder straps of another contraption that he hoists onto his back.

"What's that?" I ask.

"Herbicides," he replies.

"What for?"

"What for? To kill all this shit that's growing on your lawn. I'll probably need to do a few treatments. This lawn's a real mess." I know he's not using over-the-counter herbicides, but illegal farm chemicals that will blister my bare feet.

"That damn Chinese elm tree," he complains. "Whoever decided to plant these all over the city must have had rocks for brains. They grow twice as fast, but they make a bloody mess in people's yards." The Chinese elm spits seeds into the air in the spring that flutter to the ground and stick to decks and cars and feet. "You should get rid of it."

"But it's on city property."

"Planting these trees is like planting dandelions on your lawn because you want flowers." He finishes coating my lawn with chemicals. "Let's unload these leaves," he says, getting into the truck.

"We should also see about getting this lamppost removed," Mom says, taking off her gardening gloves, gesturing to the street light.

"What!? Why?"

"Having a lamppost in front of your house is like having a poisonous dagger pointed at you. The only way to counteract it if you can't get rid of it is to plant a jade tree in front of your door."

"Oh." This valuable information must have come from the feng shui book she ordered from the Home Shopping Channel last month. At least she's moved on from her glittery shirt-making phase.

We pile into the truck of leaves to drive to what I assume will be a leaf depository. Instead, Dad drives to the highway on the outskirts of the city and steps on the gas until the truck reaches 120. The plywood begins to shake. I slide way down on the seat as a trail of leaves sprays out behind us. A few minutes later the truck is empty. No bagging.

Dad moves around the house with determination as he sets traps to try to catch Buddy.

"I sealed up the hole in the closet, so I don't know where the little bugger is coming in." Dad tests the traps with a stick. I decline to tell him that Buddy insists on using the front door.

"I'm going to set one in the closet and one in the basement. These live traps are supposed to be pretty good," he says, scratching his grey stubble.

"I'll keep checking them and call you if I find anything," I lie.

"When we get him I'm going to take him for a little ride out to the country. I've also set a few mouse traps in the basement because there's mouse shit down there."

Mom's cleaning the caked mud from her shoes and from the way she rubs her temples, I can tell she's had enough of my house for one day. Perhaps she was feeling poisoned from the lamppost in front of my house. I don't bother to remind her that she's shown up of her own volition, and that I would have gladly spent the day drinking coffee and reading the paper.

"Thanks." I walk them to the door. When I return to the kitchen, Buddy is pacing back and forth.

"Does he think I'm stupid enough to get caught in one of his dumb traps? Really! He's gotten a little out of hand, don't you think? And why are you thanking him, anyway?"

"Who cares? Just ignore them."

"This is where I live. I think it's offensive, quite frankly, to be setting traps to catch me in my own house. It's the principle. I know this is a difficult concept to grasp for someone who doesn't stand up for herself."

"What are you talking about?"

"I read Adam's last letter about moving back in here."

"Stop reading my mail."

"And what did you tell him? Did you say no? Of course not."

"I was going to. I just haven't gotten around to it yet."

"He is not moving back in here. And you need to tell him that in no uncertain terms."

"I will."

"If you let him move back in, you're finished. And change the locks."

"Okay, okay. Have you been talking to my therapist?"

"I can't believe you pay money to see that woman when you have me here," he says.

"Are we done here? I'm tired and I want to go to bed."

"Yeah. Can you open the cupboard first? I need a snack." I throw a few crackers on the floor and head up to bed.

Baba has spent the week cleaning out the chicken coop. She patched up the holes with old boards and chicken wire, and swept the mouldy dust and hay from the floor. She spread a layer of fresh straw across the floor and hung a heat bulb from the ceiling to warm the chicks through the cool, damp nights.

When I arrive she is rummaging through the garage. She pulls out a flat, plastic crate to transport the chicks, wiping the dust off the crate with a wet rag.

Against my better judgment I agreed to take her to the Hutterite colony to get her chickens. Dad will kill me. She's got spring fever and she just wants to add a little life to her dull world. Don't we all? I can't blame her. Dad will still kill me.

Another reason I agree to take her, aside from her begging and bribing, is that I like visiting the Hutterite colony. They all look so wide-eyed, with pleasant smiles, like they've been injected with happy drugs. When we arrive, a woman wearing a dress stamped with tulips greets us.

"Hi, we're here for the chicks. We called," Baba says. I wonder if life can really be this simple and happy, or if this pared-down colony existence is just another veneer.

She leads us to a metal barn. "They're in here. You can pick which ones you want." She speaks slowly as she swings the door open. The high metal ceiling echoes with the squeaking of thousands of chicks. In front of us lies a yellow, pulsing fleece carpet.

They huddle and cower as Baba's bony hand plucks them, one by one, and places them into the crate. They're wide-eyed and oblivious to the horrid fate that awaits them.

"Pick some," she tells me. I hold one up and put it to my nose. I'd forgotten how good they smell, like milk and fresh straw. I place it into the crate, forcing from my mind the thought of its

little head being lopped off in a few months. Baba pays the Hutterite woman, after quibbling about the price, and we bring the
chicks back to the farm. She dumps the crate into the chicken
coop and the chicks tumble out, rolling on top of one another.
Butch sniffs at the chicks, and Baba cuffs her on the side of the
head so she understands that they're not her dinner. Life is restored
to the farm. Baba grins. She forgot to put her teeth in again.

"You want to make some Easter eggs this afternoon?" Baba
asks. "It's time we get going on them."

"Sure." Today the chicks come first and then the eggs. Back
inside I spread newspaper across the kitchen table. Baba places
some candles, a chunk of beeswax, and the grey plastic box with
our supplies on the paper. I set a candle in the holder and light it
with a wooden match as Baba returns from the fridge with a car-
ton of large, white eggs. Twelve clean canvasses.

Baba taught me how to make *pysanky* when I was five years old.
My tiny hand clutched the wooden shaft of the *kiska*, scraping
the metal tip across the egg, leaving a wobbly trail of wax behind
to harden on the smooth, white surface. I packed more beeswax
into the *kiska* and heated the tip in the candle flame. Just as I
brought it up, blobs of black wax bombed my egg, marring the
pattern I'd created.

"I ruined it."

"Well, you sort of did, but keep going anyway. Make the mistakes part of the design," Baba had said.

"Okay. But it won't look very nice. It won't look like yours,"
I complained.

As I'm heating my *kiska* in the candle flame, I peer up at the brown-painted kitchen cabinets. The glass display case is filled with Baba's wedding presents—teacups with gold-plated leaves, crystal serving dishes, and silver cake platters. Both her wedding and my grandfather are long gone, but the presents remain in the display case, untouched, symbols of another life, proof that Baba has not always lived on the farm alone. My eyes fix on the glass globes filled with Baba's beautiful Easter eggs. Her traditional patterns are flawless, crisp lines that form intricate stars, layered with colour, divided the surfaces of her eggs. Her designs, she has explained, symbolize knowledge and growth.

"We'll put your nicest egg into a glass globe up in the display case," Baba announced when I was seven and had been practising the art of *pysanky* making for a few years. I loved the thought of Baba unscrewing the base of the globe and placing one of my eggs into that colourful and mysterious Ukrainian world. Until now, mine had always been stored in the back of the fridge. And once I thought I'd seen Baba use one of them for a banana cake when she had run out of the regular white eggs.

Baba immersed my egg into the cup of yellow dye, the first colour in the row of cups. Yellow. Orange. Red. Some years green or blue, and then black.

I'd spent the entire day stooped over my egg at the kitchen table. Finally, it was ready for the last dye, the black one, and Baba plunged it into the cup.

"Is it done yet?"

"No."

"Is it ready?"

"No."

"Can we take it out now?"

"Would you go siddown? You'll learn patience."

At last, Baba pulled my egg from the black dye. It was dark and covered with clumps of hardened wax. She placed it into a bread pan and slid it into her warm oven. A few minutes later she wiped away the runny wax to reveal a mess of crooked but colourful lines and shapes.

"Well, at least the chicken won't recognize it," she said as she handed me my egg. As I inspected it, the warm egg slipped through my fingers and splatted on the floor.

"That's the one I wanted to put in the display case," I sobbed.

"There'll be others."

Baba cleaned up the slimy yolk and then wiped the tears from my face with the same rag.

In eighth grade Sara, Renate, and Julia spent spring break at the shopping mall trying out Pink Petal and Cherry Kiss lip gloss at Shoppers Drug Mart, fighting for space in front of the oval mirror at the makeup counter. Later, they might go to a Julia Roberts matinee at the theatre, or, if the fair was set up in the mall parking lot, they might have wandered around in their tight Calvin Kleins, pulling at cotton candy, luring the tenth grade boys toward them. I wasn't with them. I was at Baba's farm making eggs. All afternoon we listened to the stories that blared from the television in the living room—"Another World," "General Hospital," "Days of Our Lives." I was privy to all of the tragedies of life from a very young age: sex scandals, kidnappings, car accidents, and comas were the soundtrack to our Ukrainian Easter egg painting.

I perfected Baba's patterns and experimented with new designs and colours. I looked up and caught Baba admiring my steady hands.

"Have you got your visitor yet?" Baba asked. Baba's conversational pinball sent me flying from one topic to the next.

"Who?"

"Your monthly visitor. Your period."

I gagged and felt my mouthful of coffee being forced out through my nose.

"No," I mumbled.

"Well, don't worry. I was almost sixteen before I got mine."

Thankfully, a Huggies commercial interrupted what might have been an embarrassing talk with Baba.

"Why do they show those kids running around in diapers? That's where these men get the ideas to molest kids," she said, dipping her *kiska* into the candle flame. "They don't have to show naked kids to sell diapers." She had developed her own logic to explain the degenerative state of the world. Seat belts were a money-making ploy for the NDP, church attendance was down because the priest was using Sunday donations to buy his wife new hats, and diaper ads encouraged crime.

We concentrated on our eggs. The candle burned down too low, lapping at the curled edges of the newspaper. Flames suddenly shot up between us. Baba swatted out the flames with a tea towel, but the force of her blows crushed all of our eggs. We were left with a blistered table and colourful bits of eggshell. Baba would later use these as bingo chips at the church bazaar.

"So, how's it looking?" Baba asks of the *pysanky* I'm working on.

"Okay, but it's the first one."

"It's nice. We should take yours to the church and sell them. I can make back some of the money I donated," she says, scraping at an egg with a razor blade to fix a mistake. The wax can be removed, but traces of the mistake will always be visible on the *pysanky*.

"We'll see how they turn out."

"You can get ten dollars apiece for the nice ones."

Baba looks up from her *pysanky.* "I'll butcher the chicks in the summer," she muses.

"I don't know if it was a good idea to get them," I say.

"Your father would have me sit on this farm and do nothing all day."

"He'll be mad." I cross my legs underneath me on the chair as I inspect my egg.

"So what?"

She's beside the sink, struggling to open the packages of dye with her crooked fingers. *These* are the hands that will attempt to butcher chickens. Dad may have been right this time.

She slipped off an aluminum ladder while hanging Christmas lights last winter, so Dad bolted the lights to her house so they remain up all year. Later, I caught her up on the ladder this winter, shovelling her roof. The previous summer, she grew tired of mowing around the stump of a dead tree that Dad had cut down. In an attempt to get rid of it, she drilled a hole deep into the stump, poured gasoline down the hole, and lit it on fire. The fire melted the front end of her riding lawnmower. Now Dad cuts the grass.

She uses me as her ally in her arguments with her son. I'm stranded, balancing on the frayed tightrope of their relationship. But work, Baba says, is all she has. Pails of apples and bags of chicken feed measure her happiness. I don't want to be the one to take that away from her.

"Do you need a hand?" I ask.

"I can't get these goddamn packages open. Everything is childproof. These kids are ruining the world for everybody."

I put down my egg and *kiska* and join her by the sink. The kitchen has barely changed. The cupboards are still painted wood, the copper-coloured flecks in the countertop have faded a little. Only a white stove with its glaring green digital clock is new in her kitchen. Naturally, she hates her new stove. It doesn't bake as well as the old one, she says. I help her tear open the colour packages. I dump the powder into the lined-up cups, and she adds the boiling water and vinegar.

A few hours later I'm beginning my fourth egg and she is still struggling with her first. She rubs at her eye, but the cataract that blocks her vision is stubborn, and won't be wiped away.

"Can I finish this one?" she asks, taking one of my rejects.

"Yeah, go ahead."

I watch her out of the corner of my eye. She begins to draw a wax line around the circumference of the egg. I'm moved by her concentration and her need to connect the start and end point of this line. I can see her line veering. The points will never connect. Her hand, clutching the *kiska*, arrives around the other side of the egg, a centimetre above where she started. She sets the egg and the *kiska* down.

Her lines have become shaky. Until today she'd always been able to finish. Last year, her *pysanky* found a place in the glass globe beside one I'd made when I was a kid. Among the others in the mess of colour, our *pysanky* looked perfect. Closer inspection revealed that both were marred by blobs of unwanted wax and lines, not straight, but badly wanting to be—the desperate efforts of a young child and a woman going blind.

I brace myself for a tirade about her weak vision, the useless doctors, the medical system, and finally the useless Canadian government.

"Well, I guess that's it for me. I can't see." That's all she says. I don't know how to react. I prefer it when she blames the government for her problems. I've never seen her defeated. I always assumed that she would be barking and grumbling and accusing even as they lower her coffin into the ground. "Rest in peace" does not apply to her.

"Why don't you try to finish anyway? You always told me to try to make the mistakes part of the design."

"That's because you'd waste so many goddamn eggs. You'd take a fresh white egg every time you made a mistake. My chickens couldn't lay them fast enough." There are several white abandoned eggs in front of her that have blotchy streaks of wax on them.

"Why don't you try using that magnifying light?"

"No, it's no use." She waves her hand dismissively at everything on the table.

"Just paint them so that the chicken doesn't recognize them," I offer. She picks up one of my *pysanky* and rolls it in her hand.

"This one will be nice. You need to add some more red, though."

"You're not going to paint your own? You're just going to sit there and tell me how to make mine?" I set down my tool and blow out the candle.

She smiles, but I feel her sadness merge with my own. The traditional patterns of her eggs and her life have been disturbed. They're deteriorating. Her blindness is like stubborn wax that won't melt away. She is trapped in darkness.

I look up at the display case. The vibrant patterns, the stories and memories, mixed with the dye, are forever preserved in those *pysanky*, a Ukrainian map of our relationship.

Cavities and Wetting Dresses

"When does Adam get back?"
"Nehs weeh."
"You're not going to pick him up, are you?"
"I ohno."
"What do you mean you don't know? Of course you're not going to pick him up. And since he's back next week, you better figure it out." I'm tilted back in Renate's dental chair with my jaw cranked open. She prods at my tooth and gums with her arsenal of metal instruments. Unfortunately, getting my teeth fixed means I have to lie in her torture chair with my mouth open, a vessel where she can dump her unsolicited advice.

"Ahhow."
"Sorry."
"Wus a ig eal ih I ich im uh?"
"The big deal is that you won't just pick him up, he'll be staying with you. I can't believe we're having this conversation! Have you changed the locks yet?"

"I'n unna amorrow." Even though half my mouth is frozen, I can feel the blood ooze up and over my lip and onto my bib. She's butchering me alive. Right now I wish she was paying more attention to my dental care than my personal life.

"Make sure it happens," Renate chides. "In his mind he still lives there." She leans over me, but can't get the right angle because her stomach is too big. "This is a bit of a butcher job. I can't see that well into your mouth. Sorry, but at least your cavity will be filled. You're my last appointment. Hello, mat leave."

"Ou sill avin ex?"

"Absolutely. Sex is fucking amazing. It's about the only good thing about being nine months pregnant."

"I ann et laid."

"You think with your G spot. The last thing you need to worry about is getting laid. You need to get your life together. Don't even think the words 'Adam' and 'sex' in the same sentence."

"Alwight."

"Close your lips around this. It won't get you off, but it'll clean your mouth out." The plastic tube sucks away my bloody saliva. I wish it would just suck me away too. I don't want to deal with Adam coming home.

"Okay, you're done. So I'll see you at the dress fitting tonight?" she says, as she raises my chair.

"Uck. I omot forot."

A trip to Renate's office usually means I will have my dental as well as my emotional cavities filled. It's always painful.

When I get home, I pull out the Yellow Pages. I make the call.

Two hours later I watch the locksmith manipulate the locks with his sleek tools. Adam comes home in less than a week and I finally take the advice of *everyone* and have the locks changed.

"That'll do it."

"That's it?"

"Yup. Here's your new set of keys." The actual procedure hardly matched the emotional difficulty of making the call. It's a cold and untrusting thing to do, but this bulky man, clad in a jacket emblazoned with Heart Locks, deftly completes the operation in less than two minutes.

It's like getting a Pap smear. I will always put off the appointment for a couple of years because all I can remember is an eternity of having my feet trapped in metal shackles while the doctor, with his head between my legs, splays out my unsuspecting vagina with cold clamps and prods my cervix with a stick. In reality the procedure lasts minutes—less, if I don't distract the doctor with uncomfortable vagina jokes. Like with the changing of the locks, I build a simple physical procedure up in my own head to be an emotionally ravaging experience.

The Heart Lock man leaves. I chose Heart Locks from the Yellow Pages because I thought it was appropriate. Really it is my heart that I am trying to lock Adam out of. This is a sensitive procedure, but I know I cannot pay someone from the telephone book to do it.

I close the door. This door has been slammed and locked so many times. It needs to be closed for good.

I arrived home a year ago to a note taped on the door:

> When I hear you laughing
> You're not laughing at me
> You're not laughing with me
> You're laughing without me.
> And that says it ALL.
> (It's over. Goodbye.)
> You are my illness. You're killing me.
> Goodbye.

This time we were at a restaurant celebrating Sara's engagement last year when Adam insisted we leave. Our salads had just arrived.

"Go home, take a Valium, go to bed, and I'll be home in a few hours," I whispered. "I'm going to finish my dinner."

"You're not coming?" He pushed himself away from the table.

"We just got here. I'll be home soon." I dig into a crouton with my fork.

"Fine." He turned and walked out.

When I arrived home two hours later, I was greeted by the note and discovered that my keys would not open the door. The deadbolt was locked from the inside. Again.

Ding dong.

Ding dong.

Ding dong.

Ding dong.

Ding dong.

Dingdongdingdongdingdong.

I braced myself for another fight, but there was no answer. Adam had changed his tactics. I sat on the paved step and contemplated what to do. My parents would worry if I showed up there, I wouldn't hear the end of it from Renate, and Julia would punch Adam out. Sara was probably well into engagement sex by now. Adam didn't want me to tell anyone about his panic disorder, and I didn't want people to know how Adam treated me. We were embalmed in shame.

I drove to a Salisbury House restaurant that was open all night. A waitress with frizzy red hair soothed me with her offer of warm coffee.

"Looks like somebody has had her heart broken tonight," she said, as she turned over my cup and filled it with coffee. The tag on her green-striped uniform read Lily.

"My boyfriend is being kind of a jerk." The coffee soothed my dry mouth.

"I know jerks. I have two ex-husbands." She patted my arm, dropped a few creamers in front of me, and moved on to the next booth with her pot of black medicine. I flipped through a copy of yesterday's newspaper and attempted to finish an abandoned crossword puzzle. Nineteen down: four-letter word for a long time. Answer: ages.

The guy in the booth behind me was telling Lily about a movie script he was writing.

"It's about these bartenders and waitresses who work in this club," he explained. "It's kind of a behind-the-scenes of all the politics that go on in a bar, you know, with all the drunken regulars. I have this Hollywood connection too. I know a girl who used to date Gene Simmons. She's going to pitch it to him." Salisbury House— a late-night hangout where people come to dream or to forget about their dreams. I glanced around the room. Two women talked in low tones, another was buried in a Harlequin novel. A pair of paramedics ate lemon meringue pie. Everyone seemed to be killing time.

"So what'd he do?" Lily asked when she came to refill my coffee cup a few minutes later. Long earrings spiralled down to her shoulders.

"Locked me out." I fidgeted with my pack of cigarettes on the table.

"That one there," Lily said, gesturing across the restaurant to a woman playing solitaire in a booth, "is here every Saturday from eight in the evening until three in the morning. Her husband boots her out when his friends come over to play cards." I watched the woman flip over a three of spades. *That's what you have to look forward to, you pathetic loser,* Lily might as well have said.

The door swung open and a noisy group of teenagers funnelled in.

"There's my bar crowd," Lily groaned as she walked back to the counter. Within a few minutes, the place was raucous and the sweet blend of perfume and liquor wafted through the restaurant. I ached to be them and not me—the girls with their cropped tees and low-cut pants, nestling up to guys, maybe their boyfriends, or men they had picked up for the night. I had squandered my twenties. Wasn't it supposed to be the decade where you were old enough to appreciate life, but not old enough to be burdened by its problems? I hadn't felt good in years, and I hardly left the house anymore. And when I did, I wasn't allowed back in.

Tired, I retreated to my car, parked at the back of the restaurant. This seemed as good a place as any to catch a few hours of sleep. I rolled down the windows a little to let in some spring air and stretched out in the back seat of the Fury.

Click. Click. Click. Rings tapped on the window. Lily's face was cupped in her hands and pressed against the window of the Fury.

"Why don't you come stay with me and get a few hours of real sleep?" She pushed her words through the few inches of open window. I was groggy, my back ached, and I had no idea what time it was. I accepted her offer.

"I live just a few minutes away," she said, as she got into the passenger's seat. She directed me to her apartment.

I'm crashing with the waitress from the Sals. This could be my all-time low.

Lily unlocked the front door to three cats circling the floor of the entrance.

"Yes, darlings, I'm home. This is Scats, Barley, and Ingrid," she said bending down to rub their necks. Her apartment was small and smelled of the cats, cigarettes, and Avon. Lily pulled at the handle on the rose-coloured sofa until it slid open into a bed. She lay down a blanket and pillow.

"There you go. Everyone says it's comfortable." I lay down on the sofa bed. Lily went into the kitchen, where I heard her pour herself a drink and light a cigarette. Smoke wafted into the living room as I drifted to sleep.

When I woke up, a cat was sleeping on my head. Sun poured into the living room along with the recollection that I had spent the night in the home of some stranger I met at the Salisbury House. I pushed the reluctant cat off my face and stumbled into the kitchen, where Lily was sipping coffee.

"Morning." She was still wearing her uniform. I wasn't sure if she had even taken it off or gone to sleep at all.

"Good morning."

"Coffee?"

"I should get going."

"Here, sign my guest book before you leave," Lily said, handing me a cloth-covered book speckled with grease stains.

"Maybe I'll have a quick coffee before I head home." I took the book. Lily slid her package of Players toward me, and I lit a cigarette.

Hundreds of messages had been scrawled in the book: *Lil, thanks for not judging me (and lending me your pantyhose), Phil*; *Lily, thanks for letting me crash, Sandra*; *You rock, Lily*; *Lily, you're a great friend. I don't know what I would have done without you, Jocelyn*; *Lily, Thanks for not taking advantage of me, when most women would have, Steve*; *Lily, Don't take this the wrong way, but hopefully I won't be spending too many more nights here*; *Thanks for helping me get back on my feet, Trish.*

Lily obviously provided a refuge for displaced people—an admirable pastime, but I badly needed to leave her tiny, trinket-filled apartment. I didn't want to be another refugee in Lily's camp of screwed-up people.

"Thank you for everything. I should get home." I set the book down.

"Hope everything works out for you."

"It'll be okay."

"Wait, you didn't sign," Lily said, handing me a pen. I didn't want to sign. I didn't want to leave any traces that I had been here. I wanted to keep my turmoil buried within me. I reluctantly took the pen from Lily.

"It's okay." She smiled. "No one signs their real name." I realized that she never did ask me my name. I left a nice message about her pull-out sofa and signed it "Olga."

When I arrived home Adam was sitting on the steps. He leaned back on his hands, with his legs stretched out and crossed at his ankles. He was still wearing his T-shirt from last night and looked like he hadn't slept.

"Where were you?" he asked. A cup of coffee rested beside him.

"What do you mean 'Where were you?' You locked me out." I threw the note at him.

"Sorry. Where did you stay?" He wore a soft, melted smile on his face. The familiar look that admitted he'd crossed the line, the look he knew would garner my forgiveness. "I watched you from the tree." He took a sip of his coffee.

"What?"

"I climbed out of the window and into that tree and waited for you to get home," he said, gesturing to the Chinese elm.

"And you watched me trying to get into the house from the tree?" I wanted to kick him in the shins, but I smiled instead. Him in the tree waiting for me; me at the strange apartment all night. It was ridiculous what we'd become.

"These anxiety attacks make me do crazy things. It's like I can't control myself." He offers me his coffee cup and I take it. There's too much cream.

"I'll say. You need help."

"I'm sorry. It's like I want to hurt you. I can't stand it when you have fun and I feel shitty." His smile disappeared and his voice trembled a little.

"You can't do shit like that anymore." I swatted at his socked foot.

"The tree wasn't all that comfortable, you know."

The apology, peppered with humour, concluded the episode and signified a much-welcomed return to normality. It was over. For now. When things were uncharacteristically docile for a while, or when I was so lonely that the plants were making good company, I ventured out, but only furtively. Sometimes I'd go for a quick coffee after school. I lied about where I was—working late or at a meeting. Other times, I'd make desperate phone calls to forbidden friends, and hang up, mid-conversation, when I heard the front door open. Living my life in secret, in order to evade the attacks and anger.

Liar.

Whore.

Cunt.

His shouts were like doors slamming.

Why can't you just be happy with me?

Why do you do these things when you know how much pain they cause me?

These pleas drifted around the house like dust bunnies I would eventually chase and sweep up.

I hear banging upstairs as I test my keys in the new lock. It's Buddy.

"Get me out of this thing." Buddy is circling around inside the live trap. I laugh. "Really funny. Would you open it up now?"

"Okay, but I thought you were too smart to get caught in one of Dad's dumb traps?" I bend down, unlatch the trap, and open the door.

"I thought I could get at the peanut butter without setting the trap off." Buddy jumps out and shakes himself off.

Buddy and I settle into our usual spots on the steps, with Buddy working on a bag of mixed nuts and me sipping a glass of wine. A yellow city truck pulls up in front of the house.

Over the past week, the leaves on Adam's spying tree, the hated Chinese elm, have dried up and fallen off, and the branches have turned brittle. I interpret this as an obvious symbol of the dying relationship.

"Hey, how many City of Winnipeg workers does it take to inspect a tree?" Buddy asks.

"How many?"

"Four. Three to hold down the tree and one to inspect it." Buddy chuckles, a wheezing noise. I light a cigarette.

"Your jokes aren't really funny," I tell him after exhaling the smoke.

The city workers emerge from the truck. One measures the circumference of the tree, another screws something into the trunk, a third touches the bark of the tree and takes notes, and the fourth lights a cigarette.

"It looks like Dutch elm disease," one says.

"Yeah, but it doesn't usually touch Chinese elms."

"It's odd."

"Dutch elm disease my ass," Buddy scoffs. "I was napping in that tree a week and a half ago when it started to vibrate. Your dad was drilling a hole into it. He drilled a two-foot hole into the tree's roots and then he dumped a jug of farm pesticides into it."

"What?"

"Yup, saw it with my own eyes."

"Let's flag it," says the city worker with the cigarette. "They'll take it down next week. Can't take no chances." The orange flag tied to the large trunk of the tree flaps in the wind as the truck pulls away.

"After he killed the tree, Walter sealed up my hole into the house. It took me half a day to chew another one," Buddy complains.

I'm glad the tree is going.

"It fits," I say, holding up my arms in mad triumph. Elly, the seamstress, winks at me.

I came by earlier in the day for a private fitting. The dress was loose, as she suspected it would be. She took it in an inch.

"Unbelievable," Sara exclaims, delighted. She inspects us. "They look beautiful. You look great." Julia and I do anyway. Renate only holds hers up against her protruding belly so that Sara could see how our feet would look in the matching shoes she has just billed us for. "Lovely," she declares as she examines three pairs of feet stuffed into peach satin shoes.

Suddenly, before anyone realizes what's happened, one pair of shoes is soaked, as is the front of Renate's dress.

"Shit!" Renate moans.

"Oh my god, your water broke! We're having a baby. It's about fucking time!" Julia squeals.

"The dress!" Sara makes little attempt to conceal her horror.

"Don't even start," I warn her. "I'll call Calvin," I tell Renate.

"I'll take care of the dress," Elly says, handing Renate a towel.

We rush to the hospital, and three hours later, Renate delivers a seven-pound baby girl named Rachel. She's pudgy and pink and beautiful and for a moment I ache terribly for a baby. Then Rachel lets out a chilling scream and I'm yanked back into reality. Maybe I don't need one after all.

I smuggle a bottle of cheap champagne into the Women's Pavilion at the Health Sciences Centre. Calvin, Julia, Sara, and I toast Rachel's safe arrival and Renate sneaks a few desperate sips of champagne.

One baby down, one wedding to go. I might actually survive these life-altering events of my friends.

Renate swaddles her new baby while Sara natters on about final wedding details. It makes me realize that I miss Adam. It would be so easy to welcome him back into my life when he comes home, to pick up where we left off, without all of the bullshit. I know it'd be easier than starting over. Life-affirming moments, like the birth of a baby or a wedding, can gloss even the most desperate situations with hope.

"I'm meeting my mother on Thursday," Julia announces.

"That's fantastic," Renate sighs. "I finally meet my daughter and now you get to meet your mother." She strokes Rachel's tiny hand.

"Yeah, the agency set it up. I've decided that I'm going to embrace this whole Métis thing, you know? Maybe I'll get to go to a powwow," Julia exclaims. "You guys were right. There's this whole other world for me and Emma."

"Are you nervous?" I ask.

"Fuck, yeah."

"Do you need me to come along?" I offer. "I could just wait in the car or something."

"I should probably do this on my own."

"Even if you're nervous, you've got Emma with you. She's so young—she'll always just know her as her grandma."

Sara glances at her wristwatch. "Visiting hours ended ten minutes ago. We should probably go."

The next day, baby Rachel is moved into the infant intensive-care unit because the doctors have noticed that she is having difficulty breathing. They run tests and discover that Rachel has a tiny hole in her heart.

"They say that surgery will completely fix the problem. She's strong so she'll do okay with the operation," Renate tells me nervously as we sit beside Rachel's basin in ICU. A plastic tube invades her nose and another is taped to her wrist.

"She's so tiny. It seems unfair."

"I think maybe I'm being punished because I had the abortion. Some sort of twisted fate. I sacrificed a healthy baby, so now I get a sick one."

"Renate, this has nothing to do with that. It just happened. Besides, look at David: he's perfect. How do you explain that?"

"I know. I'm just trying to understand it."

"Stop it," I say. Renate drops her face onto my shoulder and I rub the small of her back. "She's going to be all right."

"I want you to be her godparent," Renate says, rubbing her eyes.

"Me?" I stifle my laughter. "I'd love to, but don't I have to believe in God, or at least in something?" I can't get my own life together and Renate's asking me to provide Rachel guidance.

"You're spiritual in your own way."

"I'd love to. Sara will be pissed."

"Fuck Sara. She's got a wedding, I've got a baby, Julia's got Emma—you need something."

"Is this a sympathy project?" An attempt to fill my empty, pathetic life?

"No way."

"So, is Sara still making you do the wedding?"

"Yup, she won't let me out of it. She says it will be good for me to get my mind off things."

"And she won't have to cut a groomsman from the roster. If you can't get out, then I don't stand a chance."

"Nope. Hey, will you stay with her and hold her hand for a while? I have to meet with Calvin and the surgeon in a few minutes."

I'm not sure I'm the best choice for Rachel. Part of my problem is that I don't believe in anything. Perhaps I wouldn't have landed myself in this mess with Adam if I was more engaged in something that I cared about. Adam has strong convictions and I have none. I think people need to buy into something either in this world or beyond. Nat wasn't rooted in anything either so she latched on to Aki's beliefs. I realize it's dangerous not to have your own convictions. Without them, you become someone else's prey.

Rachel grabs onto my pinky with her tiny hand.

"Rachel, you're only two days old and you have a little hole in your heart. And you haven't even met any boys yet." I'm already an embittered man-hating godmother. But it's my duty to provide her with fair warning about the real world. I will talk to her about self-respect and the importance of never letting that go just because a cute boy comes along.

I feel connected to Rachel as I look into her watery blue eyes. She looks strangely wise. I should be giving her strength, but it feels like she is passing her strength onto me. "You need to stay tough, kiddo. You have a fight ahead of you." She rolls her head sideways. "I know, I know, I should talk." Rachel and I make a pact right there to stay strong. I seal our agreement with a kiss on her blotchy forehead. "To the healing of hearts."

Calvin and Renate return from an optimistic meeting with the surgeon. He's performed the procedure many times, successfully. Other than her heart, Rachel is a healthy baby. I leave Renate and Calvin gazing at their daughter.

Family Plot Lines

Mom is getting impatient and frustrated with the Natalia situation, and she still doesn't know about the baby. I can't bring myself to tell her. It would destroy her, and besides, she can't do anything about it anyway. I try to explain to her that it's Nat's decision to stay in Iran, that she'll come to her senses eventually. Mom says that until I'm a mother, I will never be able to understand. She's probably right. I haven't received an email from Nat in a while, but I'm trying to respect her decision. She doesn't seem to be in any immediate danger, and I know she needs to come up with her own answers. We all do, though it's easier to impose unsolicited solutions onto those we love.

Mom insists that I accompany her to the police station. It's not how I'd planned to spend my Saturday. She thinks that I'm withholding information that might help bring Nat home. True, I am withholding information, but I doubt that Aki taking a second wife in Iran, where it's legal, and Nat expecting a baby with her husband, will strengthen her weak claim that Nat has been abducted by a crazy man.

"I'd like the police to help me bring home my missing daughter," she says to a skinny officer behind the desk at the police station. She'd gotten the idea of reporting Natalia's absence from an episode of the TV show "20/20."

"How long has your daughter been missing?" He starts to fill out a report and motions Mom to sit down.

"Eighteen months." Mom is gripping the edge of the desk so tightly her fingernails are white.

"Is this the first report?"

"Well, yes."

"How old is your daughter?"

"Twenty-six."

"Name?"

"Natalia Lasko." Mom watches carefully as he writes down her name. She might jump on top of him if he spells it wrong, as though a clerical error is the only thing that is keeping Nat away from home.

"And you have no idea where she is?"

"Well, she moved to the Middle East with her boyfriend," Mom says. I nudge her. "And she married him, so I suppose she's his wife now," she whispers. She can barely bring herself to say the word "wife."

"Have you had contact with her?" The officer puts down his Winnipeg Police Service ballpoint pen.

"No. My daughter has." She motions to me hunched behind her. I wave.

"In your communications with her, is there any indication that she's in any danger, or being held against her will?'

"No," I mumble. Mom glares at me.

"We think that she's been brainwashed by this lunatic she's married to." Mom rises out of her chair, like she's preparing to lurch at this skinny man. Her Dior scarf dangles over his desk. "He has a triangle tattoo on his neck!"

"If she's twenty-six years old and left of her own free will and she doesn't seem to be in any danger, there's not a whole lot we can do."

"I don't know what else to do. I know she's not okay." Mom slumps back down in the chair. "You were my last hope and now you're telling me that even you can't help me." Mom digs through her purse until she finds a tissue. According to "20/20," some eager-beaver detective was supposed to open a special file on Nat and make it his mission to bring her home and get a promotion out of the whole thing. The desk duty officer, who is probably more used to dealing with speeders contesting tickets, rests his wrists on his desk, hands open and empty. Then he opens the desk and offers Mom a card.

"This is a group that helps families in crisis. Why don't you try giving them a call? You might find it helpful." In other words, let him get back to his coffee and doughnut. Mom reluctantly takes the card and we leave.

"Take me to Wal-Mart. I need to get some things." This is the way Mom deals with trauma. She buys things. Lots of things. Things she doesn't need. Some people eat, others drink, Mom buys stuff. She pulls at the frayed ends of her scarf as we walk outside. We arrive at Wal-Mart and she lets the metal cart lead her around as though it's remote operated and she's attached to it. She throws all sorts of stuff into the cart—bleach, plastic storage bins, mops. "I've been meaning to get new mats for my car for ages." She also tosses one of those fuzzy steering wheel covers into the cart. And then deer whistles to attach to the hood of her car.

She spins 180 degrees with her cart and heads toward the cosmetics section where she grabs everything she will need to reconstruct her face—anti-aging creams, exfoliants, three different shades of lipstick.

When useless things begin to slip and slide over the edge of her cart, we head for the checkout.

As we stand in the long checkout line—our overflowing cart ensures no one stands behind us—Mom throws *Good House-keeping* and *Cooking Lite* into her cart. *Good Housekeeping* slides off the case of Coke and falls open on the floor between us. We both bend down to pick it up, and the headline "How to Know If Your Children Are Happy" leaps out at us. It triggers an emotional land mine in Mom.

"My daughters aren't happy," she sobs. "I don't know what I've done wrong." She's bawling and drawing the attention of all the Wal-Mart shoppers and cashiers. I'm torn between comforting her and wanting to move to the next line. "Anna, how did this happen? You're both such lovely girls." She's draped over me like a wet towel. *Oh God, please don't pull me into this. Not now, not at Wal-Mart.*

"Assistance at cash two," blares over the PA system. *That would be us.*

"Please stop crying," I whisper.

"I can't. I feel so horrible. All I want is for you to be happy." Dick: Assistant Manager, as his happy-face tag reads, arrives, apparently to save us.

"Is everything okay?" Dick asks, handing my mother a tissue.

"Everything is fine." Not only am I ignored, but Dick glares at me as though I'm a pathetic excuse for a human being. I want Dick both to fix Mom and to bugger off.

He walks Mom to the end of the store. I trail behind them, pushing the cart, a little disturbed that the Wal-Mart guy is doing a better job of comforting my mother than I am. I can't even keep up with them as Mom's cart wobbles along like a truck loaded with cement blocks.

None of this stuff will make Mom feel better. As Mom starts telling Dick about Nat and Aki, Dick nodding his head vigorously as he listens, I head through the checkout.

By the time I load her things into the trunk, her tears have dried.

"I'm so sorry. I don't know what came over me. It's all this business with Natalia."

"It's okay," I reassure her. "Are you hungry?"

"A little."

We go for sushi. I finally tell her, between pieces of sashimi, that Adam and I are ending our relationship, and more or less everything that's been going on. She listens and takes slow sips of her white wine. Her face is softened by the dim lighting of the restaurant, or maybe it's my honesty that relaxes her.

Parent-child relationships are strange. My parents spent twenty years trying to protect us from all of the shit in the world. I, and now Nat, have spent the following decade trying to shield our parents from the tragedies of our own lives. Then it starts all over. Dad tries in vain to protect Baba from the hazards of old age, while Baba defies Dad's efforts. It's an odd dance where one is always trying to lead the other around blindfolded, through a room full of swinging axes. And we've called it love.

"With everything that's going on with Nat, I didn't want to worry you even more." I sip my wine.

"I've known that you're not happy. With Natalia not talking to me, I didn't want to push you away too. I'm relieved that you've told me. And tired." Mom runs her hand through her hair. Then she tells me, in a cheery tone, that the Shopping Channel has the fall line coming out soon.

"I have to get going. I promised Baba I'd take her to a funeral this afternoon," I say, after we finish eating.

"She didn't mention anyone dying to me."

"I doubt she knows them personally."

"Are you sure this is the right place?" I ask Baba as we pull into the empty parking lot of the funeral chapel.

"Yeah, this is it."

"And you're sure it's today?"

"Yes."

I drive her to funerals about once a month, even though her relationship with some of the dead people is a little loose. Baba is a certified member of the Funeral Club. Funerals are social occasions—her own included. Sometimes I think she is shopping around for ideas.

Normally I would drop her off at the funeral and spend the morning at a bookstore or in a coffee shop. She always wants me to come in with her, but I flatly refuse. A line must be drawn.

"Maybe the funeral is this afternoon?" I ask.

"Let's go. You're coming with me."

"No one is here," I protest. She struggles to undo her seat belt.

"Seat belts. Just another way for the goddamn NDP to make money." I reach over and release the buckle. She gets out of the Fury and heads toward the entrance of the funeral chapel. I follow her inside the empty funeral home, knowing there's no funeral. Funerals are one of those rare events that never get cancelled.

"Hello, you must be Mrs. Lasko." A gentle man in a grey suit greets us. "I'm Peter Babinsky." He takes my grandmother's hand and gently shakes it.

"Hello."

"It's nice when people bring family to these appointments." He looks at me.

"Appointment!"

"Your grandmother is going to pick out a casket and make her funeral arrangements."

Shit! She's pulled me in here to help plan her funeral. It's dim inside and the ceilings are low. The smell of the place makes me nauseous. It's too warm. I take off my sweater.

"I'm interested in picking out the coffin first," Baba says, clutching her purse. She is wearing her newest polyester suit. She reluctantly got it eight years ago for her seventy-fifth birthday party.

"Well, let's take a look. Right this way." Mr. Death leads us into a room filled with open, empty caskets.

"You could have told me the truth," I mutter to Baba.

"You wouldn't have brought me." She's right. I would never have agreed to bring her if I'd known she wanted to plan her own funeral. I can't stand funerals. I ignore Baba or change the subject when she talks about her death. It seems morbid to me that she would want to spend time planning her funeral while she's still alive, especially since she doesn't have a lot of time left. Baba approaches her death the same way Sara approaches her wedding—it will be a major social occasion that others *will* enjoy.

"This one is very popular," Mr. Death says. Baba runs her hand along the mahogany surface. I shift behind her, uncomfortably.

"Soft," she says, touching the satin interior. "Do you remember your *Gido*'s funeral?"

"Sort of, I was only four."

I remember the oily, soapy smell that loomed around the coffin. I thought *Gido* had farted. Now I know that it was formaldehyde and that dead people don't fart.

"I'll have to find the pictures from his funeral," Baba says, taking my arm. "You looked at him in that casket and said, 'Baba, he looks so cozy.'" In my family it seems that confronting death is as important as revelling in life. We have photographs documenting each and every family death: close-up shots of the corpse, a parting photo of the once happily married couple, grandchildren with deceased grandparents, four-generation photos—with the first generation lying in a casket.

"This series, over here, has very plush interiors," Mr. Death says, interrupting our Kodak funeral moment.

"This is nice. I'd like to try it out," Baba says.

"I'll get a stepstool," Mr. Death tells her.

"Does it really matter? You're not going to know the difference!" I protest, but the funeral director takes her by the elbow and helps her onto the stool. I'm speechless as I watch the scenario unfold. This guy will stop at nothing to make a sale. The casket shakes a little on its stand as she stumbles into it, landing on her side. She rolls over onto her back, tucks her purse beside her, folds her hands neatly in front of her, and closes her eyes.

"How do I look?" she asks, as though she is trying on a dress. I stiffen. I want to tell her that the coffin makes her hips look wide to break the tension, my tension.

A new wave of nausea hits me as I watch her lying still in her coffin. She is trying not to breathe so she'll appear properly dead.

"I'll take it," she says, opening her eyes.

I park myself in a little side room where they put people who become too hysterical or ill during a funeral, while Baba goes over the details of her big day. I can hear them discussing flowers, the type of reception, and how many people she expects will attend. It's a lot like the wedding conversations I've had with Sara. Finally, I hear the funeral director say, "I'll get the paperwork. It'll just take a few moments."

After Baba fills out the forms, we stroll into the cemetery and walk over to *Gido*'s grave.

"He died twenty-five years ago," she says. "I'm ready to go too. I've lived a long time without him. Don't you think twenty-five years is long enough?"

"Yeah."

"This is my plot." She steps onto the plot beside my grandfather. "This is where I should be."

"You're doing okay, you know. There's no rush. He's waiting for you."

"I'm just saying that I'm ready. And I wanted you to know. That's all."

"Okay." We walk back to the car in silence.

"We might as well go and pick out a burial dress while we're at it," I suggest as we drive away.

By the time I arrive home I'm feeling lonely. I know Baba won't live forever, but I didn't expect to be confronted with her death in such visual detail. I try to push thoughts of Adam out of my mind. It's in these moments of weakness that I end up calling or emailing him. I pour a glass of wine and notice my computer screen flashing. Nat is online. I send her an instant message.

[Anna]:
how's the pregnancy? aki have any new wives? coming home anytime soon? i'm worried about mom because she's worried about you. how r things? need an update.

[Nat]:
i feel bad about mom. . . . i'll have to tell her everything that is going on, but it seems beyond her comprehension. i still believe in Allah. thought that Aki and i were on the same page. . . . there are many pages of Islam and I've only read a few.

[Anna]:
i'd return the book and find a new library.

I had assumed that when Aki got Nat pregnant and then took another wife, she might have been turned off from the whole Muslim thing. If anything, she seems to have become even more devout.

[Nat]:
just because Aki has another wife doesn't nullify the fact that we still want to spend our lives together worshipping Allah. i can't keep refashioning my life according to everyone else. when I took the Shadaha i experienced something that i had never felt before.

[Anna]:
what the hell's a shadada?

[Nat]:
It's a declaration of faith. When i took the Shadaha i finally felt at peace—like i could stop searching . . . even if i don't agree with EVERYTHING that Allah says.

[Anna]:
like the part about women not being equal and men having multiple wives?

[Nat]:
that's such a simplistic view. i submit to it because i feel and know that it's for the best. it still feels right.

[Nat]:
are you getting the Adam stuff sorted out?

[Anna]:
I'm working on it, nat. don't change the subject.

[Nat]:
i'm sure you're working on it . . . funny thing is that your life is still more screwed up than mine.

[Anna]:
Okay, sis, gotta go.

Natalia is starting to make sense. This can't be good. I wish that she could have found her peace in something less foreign, something that respected the rights of women and didn't pull her halfway across the world. I want her to come to me for advice about stupid problems like which bar she should celebrate her birthday at or which bra makes her boobs look better. I doubt she even wears bras these days. I selfishly still want her to be the sister who shops at the Gap with me and shares big slices of peanut butter cheesecake at Baked Expectations because that's what I need right now. But I understand her need for inner peace—I'm looking for it too, and I guess I'm a little jealous that she's onto something. We all find it in different places—Natalia through religion, Mom through shopping, Baba by planning her funeral, and me? I don't know yet.

The Great Escape

I ask Dad to come over and help take apart the bed frame that Adam made. It's time I start preparing for Adam's return. The sooner I get rid of all of the emotional stakes that Adam has driven into the house, the better off I'll be. It'll be easier to banish him from my world. This is my theory anyway.

Taking apart the bed he built seems like a good symbolic place to start. I was prepared to do it with a saw and a sledgehammer, but Dad was a bit more civilized about the whole procedure. At least he was when we started.

A few minutes into the job, we realize this bed was never meant to be dismantled. Like this relationship. It is then that the lump starts to form in my throat. Where there only needed to be one or two screws driven into the hard and unforgiving wood, there are eight. As we pull the difficult screws out one by one, I picture Adam grinding them in and my eyes well up.

"Holy Christ, there's a drill bit stuck in here," Dad grunts. As we pull the bed apart, I feel the relationship being ripped apart all over again. I excuse myself and go to the bathroom to cry. Dad is too busy swearing at the frame to notice my absence.

Piece by piece, as the bed comes apart, I unravel. I'm dismantling everything I have known for the past ten years. Like the relationship, the frame is flawed, but rooted in time and memory. Adam had used the bed to build our relationship, but it is also the place where I sabotaged it.

Andrea was my teaching assistant last semester, in a class of tenth-grade repeaters. We bonded over cigarettes behind the school—the repeaters and us, shivering in the cold, sucking on frozen white Players stubs. Her hands were always warm when she passed me her smoke, even when we were outside in twenty-below weather. She was lean and strong.

Andrea would drive around with me for entire lunch hours, while we chain-smoked, bought Tim Hortons coffees, and talked about my life with Adam. She had short dark hair she would run her hands through, and a mole on her left cheek that I always wanted to touch. I gravitated toward Andrea's warmth—she made me smile and want to tell her things I didn't share with any-one else. She never told me what to do, unlike my other friends, or my sister. She listened and nodded and bit at her nails some-times, and occasionally brushed my hand with hers. My friend-ship with Andrea grew strong, laced with something intoxicating that I didn't understand.

"Let's go out," she said one afternoon, about six months ago. She tossed her cigarette out the window, gripping my shoulders with both hands.

"When?"

"Tonight." She shook my shoulders and my head bobbled. It had turned into a bitter winter, and we shivered as the Fury never seemed to heat up properly. It was during one of these frigid car rides, earlier in the week, that she had told me that she'd taken a job teaching English in Japan. I'd known Andrea only for the few months she'd assisted in my classroom, but I knew I would miss her. She was one of those people in life with whom you briefly cross paths, but the moment at which your lives do intersect impacts you deeply and you spend the rest of your life wondering about that moment. If I hadn't met Andrea, would things have turned out differently with Adam? And if I hadn't ever served Adam at that university café way back, where would I be now? Is life just a series of chance moments that play out? Maybe it's our level of consciousness in life that dictates whether we allow chance circumstances, whether they be fatal or serendipitous, to shape us, or whether we ordain our own destinies. If the latter is true, I'd need to wake up and give my consciousness some spine.

"Okay, let's." I said I'd had enough of being trapped in my house, and it seemed like months since I'd been anywhere. We went to a trendy bar in Osborne Village. And then another. And then another. I knew Adam would be enraged, but I didn't care. Andrea pulled me onto the dance floor and we swayed with the crowd, sucking on sweaty gin cocktails. We finally staggered home, snow crunching and squeaking under our feet. Andrea couldn't drive home in that state, so I pulled her into the house to crash on our couch.

Adam was there, agitated, pacing, waiting to rant at me for staying out so late, for going out in the first place. He ignored Andrea when we came in. She leaned against the wall behind me, silently staring Adam down. I chipped at my nail polish, tore at my cuticles, and waited for his tirade to end.

After it was over, Adam sat down on the couch, where he would spend the night, and Andrea and I went upstairs and fell into bed. For the first time in this bed I felt calm and warm.

During the night I awoke to feel Andrea's lips brushing against me, stirring something within me that had been dead a long time. Her warm breath melted away the layer of frost that had settled on my skin. I felt warm for the first time in years. It didn't matter that

Adam was downstairs. Of course, there would be explosive consequences, but on some level I guess I was trying to blow up our relationship; it was easier than walking away. We always wonder how someone gets to the point where they go postal rather than just quitting a day job they hate. I understood what it meant to not take responsibility for your life and your happiness, to reach your breaking point and then snap. I was snapping.

Andrea's gentle hands reached for my back and I felt my spine arch toward her. I touched every part of her and she every part of me. At first toes, thighs, shoulders, eyes—then other parts that ached and screamed. I was filled with strength, and courage, and life.

Naked, huddled in bed, wrapped in Andrea's warm strong body, I drifted into a peaceful sleep.

The Lesbian Patrol Commission could charge me with fraud—I'd temporarily dipped into their cause to satisfy my own needs. I thought about plane crashes where the survivors ate the flesh of their deceased companions in order to save their own lives. Others perished because they refused to participate in what would have been savagery in any other circumstance. I learned that my will to survive was strong. I would have eaten those around me to survive. I reached out to Andrea to survive. I loved her for making me feel alive and human—until the morning.

The door swung open. There stood Adam.

"Where are the cigarettes? I need..." He trailed off when he saw the heap of clothes on the floor. A frigid, stark reality swept into the room and I was jolted from my gentle sleep. Adam slammed the door. He stormed down the stairs.

I could feel Andrea's body tighten around me. I swallowed down hard on the guilt and nausea. I convinced Andrea that I would be okay, that I needed to deal with Adam alone. We got dressed and went downstairs. She let go of my hand, slipped away. She and Adam scowled at each other as she passed through the kitchen and out the front door, each thinking the other had committed unforgivable acts.

A battle waited.

"How could you?" Adam sat in the chair and shot his words at me the moment I walked into the kitchen.

Silence.

"How could you do this in our own house? In a house we built. In a bed I made for you." He rose from the chair and moved toward me. Sunlight fell through the windows. The kitchen was too bright.

I had no excuse that he would accept or even understand.

"You cheated on me." He was inches from my face. "How could you do this to me? Fuck!" His raised voice snapped the tension of the kitchen. The bags around his eyes were swollen and moist.

"I'm sorry." I wished my first independent act in years could have been different. Why couldn't I have just broken it off with him? Instead, evidently I needed to cause him pain. I took back my power and then used it against Adam.

He left. I was simultaneously filled with shame and rage. I collapsed on the couch, my legs a couple of overboiled noodles. Ten hours later, after I'd smoked three packages of cigarettes and stolen some of Adam's Valium pills, he returned home, drunk, desperately clinging to a box containing a dozen beers that he clearly did not need. He stumbled in and fell on the living room sofa, feebly ripped at the box and pulled out two beers. He removed the caps with difficulty and held one out for me to take. I watched him without trying to see him, my eyes motion detectors, scanning for movement. When I didn't reach for it, he set the bottle down and hoisted his own beer into the air.

"Here's to you," he sneered, and wiped his running nose. "Better yet, here's to us. And to our future." I ripped into my cuticles with my teeth.

"C'mon, have a beer. We're celebrating your liberation." His tone was quiet, but growling. I'd rather he hurled his bottle at me. I'd never seen him like this before. It was my turn to leave.

"Hey, where ya going? Don't you wanna celebrate with me?" he slurred. The door slammed shut behind me. I spent the night driving around in the Fury. I drank coffee at Salisbury House and bought cigarettes at Domo, but mostly I just drove because the road gave me something to focus on. I began to pass familiar cars whose drivers, I was certain, were in similar predicaments. Maybe I should open an all-night coffee shop exclusively for people in these situations.

As the sun started to come up, I went home, like an exhausted night prowler. Adam was passed out on the couch. Beer bottles were lying on the coffee table and all over the floor, like toys that children had forgotten to pick up. Cigarette butts overflowed out of a single ashtray, while others were drowned in the inch of liquid at the bottoms of his beer bottles. I slipped up the stairs and crept into bed. My eyelids scraped over my dry eyeballs, burning as they closed, as I fell asleep.

I opened my eyes to Adam sitting in front of me.

"I tried to kill myself last night," he said, stroking my hair. "Because of you. How would you like to live with that the rest of your life?" His hand collapsed on my chest and he clutched my T-shirt. My head felt like someone had pumped it full of air while I slept. It was trying to float upwards, but my lead body was tugging it down into the bed. My stretched neck ached from the struggle. I couldn't concentrate on what Adam was saying.

"I tried to kill myself because of you last night," he repeated, in a dead, flat voice. I understood that much.

He rose, walked to the bedroom door, and then turned. "Why are you so indifferent toward me all the time? You do things to sabotage us." I threw the covers off. The small of my back was aching from the night spent hunched over the wheel of the Fury.

"So do you. You do things that destroy me too, like calling me names all the time, like refusing to kiss me, like accusing me of seeing other people when all I ever do is stay in this house. I don't want to do this anymore."

"You're a quitter. You quit everything. You quit the house, and now you're quitting me." He slumped against the door frame. His voice softened, and his tone became self-pitying. Anger wasn't working, so he was trying guilt. Excellent strategy. We both knew my weakness.

"We don't even like each other anymore," I said. I followed a crack in the plaster ceiling with my eyes until it veered off in different directions.

He sat down on the bed beside me and whispered in my ear. "Why don't you want to make this work? There's no point living without you."

He can't live without me. Of course. I can't leave. I fell for this every time like a mouse going for a mouldy piece of cheddar. When we're healthy, we say that we would never want to be hooked up to a machine to be kept alive. But we can never bear to flip that switch on someone we love. Any life—no matter how poor and dependent it is—is better than no life at all. Adam and I continued our relationship, hooked up to relationship life-support. We couldn't bring ourselves to pull the plug.

"You need help," I said. And for the first time I recognized that I needed help too.

I found the number in the phone book to a Crisis Centre that I'd heard about and secretly placed a call. Within a few hours two people showed up to "assess" Adam. They were wholesome and could have just as easily passed for door-to-door Mormons. Adam looked like he was going to throttle the lot of us, but within minutes they diffused his anger. This was their job and they were good. It helped that some of Adam's artist friends had talked about this place. I left to find cigarettes.

"I get panic attacks," he was telling them as I came back into the room.

"And he tried to kill himself," I added. Adam glared at me. The couple looked at each other and nodded placidly. They'd just come from another version of us in the suburbs—perhaps one with an SUV and more RRSPs.

"And it feels like I'm going to die," he explained.

"He's addicted to Valium," I couldn't help adding as I lit a cigarette. Adam leaned back in his chair and crossed his arms.

"Maybe you should let him tell us about it," the young woman, dressed entirely in taupe cotton, suggested. I went to the kitchen and made coffee. By the time I came back, they were handing Adam a card.

"We'll call the Centre so they will be expecting you. You will have to commit to staying for a minimum of twenty-four hours so that they can do a proper assessment."

It will take a lot longer than twenty-four hours.

Still, I was relieved to have a whole day away from all of this.

A few hours later, after Adam had packed his duffle bag, I dropped him off at the Crisis Centre. As I watched him walk up to the glass doors, surrounded by clusters of people smoking, I gripped the steering wheel. If I loved him, I wouldn't shift the

Fury into drive. I could tell by looking at this grey, boxy building that this was where desperate people went, people who have been abandoned. I quickly pulled away before my guilt cast me into the building like a fishing hook to chase after Adam, to take him into my arms, to tell him that we could get through this and everything would be okay.

The next day I went to a women's clinic to see a counsellor. I didn't know what else to do with myself. I couldn't bear to be in the house, and I was getting nauseous driving around. I learned later that the Fury had an exhaust leak that was filtering into the car. I had thought that the nausea I often felt was because I was thinking about leaving Adam. *Maybe if it weren't for that damn exhaust leak I would have left a lot sooner.*

I sat down with a woman who gave me a Styrofoam cup of black coffee. I tried to explain the situation through tears that smeared mascara all over my face. *Should've worn waterproof.*

"And then he walked in ... wanted smokes ... he was really mad ... in my car ... Crisis Centre ... suicide ... Valium ..." *This is not going well.* The woman made a call and then said she was going to send me where there would be more help for me. She wrote down an address on a piece of paper. I was hoping it would be a Starbucks.

I arrived at what looked to be a generic apartment block from the outside. I was buzzed in after giving them my name. A sign inside said "Welcome to Osborne House." Before I could figure out what this place was, I was shuffled through the front area and into a room. A piece of paper on the table read Women's Shelter.

"How are you?" The woman smiled before I could leave. *I should not be here. This is a place out of a bad Julia Roberts movie.* I took comfort in knowing that Adam was probably trying to plot his own escape from his institution.

"How are you?" she asked again.

"Fine."

"I'm Brenda. Why don't we start by you filling out this ques-tionnaire?" I filled out a questionnaire to determine if I was in an abusive situation. *Does your partner belittle you? Yup. Does your partner accuse you of being sexually provocative? Check. Do you feel controlled? Tick.* I aced the quiz. I told Brenda about the events of the past few hours, days, months, and years.

"Why don't you stay here for a few days?" she offered.

"No, thanks. I'll be fine." *Not a chance, Brenda.*

I wanted to hate Brenda, but she was too nice. I hated that this shelter existed, that the world needed places like this. And most of all, I hated that, somehow, I'd ended up here.

"Well, will you promise me that you will keep a packed bag in the trunk and come back any time you need to?"

"Okay." See you later, weak women. I'm going home.

At home the humming refrigerator kept me company as I waited by the phone for Adam to call, which he did exactly twenty-four hours later. He'd been sitting by the phone too, patiently waiting until they allowed him to use it. We were relieved to be reunited. It didn't matter that we behaved like two fighting roosters with razors attached to our heads.

We sat on the couch, smoking.

"I got a job offer. In Germany," Adam said matter-of-factly. "I didn't want to take it. I wasn't even going to tell you. But now, I don't know. Maybe I should think about it."

"A job." I never thought I would hear those words coming out of Adam's mouth. An angel had just floated down and deliv-ered us our salvation. "Of course you should take it. We need time apart. This—us—it's not working."

"I don't want to lose you."

I should have ended our relationship then, but of course I didn't. I couldn't. I wasn't sure I could ever break free of Adam, but I would have time to think—and suffer through my friends' attempts at interventions.

Adam took the job in Germany.

Coming and Going

A gainst my better judgment, I go to the airport. It's almost empty except for a few people standing around waiting for the plane. A man a few yards away holds a bouquet of flowers, cheap Safeway flowers. Another woman cuddles a baby in her arms. I buy a coffee at Tim Hortons to calm my nerves while I wait for Adam's flight. The anticipation of seeing him causes me to gulp my large coffee down in about two minutes. Why am I here? I should not be here. But I want to make sure he's okay, that he's accepted the breakup. I still need him to be okay, even when I'm dumping him. I need to see him get off the plane, to be sure he hasn't decided to jump off a bank building in Frankfurt, even though I know by now that the suicide threats were always empty, a way to control me. Besides, Lorna would say that if he wants to jump off a building because I'm making a decision that's best for me, that's his choice. We are all responsible for our own actions. That piece of wisdom cost me a mere one thousand dollars in therapy appointments. And yet here I stand on the polished floor of the airport, waiting for Adam. So, did I learn anything after all? Of course I did. I just choose not to heed my newfound knowledge.

My cell phone echoes through the vacant terminal.

"Hey," I answer.

"Where are you?" Renate barks.

Silence.

"Nowhere. Why?"

"Are you at the airport?" *Fuck.* She probably wrote Adam's arrival time down in her day planner so she could call me to check on me.

"No. I'm not at the airport."

"Final boarding call for Flight 147," a nasal voice announces over the airport PA.

"Christ, Anna, what are you doing there?"

"It's fine. I'm not taking him home. I'm just picking him up. It's the least I could do."

"Where are you taking him?"

"I dunno. Plane's in. Gotta go." I turn off my phone before she can redial my number.

People have trickled off the plane and the escalator is depositing them into the waiting area of the Arrivals Terminal, where they are met by people who love them and will take them home. I really should not be here. This will send the wrong message. I will leave.

Too late.

I see Adam's boots first, his jeans, ripped, his leather jacket, and finally his face as he descends. His hair is cut short and he's clean-shaven. He grins when he sees me and strides to where I'm standing. His gait still has a spring to it. He envelops me in a hug and I awkwardly reciprocate. To someone standing on the observation deck above we could still be lovers. Only I can feel the awkwardness of many bad years wedged between our bodies. He looks at me with clear eyes when I wiggle free of him.

"How are you?" I break the silence he is trying to impose. In his mind the scene is unfolding in slow motion: the long-separated lovers finally reunited. Adam always makes every moment bigger than it is. Always has.

"You feel good."

Actually, I feel like shit. I try to resist his easiness, but I can feel myself slipping. I understand now why everyone told me not to come to the airport. My determination to evict him from my life is beginning to melt. I'm a Popsicle in a sauna. My judgment is clouded with habit and guilt and obligation to honour the memory of our relationship. I look squarely at Adam; I don't feel attracted to him anymore the way I used to. I don't feel any hope about resurrecting our squalid relationship. But I feel a duty to respect our history because I've spent a third of my life with Adam.

I cannot let him sense this weakness and lure me back.

"How was your trip?"

"I knew you'd come." I had told him that I would try. I look around for a familiar face and realize that he hasn't arranged for an alternate pickup. No one is here but me.

"How was your flight?"

"Long. It's good to finally be home. It's so good to see you, for you to be here." *Stop trying to turn this casual moment into something bigger than it is.* It means nothing, but Adam's acting like I've bought him the Arrivals Terminal as a present. I thought coming to the airport might be part of my closure. To Adam it is the beginning of a new chapter. *Ugh.*

"How was the museum work?" I fill the space between us with practical questions as we wait for his backpack to appear on the carousel.

"I liked the work, but the guy who owned the museum was a rich, pompous asshole." Adam has never had a boss he liked. "Why hire artists if you're not going to give them creative licence? But how have you been? You look great!" Adam stands with his legs crossed at the ankles, his thumbs hooked into the pockets of his jeans. He's a little thinner, but he still fills out his jeans nicely.

"I'm all right." *I was doing better before you stepped off the plane and I'm regretting having come to the airport. Other than that, I'm good.* I feel my old pushover self creeping back and the monkeys are doing acrobatics in my stomach again. *Bastards.* Adam sweeps his backpack off the carousel.

"So, where to, Mister?" I casually throw out the question as we walk outside.

"I didn't get a hold of Dave, so I thought I would stay at the house until I get things figured out. I hope that's okay," he states more than he asks. *No. Not okay. No ride and no place to stay!*

"I thought we'd settled this. You were going to stay with Dave." I ram the buttons at the parking pay station.

"I didn't want to impose. I'm going to find a place to stay. Just give me a few days. Okay?" *You didn't want to impose on Dave? What about me? What about the last ten years? No. Not okay at all. And it's costing me parking money to put you back in my life.* I snatch my receipt from the machine.

"No, Adam. It completely flies in the face of our ending this relationship if we move back in together."

"Where am I supposed to go? I've spent years working on and living in our house and now you expect me to have somewhere to go just like that?" He snaps his fingers on the last word.

"It's not a good idea. You agreed and now you're reneging."

"It's just for a little while until I get some things in place." He tosses his backpack into the trunk of the Fury.

"Adam . . ."

"Please, Anna, can't we just do this? Can't you do this for me? After everything, this is not too much to ask. It won't be for long. I promise."

This is a bad idea, but unless I drop him off at a park downtown, I have no choice but to bring him home with me.

"I guess so, but please make some other arrangements. Where will you sleep?" I pull out of the parkade and onto the street.

"I suppose the bed's not an option?"

"The couch. It's not all that comfortable, so you really should find a place." I can't believe that I'm letting him back in the house. Lorna is not going to be happy about this at all. I should have programmed her number into my cell phone speed dial.

"I've slept on the couch a lot, remember?" We drive in silence for a few minutes.

"It's so hard to let go, you know?" Adam finally says. This is exactly what I was afraid of. I need to see Lorna, but there is no way I can tell her that Adam is living with me. If I completely ignore her advice, I wonder if the appointments are refundable.

"Adam, promise me that you'll find somewhere else to go soon. I really can't do this."

"I will. But don't forget that it is our house."

"And we'll sort all that out." I concentrate on the white dashes on the road, but I can feel Adam looking at me.

"Thanks for picking me up."

When we arrive at the house, Adam sets up camp in the living room. The way he pulls his baggage apart makes it look like he doesn't plan to leave anytime soon. I pour a glass of wine and go upstairs to draw myself a bath. The bath warms my skin and the wine relieves the tension inside my chest. Nothing has changed. Adam is back in my life and I have that familiar sinking feeling. I cannot say *no* to him, and yet I know that my happiness and future are at stake. I cannot go down that familiar easy path of avoiding standing up to him. I will face him once and for all, accept that it will hurt him, and walk away. I will get on with my life. But not tonight.

I dunk my head under the water and stare at the blurry wine glass in my hand. I close my eyes. When I open them, Adam's face is staring down at me. I lurch up and try to cover myself. The cheap lavender bubbles have long evaporated.

"What are you doing?" I accidentally splashed some wine into the tub and the red liquid swirls and stretches out in the clear water. Adam has helped himself to my wine and holds a filled glass.

"I've seen you naked before, you know." He makes a good point, but I still feel exposed and awkward.

"I just need some space."

"Sorry, just thought I'd have a drink with you." He lifts up his glass. And now *I* feel like the asshole. Over the years, Adam has honed his passive-aggressive bullshit, so that he can smoothly make me feel like the bad guy simply for wanting to take a bath, alone, after we've apparently broken up. "We have a lot of memories in this bathroom." He fiddles with my toothbrush. "Remember when we were building it and you got tired of holding up the drywall and you let it crack on my head?"

"It was an accident," I say.

The next morning as I'm rushing about, collecting my things for work, Adam walks into the kitchen wearing only his underwear. *My God, he looks good.* He has a steaming mug of coffee in his hand.

"Morning. Coffee?" he says, offering me the cup. He knows all of my weaknesses.

I take the mug and take a giant gulp. "Maybe you could put some pants on?"

"Oh, yeah, sorry. You're going to work?"

Real people have jobs.

"Yeah. Are you planning on looking for work now that

you're back?" I take one more swig of coffee before setting the mug down.

"Not right away. I'll live on my savings for a while."

Does he mean me?

"Have a good day," he says as he heads upstairs.

"Where are you going?"

"I thought I would crash up in the bed for a few more hours since you're not using it. I forgot how bad that couch is." I'm nervous about the idea of him sleeping in the bed, but I can't think of a single reason to refuse him. "Oh, do you have an extra key? I noticed the locks were different, and I wanted to get some things done today." I set a key on the counter and slip out before he realizes the bed frame has disappeared.

"You gave him a key to the changed locks? What are you—an idiot?" Ted says, stuffing his sandwich into his mouth.

"Thank you. Yes, I know it was dumb. What else could I do? I didn't want to get into an argument with him about it." I stab a french fry with my fork.

"Why did you change the locks?" my sweet student teacher, Liz, asks.

"Because I didn't want my ex back in my life." I'm sure good Christian girls don't have these kinds of problems.

"Except now he's living with her," Angelo chimes in. "Thanks for putting my truck in the *Buy and Sell*. A little originality would be refreshing, Lasko. I still have those forty-plus women who like cats and long walks calling me for dates."

"So, Anna, you're technically right back where you started then?" Ted says mockingly.

I'm not back where I started because now I know better. Before I didn't get it and I actually believed we could work it out.

Now, I know we're through—I just can't quite seem to go through with ending it. I can't explain this to my colleagues or my friends. When you stand at the edge of a tall diving board or on a cliff high above the lake, you know you're going to take the leap, but you have to mentally prepare. You have to convince yourself it will all turn out okay. All the little figures splashing around down below jumped and they're fine. But if you stand there and think about it for too long, you'll sheepishly creep backward and never take the plunge. I will jump.

Julio, Goth Girl, Fan Fiction, and Craig are waiting for me in my classroom when I arrive. Craig is cleaning out the jam between his toes, much to the disgust of the other students. He jumps up when I walk in. I let Craig read the next instalment of Argamyte's adventures because he's frantic with excitement.

Argamyte, it seems, is consulting a self-help book to help him ward off the villains and restore order to the world. Argamyte, we learn, is a victim of violence. His father beat him mercilessly as a young boy, Craig tells us. I suggest to Craig that Argamyte must face his own demons before he can restore order to the world. Perhaps he could find and confront his father in the next chapter. Craig is thrilled with this idea and begins ferociously writing, his bare feet curled up beneath him. I decide that, like Argamyte, I will face my demons and force Adam to move out.

At home Adam has cooked an impressive pasta dinner. He hasn't cooked for me in years. *I can't ask him to leave now. I'll do it after dinner.* The last time Adam cooked supper he made a spicy Italian dish. We tried to make love afterward on the kitchen floor, except Adam hadn't washed the hot peppers from his fingers. I thought my vagina had caught fire. I ended up on my back in the tub with my legs up in the air while Adam poured four gallons of milk over my flaming crotch to try to cool it off.

"Thanks, but you don't have to make dinner."

"I wanted to. How was your day?" he asks as he lights a candle. *Enough with the romantic bullshit.* Adam is recreating the good parts of our past. Parts that haven't existed for a long time.

"Fine. Uneventful. Yours? Any luck finding a place?" I fake a coughing fit in an attempt to extinguish the candle. The flame flickers and sways but refuses to burn out.

"I might have something. Anna, why can't it be like this?" Adam leans into me. I can feel his breath, smell the soap he used this morning. "I know it's hard for you to believe, but I get it now. I screwed up and I've had time to think about it." I wish this is how our relationship could be. And I wonder if it's possible.

"This is great pasta." I go to the counter and pour myself some more wine and turn the dimmer up on the lights.

"Thanks. Do you want to go to a movie tonight?"

"I should probably do my marking." *And make you move out.*

"Early movie. I'll have you home by 9:30."

Since you don't have a car and I'll be driving, I'll have myself home by 9:30.

"Adam, for what it's worth, you do seem a lot better and different," I say. "Okay, I'll go to a movie." I feel like a child doing something illicit, like drawing on the walls. We will definitely talk about moving out after the movie.

Adam changes into his unripped jeans for our "date."

"Hey, Anna," a voice says behind us in the lobby of the cinema. I turn to see Sara and Jeff standing there. Winnipeg is too goddamn small. Of all the people I could run into, it has to be Ken and Barbie.

"Hi, Sara. Hey, Jeff."

"We're taking a night off from the wedding planning," Sara says. She smiles placidly at Adam and glares at me. Her one night off in a year had to be tonight.

"Hey, you're back. Welcome home," Jeff says, shaking Adam's hand.

"We're just here to see a movie," I say. Awkward silence. "I guess we should get going. It's gonna start soon."

"Well, I'll probably see you guys at the wedding. It's only a couple of weeks away now," Jeff says. He is lean with a handsome, chiselled face—but daft as ever. But then again, Sara probably hasn't filled him in on anything not related to their stupid wedding, like my pending breakup.

"We're not together," I clarify. Jeff, confused, rubs his jaw.

"Anna's going to be busy with the wedding party stuff all that day," Sara says, attempting to dissuade Jeff.

"Well, Adam, you should still come," Jeff says. I think there is more substance in my bag of buttered popcorn than there is in Jeff's head. Renate, Julia, and I joke about Jeff being a bit on the thick side, but this could be the topper on their wedding cake. What part of "We're not together" did he not understand?

"I'd love to."

Of course he'd love to. I shoot Sara a glare and she lifts her shoulders helplessly.

When we get home, Julia is in front of my house, sitting in her car. She blasts her horn and I climb into the passenger's seat. Adam heads into the house. He has a key.

"I've been dispatched to find out what the fuck is going on," she says. I roll down the window and light a cigarette, taking care not to blow smoke in the car. Emma is sleeping in the back.

"What?"

"Don't what me. You were on a date with Adam."

"It wasn't a date."

"First off, you're not to go on dates with him. Second, why is he still living here?" My cell phone rings.

"Fucking hell!" Renate starts yelling into my other ear.

"Look, I've just gotten the lecture from Julia, so save it. Actually she's in the middle of it, so I'll have to call you back. How's Rachel?"

"She came home today. Don't try to change the subject."

"I'll call you tomorrow." I turn off my phone. Julia steals drags of my cigarette. She quit smoking when she had Emma, but not quite.

"Rachel's home."

"Yeah, I know. What is going on with you these days? Are you going back to him? If you are, tell me so I can stop wasting my time. Jesus, Anna."

"No, I'm not going back. When I'm in this car I know that, and when I'm in my car or at work I know, but when I get back into that house I don't know what happens. He seems like he's better and I don't want to hurt him."

"You're smart. You know that it won't work. Even if he swallowed a truckload of happy pills and he's better, which I doubt, you have bad history and karma. Let logic prevail. Just because he's better does not obligate you to go back to him."

"I know."

"He owns you. He can't live here."

"I know. He says he's looking for a place."

"Bullshit. Look, I have a massage client who owns an apartment block on Grosvenor and he needs a caretaker. Free rent, plus a couple hundred extra a month to call a plumber if a toilet backs up. This should be right up Adam's alley. It's free."

"I'll tell him about it. At the movie, Jeff invited him to the wedding."

"What? That guy is a fucking brick on a leash. God, I hope he's great in bed."

"Adam's going." I toss my cigarette onto my lawn and roll up the window.

"We'll try to get him uninvited," Julia says, fiddling with the stick shift.

"Thanks, Julia."

"I met my mom tonight."

"I'm sorry. I've been so wrapped up in my own bullshit that I forgot to ask you about it."

"It's okay. It wasn't even that big of a deal."

"It's a huge deal. What happened?"

"Nothing, really. We talked. She's got five other kids and, like, thirteen grandkids, so it's not like she's been waiting her whole life for a grandchild. We're going to see each other once in a while, and I'm going to meet my half siblings. Em will meet her cousins."

"This sounds good."

"Yeah, but I started to build up this whole reunion in my head like it was some fucking Hallmark commercial and it isn't like that. I asked her about being Métis and she said 'What do you want to know? I'm glad you don't look Indian. Your life would have been a lot harder.' Not exactly what I wanted to hear."

"What'd she mean by that?"

"She said she was glad when she heard I went to a Canadian family of Italian descent. Being Aboriginal has been a pain in the ass for her. It's not something I should worry about embracing, she says."

"Do you look like her?"

"Maybe my eyes."

"You know, even if your mom doesn't celebrate her culture, it doesn't mean that you and Emma can't. I know you were excited about it."

"I dunno. The whole point was that it was part of my new family."

"We're your family. We'll have one of those smoke ceremonies. We can look it up on the Internet—like how you guys ran the intervention."

Julia glances at her watch. "I have to get going. Deal with this Adam bullshit! I mean it. What's going to happen when you go back in there?"

"I'm going to tell him about the apartment block and insist he move there."

"Good. Okay, I gotta get Sleeping Beauty back there to bed," Julia says. She reaches over and gives me a sideways car hug.

Julia is like the cleanup crew for the Emotional Mafia. Her tactics are severe, but effective. I return to the house and tell Adam that he must move out within a week. And only as I say these words, and mean them, do I realize this breakup is as much about me as it is about Adam. I've wanted Adam out of my life for years now, but the thought of Adam being gone forever makes me queasy and I go to the bathroom to throw up. I slump down, clinging to the porcelain bowl; my bad relationship with Adam is my thing, and over the years it's become part of my identity. *Anna—oh her, the one who dates that crazy guy. I don't know how she does it.* Dumping Adam means losing a part of myself. It means I don't get to be the relationship martyr anymore.

I pull myself up, rinse my mouth, and prepare for an argument with Adam about his being forced out of the house. I hear the front door slam as I come out of the bathroom. Adam is gone and there will be no confrontation. How anticlimactic.

I am reminded of when I was growing up and how little things Nat and I did would really set off Dad. If we mouthed off or stayed out an hour past our curfew, we would sit through a lecture about respect or responsibility. So when I smashed up the family car, and when Nat was playing around with candles and set her bed on fire, we feared our father's reaction. But in those situations Dad didn't even raise his voice and there was no tirade. We didn't understand it at the time, but he knew that those experiences were terrifying and blatant enough to teach the lesson—there was nothing more to say.

I think Adam finally realized that our negative experiences—everything we've been through—were too powerful, so there was nothing more he or I could say.

"I keep feeling like I am a prisoner on death row and the Governor is going to call off the execution at the last minute," Adam says. He is supposed to be moving out today.

"You must have done something pretty bad to land yourself on death row." I try to break the tension with humour. He refuses to look at me as he begins to pack. He slides past me, eyes and head down. There is not even the slightest bounce to his step. I don't want the prisoner to die, but I can't reverse the sentence. I try to act casual and cheery because I don't want him to know how hard this is for me. I can't let him sense that there may be an opening. He will find it and crawl through.

Adam begins peeling back the layers of himself that have stretched and grown over everything in our house, a layer of skin marred with the barely crusted scabs of our relationship. I stand in the living room watching him and everything inside of me burns as he pulls apart our home. I feel waves of nausea.

Adam tugs a lamp cord out of the socket. He unhooks and slides one of his framed photographs of us from the wall. He pulls apart the vines of our separate plants that had grown together. Things that breathed life into the house and the relationship are cast into flimsy cardboard boxes. We can all be reduced to travellers carrying cardboard boxes.

"Do you want this? I'd like to take it," he says, pointing to an antique footstool we'd bought together at a garage sale. He had probably picked it out and I'd paid for it. That's usually how it went.

"No, take it. Take whatever you want." I leave. I cannot watch.

"This will be the perfect distraction to take your mind off this Adam shit." I'm in Julia's car, and we've just had lunch—mine was liquid. She called me and said she'd be picking me up for lunch and then she had something she wanted me to see. I have no idea where we are going.

"Tell me when we're there." My head is pounding. I close my eyes.

As she's driving, Julia gives me the update on Emma's developmental progress. Yesterday she smeared the contents of her diaper all over herself and her crib. A redecorating effort, Julia calls it. Her birth mother is spending lots of time with Emma and she's met one of her half siblings.

"They all seem really nice. I don't know how much I have in common with them. But I've just decided to take it for what it is. And it's cool to see Emma playing with all her new little cousins."

When I open my eyes, we're at the airport. "What the hell are we doing here?"

Julia buys me a coffee and we grab a bench by the security check at the departure gate.

"There he is."

"Who?"

"Phil."

"That guy who called you fat?" He carries a duffle bag as he approaches security. He's still wearing the Blue Bombers sweatshirt. "What's he doing? What are we doing?"

"He's off to Toronto to meet his latest Internet amour."

"How do you know? Are you still emailing this asshole?"

"Sort of. I'm Jessica. The slim, beautiful woman he's off to meet in Toronto."

I laugh, spitting coffee all over my jeans.

"I only wish I could be at the arrivals gate in Toronto to see his face," she laments. Julia's vindication is almost enough to make me forget that Adam is at our house dissecting our world, peeling apart our lives. Julia lends me a pair of pyjamas that evening and insists that I stay the night. Adam won't be nearly finished packing and she's still worried that if I go home, I might renege and tell Adam not to move out.

I arrive home the following afternoon just as Adam is loading a dresser onto the back of a pickup truck with the help of our friend Wayne. Wayne looks at me and turns a little red, as though he's been caught stealing from my home. Our friends will be divided up like the furniture. Adam got Wayne.

"I'll meet you there," Adam tells Wayne. Wayne slinks behind the wheel of the truck, starts the ignition, and drives off.

"That was the last load," Adam says. We walk inside the house together. For the last time. The rooms feel emptier. We stand in the kitchen. The refrigerator and the lights hum. The last time we stood together in the kitchen this calmly and silently was when we were deciding whether or not to buy the house.

"I guess that's everything then," Adam says quietly.

"Yeah."

"Do you mind giving me a ride to my new place?" He's moving into Julia's massage client's apartment building seven blocks away. He can easily walk. But I drive him because with this simple car ride we will cross the finish line of our relationship.

We drive in silence. I swallow hard and chew the insides of my cheeks. There's blood. I stare at the road and the passing cars. I concentrate hard on finding a pattern in the colours of the oncoming vehicles. Red. Green. Blue. Blue. Grey. Anything to avoid Adam. Silver. Green. Brown. No pattern.

I pull up in front of the glass doors of his apartment block.

"I'm sorry, I wish all this could have been different, I really do." I feel my lunch, curdled and sour, rising up at the back of my throat. I don't want him to get out of the car.

"I know. It's okay." His hands rest helplessly on his knees, hands that were always plucking guitar strings or pounding wood. His head is slumped back on the headrest and he gazes straight ahead.

Then, he opens the door, gets out, and slams it shut behind him. He walks through the glass doors, his steps heavy. As I watch him walk down the corridor, I feel like I am dropping my kid off at day care, but knowing full well that I never intend to pick him up. Relationship over.

I return home. As I wander vacantly around the house, I stumble over missing chunks, bits of my life gone. Mirrors have vanished, sucked up by the very images they used to reflect. Piles of laundry are no longer there, just the lingering odour of Adam's sweat and cologne. Stacks of books that we'd read and talked about have disappeared, leaving the ideas and knowledge suspended—

no longer attached to the books, no longer invisibly connecting us together. Dark square patches on the walls that were once protected by Adam's steel-framed industrial photos are exposed to the paling rays of the sun. Gaps. Sharp, chilling gaps. If I venture too close, I cut myself, like touching the crisp edges of a broken window. I curl up in the bed. The bed frame is gone, and now Adam is gone.

The phone rings throughout the day. I don't answer it. My friends leave congratulatory messages. "You did it!" "Way to go!" "You're free. Congratulations!" "The bastard's gone. Let's celebrate." I turn off the ringer.

It's empty inside the house. Inside me. The refrigerator still hums, whines for Adam. I run the dishwasher to break the pain and silence, even though it's almost empty. The appliances offer me comfort.

I move empty picture frames from one room to another. I will buy a bathmat for the bathroom floor. It's a small step, but it will warm my feet when I step out of a long, slow bath. I remove the mirror. I don't want to face my reflection. The empty, blank space on the wall is more comforting than the image a mirror would reflect back at me. Until I feel better, I've pasted up a picture of a supermodel. *That's me. I'm beautiful. Who needs a mirror?*

Favours

"This is so disgusting," Sara whines.

"Oh, come on, how many times will you get married?" Julia huffs. "This is like the only chance in your life you'll get to have a lap dance. This is the closest I'll come to getting married, so I'm getting one." She readjusts the plastic penis on Sara's head.

"It's *my* stagette and I don't want a stupid lap dance."

"I'm with Sara on this. This place is horrid," Renate chimes in. "I've left my children in the hands of a sitter for *this?*" Just behind her head is a flashing neon sign of a naked man. Every time the sign flashes the penis gets bigger, until it disappears and then lights up again.

"I'd like to see the naked guy all over Sara," I say.

"Fine. But for the record I WANTED to stay at Earls and drink margaritas," Sara barks.

"Be glad I didn't strap a blow-up doll to you. I was going to," says Julia. Music blasts and a male dancer emerges in an animal-print thong. Within about ten seconds he's ripped it off— so much for suspense. Sara thrusts a five-dollar bill into my hand. "Give it to him for me. Maybe he'll go away."

"Forget it." I toss the money back at her. "It's your stag." Our reluctance encourages the stripper. He's pumping and thrusting himself all around Sara.

"Do it!" she demands. "You're the bridesmaid—you're supposed to do these things." Julia, whose idea it was to come here in the first place, is busy ordering a round of shooters. I'm sure she'd gladly have dealt with the five-dollar bill.

"Fine." I snatch the bill, annoyed, and thrust it into the guy's hand. As he drops his skimpy little leopard-print number onto our table, I look up at his face. It's Anton. Anton, who always corrects me, from my first period twelfth-grade class. Anton, who should be at home reading *Grapes of Wrath* for the fortieth time.

Why would one of my smartest students take his clothes off for money? When I started teaching, I would have taken the time to find out the answer to that question. I'm not so jaded that I don't recognize that there is a terrible story here. This is a deeply troubled student. I'm sure Liz, my student teacher, would find out Anton's motivation for strutting around in a thong. If only teaching were just about comma splices and run-on sentences, but it's not. I'm barely able to handle my own emotional problems, so how can I tackle those of my students? I'm a deeply troubled teacher and I need to leave this profession as quickly as I'm about to leave this bar.

Our eyes meet for a split second. And in that second it is mutually understood that neither of us will ever speak of this.

"I have to go," I say, grabbing my purse.

"What! Why leave? There's four more dancers," Julia insists.

"YOU have to stay, Anna," Sara snaps. She is clearly not having fun.

"I teach that kid." I turn and walk out of the bar, making every effort possible not to see Anton, who has moved to the opposite side of the bar.

At home my computer screen is blinking with a message from Nat. I'll refrain from telling my newly Muslim sister I've just watched one of my students strip.

[Nat]:
i'm having my baby in two weeks. Aki will be away on a religious pilgrimage. i might have come home if i'd known i'd be alone. i'm not allowed to fly this close to my due date.

I wonder if the pilgrimage is to his other wife's house, or maybe to find wife number three? She can't go through this alone. I make a decision.

[Anna]:
i'm going to come down there for the birth if it's okay with you. i've been meaning to get to Iran for years anyway.

[Nat]:
you'd come, really?

[Anna]:
i'll leave right when school's out. sara's wedding will be over by then.

[Nat]:
You won't recognize me, i'm bloody huge.

[Anna]:
will you come back with me?

[Nat]:
I don't know.

I fill Nat in on Adam, and on Mom, Dad, and Baba and everything else I can think of that's happening here. Before we sign off, she asks me again if I'm really planning on coming to Iran. I tell her that I am.

I go to the kitchen and pour myself a glass of wine. Since Adam moved out, it feels like I don't belong here anymore. It's unbearably quiet. I sink down and sit on the floor, my back pressed against the cold cupboard door. I feel like I've just gotten off that roller coaster that rips through the dark haunted house, echoing with screams, the one where the creepy guy in the mask tries to grab at you when you're not looking. I've been on it for a really long time, so when I finally step off, and the feelings of fear and insecurity subside, I don't know what to do with myself. It's how I feel in the house these days. I need to get used to the quiet again.

I book a plane ticket to Iran. I'll be with Natalia when she delivers her baby and then I'll bring her home. My parents will be able to sleep again and Baba will be able to die in peace. We will be connected by love and the strength of our relationships. I don't know if it'll all work out like this, but that's my plan. I finish my wine, turn out the kitchen lights, and go to bed.

"Uninvite him! It will kill me if he's there."

"She's right," Renate agrees.

"Yeah, she's liable to get back together with him," Julia adds, as she peels a dirty diaper from Emma's bum. We've gathered in Sara's white kitchen to make wedding candles for her guests. Guests such as Adam.

"He's already called Jeff to thank him for the invite and to confirm that he's coming. And bringing a date," Sara mutters as she wipes the counter.

"What?" Julia and Renate exclaim in unison. I'm too dumbfounded to speak for a minute.

After the initial shock of Adam leaving the house and my life, I have felt great—like I'd been carrying my '65 Fury on my shoulders instead of driving it, and had finally put it down. At first I felt empty driving to work in the morning without the usual anger and guilt from a morning argument with Adam. It was strange to come and go through the front door without having to concoct elaborate excuses to explain my whereabouts. Even when he was in Germany, I still felt defensive, but now it is finally gone.

But I've adjusted well, and float through my quiet and uncomplicated life, although I've wondered and worried about how Adam is doing. Is he wallowing? Should I call that Salvation Army crazy house to see if he's checked in? I had believed that Adam needed me to survive. He kept telling me he couldn't live without me to keep me tethered to the relationship. And now I find out he's dating. I feel dizzy, like I've been sucker-punched. I'm the sucker. Deep down I wanted to believe that he needed me that much. Apparently not.

"How much is he paying her?" I finally manage.

"Look, dinners have been ordered for them. It's awkward. How do you uninvite someone? You can't." I'm sure she consulted the proper etiquette for this situation in one of her nine thousand *How to Be a Nightmare Bride and Get Your Friends to Hate You* wedding magazines.

"You just do because you give a shit about your friend," I say. I realize that I've forgotten to put the candlewick into the last twenty jars that I've filled with peach wax. I don't bother redoing them, or telling Sara. There must be some use for a pot of peach wax.

"You're overreacting. It's a huge wedding—Julia, that label is crooked—I bet you won't even see him."

"Or his date," I snort, pressing string nubs into the surface of the wax. The candles will appear fine. I will appear fine. I suck back the rest of my wine and refill my glass. "I've booked a flight to Iran the day after the wedding," I announce.

Sara, Renate, and Julia abandon their jars and look up. "I'm going to try and bring Nat home."

Concrete and Cardboard

A rmed with a basket of dirty laundry, I survey the basement and try to locate a route to the washing machine through a labyrinth of cardboard boxes. The basement is home to a medley of forsaken junk that Adam, the packrat, conveniently left in the basement when he moved out.

Adam regularly arrived home with carloads of junk: lights, fans, imperial scales, and obsolete film projectors were all deposited in the basement. He liberated lumber and decrepit lawn furniture from people's garbage. No antique store or industrial garbage bin in Winnipeg was safe. My favourite item was the radiation detector, a device that crackles and hisses when it detects radiation. It was either wildly inaccurate, or there was a radiation spill in my living room.

"What? This is good building wood," he would say, when I suggested that we had no more room in our home for other people's trash. Sometimes he refashioned a ramshackle coffee table into a desk, but that too would eventually end up in the basement.

Adam's art school projects were also relegated downstairs each time he created a more accomplished piece. As he progressed through fine arts, his works grew exponentially in size. A globe that had been repainted; a life-size portrait of the Queen, nude; and welded scrap-metal sculptures rose up out of the jumble of concrete and cardboard in the basement.

Adam was not solely responsible for the disorder. My fashion cast-offs—boxes of shoes, coats, and old purses—spill out from one corner of the basement. I blame Winners discount store for this collection. In another corner I have stacked the boxes of "legacy" my grandmother has given me over the years in her own purging efforts—embroidered linen, cast-iron pots, dishes, and plastic bobble jewellery. Another small room in the corner contains broken futons I've stored for friends since our university days, furniture that has long been abandoned for sleek leather couches from Urban Barn. Adam and I even had a section of the basement dedicated to useless gifts—tape rewinders and egg yolk separators given to us by his sister.

Finding that the washing machine is unreachable, I set down the laundry basket, and begin to haul boxes of books and records up the stairs and out the front door. I drag up sculptures, broken vacuum cleaners, and baskets of shoes. I twist a reluctant armchair through the door. I collect the mousetraps so carefully placed by my father. Within an hour the pile on my lawn is substantial and the floor of the basement is visible. By evening, the basement is bare.

"Clean at last," I say, my voice echoing through the empty concrete room. I pour myself a glass of wine and sit outside on the stoop while I consider what I should do with the sprawling mess on my lawn. Buddy races down a tree and scampers up to the boxes.

"What's going on?"

"I cleaned the basement."

"It's about time." He leaps from one box to the next, inspecting the contents.

"Now I don't know what to do with it."

"Why don't you sell it?"

"Yeah? You think people would buy this stuff?" I've never even been to a garage sale, let alone hosted one.

"Are you kidding? You wouldn't believe the crap I see people buy at these sales. Got anything to drink?" he says, eying my wine. He laps up the red puddle I pour for him on the step. I think I'm fostering his dependency on liquor: Buddy, the drunk neighbourhood squirrel. I rip a flap from one of the boxes and write "YARD SALE SATURDAY' in huge letters and attach it to the front fence.

"There. Easy."

"You might want to set it up a bit—hey, I take naps in this old fur coat." Buddy has returned to rummaging through the boxes.

"I will in the morning. I'm exhausted." We go inside and fall asleep in front of the television.

"Excuse me, is the yard sale today?" a man in a brown suit with glasses inquires when I finally get up to answer the doorbell. I assumed it would be Renate or Julia dropping by for coffee and all I'm wearing is the oversized T-shirt I'd been sleeping in. Half a dozen people are already sifting through the boxes.

"Yeah, sorry, I'll be right out." I tug the shirt down so that it covers my thighs and shut the door. The phone rings.

"Hi, were you sleeping?" Mom asks. Every Saturday morning my mom calls at the same time, wakes me up, and then asks if I was sleeping.

"Hi, no. Can I call you later?"

"What are you up to today? How 'bout lunch?"

"I can't. I'm having a yard sale. I've gotta go. I'll call you later." When I return outside, pulling on my jeans, the man in the brown suit is standing beside two boxes of books waiting for me. It's a cloudy, cool day and I grab a shabby grey sweater from one of the boxes and pull it over my head.

"I'll give you ten dollars for both these boxes," he says.

"Really?" Most of the books belong to the school. Had I known they'd be such hot items, I would have grabbed a few more.

"Nothing is priced," a lady complains.

"Well, I haven't gotten to that yet."

"And how come nothing is laid out? You got to dig through these boxes. Do you have any records? I'm looking for records." She waves her pink-polished nails frantically over the boxes.

"Somewhere."

"How much for these iron pots?" a woman in a "Frankie Goes to Hollywood" T-shirt inquires.

"Two dollars each, or five for all of them." I'm getting a headache. *This was a stupid idea. Where is Buddy anyway? Probably still sleeping.*

"Okay, I'll take them," she says. "This is the worst garage sale I've ever been to." *Then don't buy the pots.* I find a roll of masking tape and a marker and start slapping prices onto everything. I'm steadily interrupted by people making offers.

Two hours later, my parents pull up in their half-ton truck, packed full of their crap. Mom jumps out, waving, in her red-and-white polka dot pantsuit. Dad backs the truck right onto the lawn.

"Hello! I wish you'd given us more notice," she says, smiling. *I don't recall giving them any notice.* Dad drags a wobbly table off the truck and sets it up. His hair sticks out in all directions and his plaid shirt hangs loose, untucked. Looks like my mother woke him up too. Mom unloads the truck. "We've got so much junk to sell."

"I'll give you two dollars for this coat," a woman says without even looking at the price. Buddy wouldn't want me to sell the coat.

"It's five."

"Two-fifty."

"Four dollars."

"Three. The lining is torn." And it's ugly.

"Sold."

"And I don't think that picture of the Queen is very respectful," she scolds as she hands me the money. I plan to give the nude portrait away as a freebie to whoever purchases Baba's china commemorating the Queen's coronation.

By now my parents have set up and overpriced all of their early nineties trinkets and broken appliances.

"We're going to go in and make coffee. Would you like some?" Mom brushes dust from her pants as though she were trying to brush away some of the gaudy polka dots.

"Yeah."

"Keep an eye on our table," Dad says, scooping up the newspaper from the step.

Adam walks through the gate. I cringe, duck down, and pretend to sort through some boxes, hoping he won't see me. He circles around the yard like a preying bird before he approaches me.

"You're selling my artwork?" he demands, gesturing at the nude portrait of the Queen. He squints to look at the price and then contorts his face. I have generously priced all of his art pieces at three dollars each.

"Well, you didn't take it. I didn't think you wanted it." I've been caught.

"How about fifty cents for these coasters?" a woman asks.

"Fine." She hands me two quarters.

"I left this stuff for you," he says. Then it should be my prerogative to sell it.

Adam picks up the gargoyle that once held court atop our Christmas tree. Its wing is broken and it looks pissed off.

"But I have no room, and there are too many memories."

Another woman interrupts. "Do you know what size these shoes are? I don't know if they'd fit my granddaughter."

"Just take them."

"Really? Are you sure?"

"Yes. Fine." *Get lost. I'm trying to have it out with my ex.*

Adam says, "You should have called me. I would have come and picked up the stuff." That's a conversation I wanted to have. *Can you come and pick up your art, art that is so precious that you left it behind, art that I funded with my salary?* I thought he would be angrier; the old Adam would have been livid, ranting and raving around the yard. Instead he stands there, caressing the broken gargoyle. He just seems disappointed.

"You can take whatever you want now. Fifty percent off," I try to joke. He doesn't laugh, just looks at me like I'm pathetic.

"It's too late. This is fitting. You never supported me. This is just another example of it." Here we go, in the middle of my first-ever yard sale. People are looking at us. Even the damn Christmas gargoyle is staring in disbelief.

"How can you say that? I paid for the tuition so you could make all this stuff."

"There is more to life than money." I feel sheepish and cheap as I sit behind a table selling off all of Adam's artwork and Baba's heirlooms.

"Just take whatever you want. I can't get into this right now."

"Excuse me, how much for this picture?" a man asks of one of Adam's photos. Adam smiles smugly. *See, people want my artwork*, his eyes say.

"Three dollars," I mutter.

"What if I just want to take the frame?" the man says. Adam throws the gargoyle down on the lawn and storms through the front gate. He pauses and looks back at me. His look says, *Look at me, I've moved on. You, you're sitting here trying to piece together your pathetic little life. See ya.*

I feel stupid standing amid all of my junk, his junk, our junk.

Mom appears on the front step. "We're invited to Dianne and Terry's for lunch," she calls.

"Don't worry about our leftover stuff. We'll come by later or tomorrow to pick it up," Dad says. He puts on his Blueblocker knockoffs and they leave.

By the end of the day most of my junk has disappeared. The items are not only recycled, they're reinvented—the thrill of some old sad basement trinket will bring cheer into a new room, a new life across town. Garage sales let people reinvent themselves at a bargain price.

My parents don't return to collect the half truckload of suburban crap, which includes many of the home-shopping items that Mom had shipped to my house in the first place. I interpret this as a sign that she is purging her own demons. Thunder cracks the silence of the neighbourhood and it starts to rain. I haul all of their junk into an industrial bin that I'd ordered precisely for this reason—and for the rest of Adam's art.

Buddy pokes his head out of a box of Mom's old Christmas ornaments. "Now we're finally making some progress," he says, before jumping out and running toward the house.

I follow him in.

The Slaughter

"We have to butcher the chickens sooner than I thought. I can't see well enough to find the little buggers to put them in the coop for the night. They're too quick," Baba says when I arrive at the farm. "My eyes are worse than I thought."

"You want to do them today?"

"Well, why not? It'll only take a few hours once we get going."

"Okay, but I have to leave by five for Sara's wedding rehearsal."

"They're on the young side. I was hoping to fatten them up a little more. But they'll do."

As she strides ahead of me toward the chicken coop, I can see that Baba has sharpened the axe and ground it into the stump.

By the time I reach the coop, Baba has already cornered a chicken. When I told her I'd help with the chickens, I had considered only the romantic aspect of helping her get back to her farm roots. I'd never envisioned rolling heads and spurting blood. Dad usually did that part.

As a child, I was used to animals disappearing from the farm; the next time I encountered them, they appeared on a tray at McDonald's. I had limited access to farm life. I was always shipped back to the comfort of the city before things got too graphic. I saw many slimy calves being born, taking their wobbly first steps, but I was never around when they took their last steps. Baba made the mistake of letting me befriend and name one of the newborn calves. Andy. One fall day, Andy didn't come running when I called him. I learned that I was forever part of a club of people who ate their pets.

The chicken beats its wings against the wooden boards of the coop, sending a spray of dust and hay into the air. Baba grabs one of its outstretched wings. It shrieks. Five chickens bolt from the coop, and Baba, clad in rubber boots, strides out in their wake, clutching one unlucky chicken by its feet. Its body thrashes against her legs. She walks to the stump and pins the neck of the chicken down. She raises the axe and lets it fall at the base of the chicken's craned neck, its beak stretched open. The corpse flaps and convulses its way into the long grass. The head remains motionless on the stump, its bulging eyes watching its own detached body dance about. Butch's jaws close around the jagged, bloody neck on the stump. Chicken heads are part of her healthy diet.

My role is to retrieve the limp body of the chicken. I find it with its white feathers freshly stained with wet, red blood. It makes me think of that William Carlos Williams poem I do with my students. The one with the wheelbarrow and the rain and the white chickens, except in Williams's poem there's no blood and the chickens don't die.

As I carry the bleeding chicken toward the coop, it twitches and spasms in my hand. Next year I'm taking her to the Safeway meat department for her chickens.

I immerse the chicken into a pail of steaming water. The heat loosens the soggy feathers and upon Baba's instruction, I tear them from the stiffening skin. I'm interrupted only to go and look for another decapitated bird in the grass.

Baba takes the naked chicken, slices it open, and removes its innards. She is able to locate and lift from the clump of slime the prized gizzard. She'll boil it for lunch. She tosses the rest of the innards aside for Butch to eat.

Baba grabs the second-last chicken. I hear the axe hit the stump, followed by a screech. But it's not the screech of a dying bird. I abandon the half-feathered corpse I am working on and run over to Baba. She's clutching her hand. She extends it for both of us to see. The top inch of her index finger is severed and dangles, attached only by a bit of skin. *Oh God!* She's going blind. I probably should've been the one doing the chopping.

Dad's going to kill me! I take a rag that we were using for butchering and wrap it around her hand. *Shit. Shit. Shit.* "Let's go to the hospital."

"No, let's finish these chickens," she grimaces.

"Are you nuts? You just chopped off your finger. We're going to the hospital—NOW." Blood is starting to seep through the rag. Her blood blends with the chickens'.

"Fine. But put these chickens in the fridge first."

I throw all the chickens into the fridge in the barn.

"Are you okay?"

"Yeah. Dammit, this has never happened before in all my life, and I've butchered thousands of chickens. It's that bloody axe." *Or maybe it's your failing eyesight.*

I walk her to the Fury, help her inside, and fasten the seat belt.

"I'm never going to die. God's just going to take me piece by piece."

I speed all the way to the hospital where the triage nurse takes one look at Baba's bleeding stump and admits her. A doctor freezes her hand and removes the dangling tip of her finger with a swift tug. It cannot be reattached, he says. He tells her that she will still be able to function almost normally after the finger heals.

"It won't look pretty when it heals, but we could get a plastic surgeon to look at it," he says cheerily.

"I don't need a plastic surgeon," Baba grunts.

"Because of your age, I'd like to keep you in here overnight for observation," the doctor suggests.

"I'm not sleeping here. I've got chickens." She struggles off the gurney, still in her rubber boots. The doctor wraps her hand and makes her promise that she will have a checkup in a few days with her doctor. There is not a lot they can do for a stubborn old woman who hacks off the tip of her finger.

We return to the farm. There is one lone chicken wandering around the blood-bathed yard, wondering what happened to all of its buddies. She decides to spare it. The two of them, Baba and the chicken, will live alone on the farm. Together.

As I get Baba settled in a kitchen chair, I check my watch. Sara's wedding rehearsal started ten minutes ago. *Shit.* I leave a message on her cell phone, explaining the situation. I know it won't make a difference. It wouldn't matter to Sara if Baba had died. This is her wedding rehearsal. She might even kick me out of her wedding party. Would that be such a bad thing? Maybe I should skip the rehearsal, skip the wedding, skip out on the whole thing. The thought is tempting, but then I'd have to stay on this farm with Baba and that lone chicken forever.

"I'm sorry, I should be staying overnight with you. But I can't. I'm late for the wedding rehearsal." I should be staying and making her tea. Her hand is so thickly wrapped that it's a useless bandaged stump.

"Go. I'm fine."

"Are you sure? I should call Dad," I say.

"Don't you dare! He doesn't even need to know about this."

Our family secrets now extend to maimings. This will be a tough one to hide. I figure by the time I tell them about Nat's baby, Aki's other wives, and my trip to Iran, they won't even hear the part about Baba's hacked-off finger.

"You're missing the tip of your finger. I think he'll notice. Don't use that hand at all. Those were the doctor's orders. I'll call you tomorrow."

"Okay." She is already at the sink fumbling with her kettle.

I speed all the way to the church. I arrive forty-five minutes late, not bad considering the day I've had. Everyone is lined up at the front of the church and turn around when I run in.

"I'm sorry, I'm sorry," I apologize profusely to Sara. She turns back to face the minister.

"We're about halfway through the ceremony," the minister says.

"Holy shit, do you ever stink," Julia whispers. "What'd you do, take a bloodbath before coming here?" I look down and see that my forearms have chicken blood smeared on them, I didn't change. *Fuck.*

Renate is standing beside Julia, breastfeeding Rachel.

"Can you do that in here?" I ask her.

"Yeah, it's a United church. Besides it's less offensive than what you've got going on. You look like you just finished some voodoo ritual." She picks off a feather that is stuck to the dried blood on my arm. The smell of chicken manure and blood wafts around the altar. Sara squints at us and looks particularly sinister through her false lashes.

"And then you will sign the register with your witnesses," the minister explains. "When they're finished, Julia and Doug will go over here and light this candle on behalf of the congregation."

"I'm supposed to do that."

"Not anymore," Renate whispers back. I've been fired from my only duty.

"Then I will pronounce you husband and wife and the wedding party will walk back down the aisle and you'll follow and you're done! Not so hard." The minister smiles.

I join up with Jeff's brother, Ron, whom I'm meeting for the first time.

"Hi, I'm Anna," I say.

"Ron," he flatly replies, stepping back, barely looking at me. A bubble appears above his head and it reads: *How did I get stuck with you?* I can tell by looking at him—not a hair out of place, perfectly tanned—he was that cocky guy in high school who walked all over everyone. At least his cologne, which he's wearing way too much of, temporarily masks the smell of the chicken blood. I trail after him examining my arms for vagrant feathers.

"How could you be late for this? How could you?" Sara tears into me when she reaches me at the end of the aisle.

"I left a messa—"

"I got your message," she hisses. "What are you doing butchering chickens on the day of the wedding rehearsal? God, you reek." She steps away from me.

"We weren't supposed to, but my baba—"

"You have no respect for anyone. Unbelievable."

"I said I was sorry."

"Go change before you come to the rehearsal dinner," she snaps. Good thing she reminded me about the dinner. I was already mentally half in my bathtub with a bottle of Merlot. I'm exhausted, but there is no way out of *this great opportunity to get to know my groomsman*, as Sara had put it. I'm envisioning an awkward conversation about hair gel with Ron as he scans the party for hot, available women.

Having My Cake

The alarm jars me from my sleep at 7:30 a.m.

June 30th.

Wedding day.

I call Baba and she says she's doing okay. She's thinking of butchering the last chicken today. Before I hang up, I make her promise she won't. I shouldn't have had so much wine at Sara's rehearsal last night. She wants us at her house by 8:00 a.m. sharp. I don't feel like getting out of bed and I definitely don't feel like being Sara's peach-coloured slave for the day. Ugh.

I should be excited and honoured to be supporting my friend on the most important day of her life, but I'm dreading it. I don't believe in weddings or marriage or even relationships, for that matter. To be a cheerleader at Sara's wedding is hypocritical and a continuation of my self-destructive pattern to participate in things I don't believe in anymore. I recite my own vow: *I will never be in another wedding party. I will never be in another crappy relationship. I will never do things that make other people happy but make me miserable. There.*

I stand in the shower, razor in hand, inspecting my armpits. Course hairs sprout in every direction. I've had no incentive to shave for the past month. I was planning on becoming one of those hairy, unattractive hippy girls to reinforce my attitude about relationships and men. I've been waiting for my unibrow to grow in. I contemplate not shaving, and donning the sleeveless dress with my unruly armpits. I imagine my delight in Sara's stunned reaction as I throw my arms up to catch her bouquet. But instead, I slice the hair away with the razor and then slide the blade across my legs until my skin is smooth and appropriate for a wedding. At least I will *look* like I want to be there.

I arrive at Sara's half an hour late.

"Good morning," Sara beams as she hands me a coffee. "Have some fruit." She looks like Eve standing there with her phoney-baloney smile, trying to tempt me with her poisonous apple.

"She's almost on time. I win," Renate says holding out her hand to Julia.

I pick away at some cantaloupe.

Ding dong. The photographer. *Ding dong.* The videographer. They set up and then document us awkwardly sipping coffee and nibbling muffins as though we are dignitaries at some significant event, like the signing of a peace treaty, rather than stars in a wedding home video that will be watched once and then stored on a dusty basement shelf. *Ding dong.* The florist. *Ding dong.* The stylist. *Ding dong.* My head.

"I look like a hooker," Renate complains about her makeup. She has creamy skin and rarely wears makeup. Julia is wearing less makeup than usual and complains that she looks like a zombie. The chipper makeup girl plucks my brows clean, chattering away about her Spanish vacation where she met her Spanish boyfriend. "Have you tried Spanish coffee? It's to die for," she coos into my ear as she dusts my face with powder. She foils my plan to look like shit for Sara's wedding and actually makes me look good with her brushes and glosses and shimmering shadows. Damn her.

When we slide on our dresses, mine, of course, is too loose.

"Renate, you help Sara. I'll help Anna pin her dress," Julia whispers, shoving me down the hall.

"It's fine. I actually don't care if it doesn't fit," I protest. "So, it's a little loose. Who gives a shit? They're all supposed to be looking at Wonderbride anyway."

"We're pinning it." Julia gets down on her knees and slides her hands underneath my dress.

"Would you fuck off?" Julia snaps at the videographer who is taping us. "This isn't *Bridesmaids Gone Wild.*"

"That'll be a nice segment for the Happily Ever After video," I say as Julia pins my dress. *Ding dong.* Sara's mother shows up wearing animal print. Renate wins another bet. We have decided the best way to survive the day will be to bet on everything from the weather, to who will be wearing what, to how many fits Sara will throw. The first fit of the day occurs when I spill my coffee. It looks as though a dog has peed all over my shoes. We then bet on how many of these fits I will cause.

An hour before the ceremony Sara emerges from the bedroom. She's stunning. The billowy skirt of her dress floods down onto the floor. Sara and her dreams are all stuffed into the beaded bodice of her dress. She's had an imperfect life and this is her chance at one perfect day. I smile and nod my speechless approval, but I can't meet Sara's eyes. She has placed so much importance on today, but soon it will be over. Once it's over, will Sara look within rather than constantly measuring her happiness by things outside of herself—like her wedding? Somehow I doubt it.

She'll ride off into the Caribbean sunset in her chariot filled with wedding cash and gifts. When all this wedding business started, my bitterness was rooted in a little bit of envy. As a little girl I was raised to buy into this. I am the Diana Generation. My mother bought me every book about the princess ever published. For hours we would pore over the pictures of her perfect dresses and matching hats. At five years old I watched that wedding with my mom on TV, live, at five in the morning. As she walked down the aisle in that million-dollar gown toward her prince, Diana made little girls everywhere believe that the fairytale was possible. All we had to do was find our own Charles. It didn't matter that he was eleven years older than Diana, balding, and a total bore. He wore the title Prince of England.

Today, Sara is living her own version of it—a perfect wedding to her investment banker.

I stayed up half the night glued to CNN the night Diana was killed in a car wreck. The fairytale had gone horribly wrong. It had to end this way. All those little girls, myself included, needed to abandon the fairytale ending. It is dangerous and deadly to cling to such fantasies. I hope it all works out better for Sara.

At 1:30 a limousine the colour of whipping cream arrives to take us to the church.

At 2 p.m. sharp the music starts. Julia walks down the aisle first.

Then it's my turn. The long burgundy carpet stretches out in front of me, a canvas of impossibility. I spot Adam and his date a few pews away. He smirks, his chin cocked high and proud. Julia reaches the front and looks back. *Okay, I can do this.* My feet remain planted. Renate prods my back with her bouquet. *Okay, okay, I'm going.* Julia's steps were confident, mine are tentative, wobbly. My discomfort extends well beyond the dress and the shoes to my own skin.

I pass Adam. He smirks at me. There are too many people and I can't get a good look at his date—I catch a glimpse of an ugly floral print. Of course Sara has invited all sorts of people from high school, whom she hardly ever sees, so she can prove her success in wifedom.

Something inside me snaps. Everything is in slow motion. People are staring at me. *She's the bridesmaid, again? Wasn't she in the last wedding we were at? How many bridesmaid's dresses do you think she has? Are you even allowed to be a bridesmaid after thirty?*

"What's the matter with you? Why'd you stop in the middle?" Julia whispers when I arrive at the front.

"You're practically holding your bouquet over your face," Renate mutters as she takes her place next to me. I thought maybe no one would notice it was me if I covered my face, maybe they'd miss my name in the program. I don't want to be the bridesmaid anymore.

"Nothing's wrong. Your tits look amazing in that dress," I reply.

"I can feel them starting to leak. I didn't get a chance to pump this morning."

Sara walks up the aisle. She's lovely. The priest tells everyone to sit down before he launches into a lecture about the importance of love in the world. The ceremony drones on. "I, Sara, take thee, Jeff"...blah, blah, blah.

When I emerge from the church, an old man, who obviously can't see well, mistakes me for the bride and heaves rice in my face. *I'm not the goddamn bride.* We take pictures at the park, downtown, at the Legislative Building. Wedding parties nearby take the exact same photos. *Insert bride and groom here.* We jump up in the air holding hands at the photographer's instruction, while he takes a dozen more pictures. As we land, the heel on one of my hundred-and-fifty-dollar shoes breaks. *Dammit.*

Renate's husband generously offers to trek to the shoe store to find me another pair of size nine peach shoes. He returns with a roll of duct tape.

"Why you all the time? Not anyone else," Sara whispers angrily into my ear as I try to reattach the heel of my coffee-stained peach shoe.

"I don't know why my shoe broke! You picked them!" *Maybe if we didn't have to jump up and down like kangaroos for these goddamn pictures.*

"Ron told Jeff that he thinks you're acting weird," Sara says. "And I think I'd agree." I'm becoming progressively less tolerant of the bride as the day drags on. The heel of my shoe is looking less like footwear and more like a weapon.

"Who's Ron?"

"Your partner." She glares at me. *Oh, him.*

"Prom King's barely said two words to me!"

"Just try to get along with him."

"Okay. Fine." I hobble into the limo and finish duct-taping my heel. It's wobbly, and dancing with Ron during the obligatory wedding party dance will be problematic, but dancing with Ron would be problematic regardless of the shoe.

At the reception my state and my behaviour deteriorate. I'm a badly dressed accessory to the bride. I feel stupid and alone.

Adam and his date are seated two tables away from the head table. Nice planning, Sara. Thanks. I am convinced that she is trying to destroy me. This entire day seems like it has been planned to make me look and feel like a failure. It's hard to tell if Adam is paying his date or not. She wears really ugly strappy shoes. Then again, I'm in no position to be commenting on someone else's shoes. Adam occasionally nods at me as he rubs his date's fake-and-bake back. She has an orange hue to her. *He went from me to that?*

I concentrate on the goldfish swimming around the bamboo stalks in the vase in front of me. Its eyes are bulging, panicked. *What a stupid idea. Fish.* Guests are supposed to take them home. They'll die because no one has fish food. Sara got the idea from a wedding magazine, which means there will be thousands of dead fish this wedding season. If a thousand out of the six thousand couples who get married in Manitoba each year implement this silly craze, and the couple have twenty-five tables at their wedding, with one goldfish per table, that's 25,000 dead fish. And this fish looks like it knows it. I drop part of my dinner roll into the vase in an attempt to feed it, but I only frighten it further. The only thing I can relate to at this wedding is this fish darting around, trapped in six inches of water.

The monkeys go crazy in my stomach and in my chest. It's hard to breathe. Beads of sweat form on my neck and forehead. I'm alone. I've spent the past ten years in a bad relationship. I believed Adam when he repeatedly told me that we were good together and that he couldn't live without me. Apparently he can. I never listened to myself. Without a second thought I've been replaced tonight by some girl with bad highlights and an orange tan. I've remained at an insipid job without even thinking about what I really want to do. I'm a bridesmaid for a high school friend whom I'm finally realizing I don't even like anymore. My sister is trapped in the Middle East with a polygamous husband. And to top it all off I have to wander around all night looking like the fucking peach Creamsicle bridesmaid that I am. This is not a good night to be having a breakdown, but I can feel it coming on like a migraine.

As I walk to the bar for my third drink, I spot Sara's pristine unguarded wedding cake. It taunts me. The only thing in the world that will comfort me right now is a piece of that cake. Well, cheesecake would be better, but a piece of this lemon chiffon will do. I take the gleaming knife and cut a huge chunk out of the immaculate white cake. I go to the bathroom, lock myself in the third stall, and stuff it into my mouth. It's sweet and it melts on my tongue. It makes me forget where I am—until I hear Sara's shriek from down the hall.

"We haven't even taken pictures of it yet!"

I shove the rest of the cake down my throat. I gag on the velvet icing. I emerge from the stall, wiping the cake from my face as Sara bursts into the bathroom, wiping tears from hers. Renate and Julia are close behind, trying to console her.

"It was probably some kid," Renate says. "We can photograph the other side. It's okay."

We enter the hall and arrange ourselves at the head table. I pour myself the last of the wine at my end of the table, though the toasts haven't even started. At least the wine is good.

"I've written a great speech," Ron says to me as he stuffs forkfuls of chicken Kiev into his mouth. It's one of the few things he's said to me all day.

"That's nice," I reply, downing the remnants of my drink.

I've barely touched my food. I'm not hungry, I'm too full of cake. Every time I look up, I have to see Adam ogling his date's breasts. It kills my appetite and enrages me. *I believed you, asshole, when you made me think you couldn't go on without me. You wasted years of my life,* I stand up and mouth to Adam. I realize I'm making a scene when Sara's great-aunt at the table in front of us starts pointing at me and whispering to her neighbour.

"What is your problem?" Ron asks snarkily as I sit down. "Do you have bride envy or something?"

"No, Ron, I don't have bride envy. Thanks for your concern."

After dessert, Ron goes to the bathroom. I reach over and pick up the folded-up piece of paper in front of his wine glass and read it. I tuck it into my purse. I've been listening to what a great guy Jeff is for two years. And if Ron's speech is so great, then he'll have committed it to memory. I finish the remaining sips of Ron's wine.

When he returns, his tan fades a few shades.

"Have you seen my speech?"

"Where'd you leave it? They cleared the tables."

"I left it right here." He turns and leaves, muttering about checking if he'd left it in the bathroom. When he returns there are beads of sweat on his forehead. The Prom King is cracking.

"Great, now what am I supposed to do?"

"Just wing it. You'll do fine."

Ron muddles and stammers his way through his speech. It would appear that public speaking in front of two hundred people without notes is, unfortunately, his one weakness. I read his speech along with him, noticing that he misses many of the key points. It was a good speech. I just can't bear to hear how lucky the bride is, how magical they are together. We all know this already, have known it for a year since they started planning this wedding. I'm just preventing Ron from stating the obvious. Petty jealousy and insecurity have turned me into a wedding monster. I guess I do have bride envy after all.

Renate delivers a moving speech for Sara, outlining her quirky perfectionist personality. Partway through the speech, Renate's baby girl, Rachel, starts screaming. I like the fact that Rachel, like me, takes the opportunity to pee on Sara's wedding. As her godmother, I won't have to teach her as much as I thought I would.

I hang around the bar for the next few hours until the bartender suggests that I lay off the wine for a while. A pair of heels beside the dance floor catch my attention. My duct-tape heel is starting to give, so I try on the shoes. They fit. I toss my broken shoes into the empty elevator and send them down to the lobby.

I eat the chocolate favours off four tables and I'm loading more into my purse when Julia approaches me.

"Come dance," she coaxes me. A tall guy with a loosened tie hovers behind her. Great, even Julia—self-proclaimed Single Woman—has hooked up. A shimmering dead goldfish floats sideways on the surface of the water in one of the vases. *Fitting.*

I'm about to refuse when I catch sight of Adam and his date, huddled together, sharing a piece of wedding cake.

That was *me.*

Seeing them sitting there, digging into a single piece of cake, makes me realize that Adam and I shared everything. I never had my own slice of cake. My misery, my happiness, my identity were all moored to Adam. I sacrificed my independence for the relationship.

We were horrible together, but we were addicted to the emotional power we held over each other, the highs and lows we could inflict on one another. It was our version of a crack habit. I couldn't walk away. I needed him to be dependent on me. Taking care of Adam became my purpose because I didn't have one; I needed to save him because I couldn't save myself.

Adam was addicted to this power that he held over me, but looking at him across the room, nuzzling with this cheap girl, makes me realize that my addiction was so much worse. He affectionately wipes icing from the girl's chin with his thumb.

She can have Adam's cake and eat it too. Not me. Not anymore.

I don't even like cake.

"Sure, I'll dance," I say, turning to Julia. Why the hell not? The floor is packed with people doing the chicken dance.

NaNe NaNe Na Na Na. I bop my head back and forth, inducing near whiplash.

Flap. Flap. Flap. Flap. I thrust my elbows out so viciously my shoulders pop.

The space around me has cleared, and eyes bore into me—

even Adam and his date abandon their cake to look up. Unlike when I walked down the aisle this afternoon, I don't care if people stare at me and I don't care what they think. I dance. I'm free. Is this how the chicken feels after its head has been cut off? They say it's an involuntary muscular reaction, but maybe the chicken is celebrating its freedom from a life of fear, bondage, and desperation.

NaNe NaNe Na Na Na. I kick off the stolen shoes. My blistered feet are soothed against the cool floor. My entire body jerks in every direction.

I close my eyes. This is me flying away.

Julia jabs my ribs and I open my eyes, breathless. The song has ended and the rest of the chickens are still standing around, eyes bulging, waiting for the next song. I walk away. The shoes lie in the middle of the floor.

Epilogue

July 1st. The day after Sara's wedding. Big hangover.
    I draft and mail my resignation letter to the school. I tell them something about teaching being a rewarding and fulfilling career, but not for me. I say that while my commitment to the profession will be tough to replace, Liz, my student teacher, will do just fine. The world will be a more poetic place.

Adam is gone and I don't have to hide from him in my classroom anymore. Maybe I'll take Craig's advice and try writing my own material for a change. Craig had found one of the poems in a poetry anthology that I read to the group. He was so disappointed that he stopped coming to the writing group. I miss the *Chronicles of Argamyte*. I hope it all worked out with the dragon.

I've been plagiarizing in both my writing and my life. I'll begin writing as a way of reinventing myself and saving myself from emotional paralysis. My heroine will be a woman in her thirties—intelligent, ambitious, funny, insecure, and lonely. There won't be a fairytale ending, but nor will her life culminate in a miserable car wreck caused by her own quest for superficial happiness. There are no princes, nor are there any villains who rule her fate. She is ordinary and her story is uncomplicated.

I live in a world where everybody aspires to be different or better than who they are, to define their happiness by things outside of their identity. A great house. A great job. A great wedding. A great family. A great relationship. I've spent a decade trying to convince myself that if I tried hard enough, I could fit these moulds. I'm going to start over and begin by finding peace within myself. I bought all those self-help books because somewhere along the way, I started to believe that I wasn't good enough as I was. These books are written to help tame the vices in our lives, but the vices make us human. I am so far from perfect, from *greatness*, that it's comical, and that's okay.

I pick up my ticket to Iran. Tears roll down Mom's cheeks when I tell her about the trip. It takes me half an hour to convince her that I'm not following in Nat's footsteps, but trying to bring her home. I don't tell Mom about Natalia's baby—yet. I hope that when she finds out about her grandchild, she'll be able to hold her and maybe the baby will bring my family together again. But if it doesn't work out that way, that's okay too.

When I tell Baba about my trip, she points out in disgust that I might miss her funeral. I promise her that I won't miss it and I assure her that, anyway, I've already seen how good she looks in her coffin.

I don't know if Nat will come home with me. I need to tell her that I walked away from Adam and from everything familiar in my life. It's not a hypocrite on her doorstep asking her to take back her life. Natalia must have learned some of her lessons from observing her older sister. I might be part of the reason she's ended up in the Middle East as one of Aki's two wives. I will fly halfway around the world to tell her that it doesn't have to be like that. If she has a daughter, I will tell her, too, the day she is born.

The last thing I do before leaving for the airport is pound a "For Sale" sign on the lawn in front of the house. I leave the details of the sale with a real estate agent, the same one who got me into the whole mess in the first place. When I told Buddy I was selling the house, he disappeared, like the fool in *King Lear*. I don't know what happened to him. I didn't get a chance to say goodbye. As I packed up my things to put in storage, I found smatterings of peanut shells in the closets and underneath the stairs. I swept them up and threw them away. The self-help books still sit on the kitchen table, untouched and unreturned.

The plane lifts off and floats above the city. Somewhere down there is Adam. I could sit on this plane stewing and blaming Adam for my having spent my twenties in a miserable relationship, but I could have walked away a long time ago. I chose not to. I know that now and I don't blame Adam.

The plane lifts higher and below us the fields stretch out, a checkerboard of gold, blue, brown, and black. Baba is somewhere down there rooted firmly on one of those prairie patches, probably re-roofing her barn. Regardless of how far I fly, these Prairies are as much a part of me as they are her.

The plane ascends higher, flooded by clouds, until it emerges and levels off in the clear blue sky. The pilot's voice comes over the speaker.

"Good afternoon, ladies and gentlemen. We've reached our cruising altitude. . . ." I've reached my cruising altitude.

Finally, I'm there.

Acknowledgements

Thank you to the Manitoba Writers' Guild and the Sheldon Oberman Mentorship Program, with special thanks to the late Obie who read a story and told me I had a book. The Winnipeg and Manitoba Arts Councils have provided financial support; special thanks to Joan Thomas for her encouragement. RETSD allowed me time to write, and the *Winnipeg Free Press* and Margo Goodhand printed the stories and columns of an unproven freelance writer. Many thanks to *Prairie Fire* and MWG for awarding me the Anne Szumigalski Scholarship so that I could attend The Sage Hill Writing Experience.

Many dear friends have read this book and offered encouraging words: Jill Kalmacoff, Jill Cooper, Trish Cooper, Geoff Ripat, Stephanie Gibbons, Leona Sembrat, Susan Taylor, Michelle English, Bev Greenberg, Liv Lunde, and Shandi Mitchell. Special thanks to Tracey Llewellyn, Kieran Hunter, and Gwen Smid for reading this book when it was still written on scraps of paper and stapled together. Techies Sean Smythe, Kathy Athayde, and Karen Strubar rescued *The Prairie Bridesmaid* one night when it disappeared into the depths of my computer, and taught me to properly back up my work. Thanks to Chris and John Syvitski and the Stellas folk for kindly lending me their cabins.

I am indebted to Marjorie Anderson for her brilliant editing; for helping me transform an early manuscript into a novel that I could be proud to send out.

Thank you Key Porter Books. Janie Yoon took on *The Prairie Bridesmaid*, and provided thoughtful editorial guidance early on. Jane Warren embraced this book and made it so much better; her editing was visionary and meticulous all at once, and always delivered with patience and humour. Marijke Friesen found the heart of this book and then designed a lovely cover. I'm grateful to Jordan Fenn, Rob Howard, and Jennifer Fox for launching *The Prairie Bridesmaid* out into the world; Key Porter has made the publication of my first novel such a great experience.

Samantha Haywood believed in this book and in me. I am so grateful for her intuitive feedback, her talent as an agent, her humour, and her friendship.

My parents have a rare ability to be supportive, open, and encouraging, but never pressuring. I am doing what I love because of how I was raised.

I am grateful to Oskar for snoring softly in my lap while I finished this novel—for letting me be a new mother and a writer.

Finally, I thank Rob—my extraordinary husband, best friend, and editor, for inspiring me to follow my dream, for helping me to edit it when it turned out to be a book, and for tolerating me when I abandoned the dishes for months at a time while writing. Because of you there is a book.

The Soundtrack

With the purchase of *The Prairie Bridesmaid*, you can download the novel's soundtrack from www.theprairiebridesmaid.com. All of the music connects to the themes and ideas of the book. Daria is eternally grateful to the artists for sharing their music.

The Artists

Sarah Slean
"No Place At All," from her album *The Baroness*
www.sarahslean.com

Scott Nolan
"Dutch," from the album *Receiver/Reflector*
www.scottnolan.ca

Snailhouse
"Birds and Bees," from the album *The Silence Show*
www.snailhousemusic.com

Jill Barber
"Hard Line," from her album *For All Time*
www.jillbarber.com

Chantal Vitalis
"More Captured Than Released," from the album *Today's Special*
www.chantalvitalis.com

Greg Macpherson
"Ukrainians," original unreleased song
gregmacpherson.com

Keri Latimer
"Careful Now," original unreleased song
www.nathanmusic.ca

DARIA SALAMON's writing has been published by *The Globe and Mail*, the *Winnipeg Free Press*, and *Uptown Magazine*, and has been shortlisted for the Writers' Union of Canada's Emerging Writer Short Fiction Award, the Larry Turner Award for Creative Non-Fiction, and the Canadian Authors Association's North of 55 Writing Contest. She lives in Winnipeg with her husband and son, Oskar.

Please visit www.theprairiebridesmaid.com.